INTRODUCTION
by Daphne Patai

For nearly fifty years, the identity of 'Murray Constantine', pseudonymous author of *Swastika Night*, has been concealed from public view. Only in the early 1980s, in response to persistent inquiries, did the novel's original publishers acknowledge that 'Murray Constantine' was in fact Katharine Burdekin. Born in Derbyshire in 1896, Burdekin died in 1963 having published ten novels between 1922 and 1940.

Intensely interested in politics, history, psychology and religion, Burdekin experimented with a number of literary structures, yet her novels, whether published pseudonymously or under her own name, are clearly the work of one hand, one creative intelligence in the process of development. Though Burdekin's feminist critique appears in her realistic fiction and even in her children's book, she excelled above all in the creation of utopian fiction, and the special vantage point afforded by the imaginative leap into other 'societies' resulted in her two most important books: *Swastika Night* (1937) and *Proud Man* (1934). When these novels first appeared, contemporary reviewers tended to miss Burdekin's important critique of what we today call gender ideology and sexual politics, though on occasion they noted her feminist sympathies, which, indeed, led some to guess that 'Murray Constantine' was a woman. With this reprint of *Swastika Night*, Burdekin's works may finally begin to find their audience.

Like fictional utopias ('good places'), dystopias ('bad places') provide a framework for levelling criticisms at the writer's own historical moment. But in imagining in *Swastika Night* a Europe after seven centuries of Nazi domination, Burdekin was doing something more than sounding a warning about the dangers of fascism. Burdekin's novel is important for us today because her analysis of fascism is formulated in terms that go beyond Hitler and the specifics of his time. Arguing that fascism is not qualitatively but only quantitatively different from the everyday reality of male dominance, a reality that polarises males and females in terms of gender roles, Burdekin satirises 'masculine' and 'feminine' modes of behaviour. Nazi ideology, from this point of view, is the culmination of what Burdekin calls the 'cult of masculinity'. It is this connection, along with the strong argument against the cult of masculinity, that set Burdekin's novel apart from the many other anti-fascist dystopias produced in the 1930s and 40s.[1]

Burdekin envisages Germany and England in the seventh century of the Hitlerian millennium. The world has been divided into two static spheres – the Nazi Empire (Europe and Africa) and the equally militaristic Japanese Empire (Asia, Australia, and the Americas). In the Nazi Empire Hitler is venerated as a god, exploded from the head of his father, God the Thunderer, and thereafter undefiled by any contaminating contact with women. A 'Reduction of Women' has occurred by which women have been driven to an animal-like state of ignorance and apathy, and are kept purely for their indispensable breeding function. All books, records and even monuments from the past have been destroyed in an effort to make the official Nazi 'reality' the only possible one. A kind of feudal society is in force throughout the Nazi Empire, with German knights as the local authorities, indoctrinators of a Teutonic mythology whose spurious nature has long since been forgotten. The women are kept in cages in segregated quarters, their Reduction complemented by the exaltation of men. This situation has led to homosexual attachments among males (Burdekin suggests that male homosexuality may involve embracing, not rejecting, the male gender role), though procreation is a civic duty for German men. Christians, having wiped out all the Jews at the beginning of the Nazi era, are now

SWASTIKA NIGHT

First

Intro

Introduction photoset in North Wales by
Derek Doyle & Associates, Mold, Clwyd
Text set by Richard Clay and Company, Bungay, Suffolk
Printed and bound in Great Britain by
Oxford University Press

themselves loathed, considered Untouchable.

Seeing the relationship between gender hierarchy and class structure, Burdekin, in her earlier novel *Proud Man*, had written that English society (which that book's fully evolved narrator labels 'subhuman') is divided horizontally by a privilege of class and vertically by a privilege of sex. In *Swastika Night* she further suggests that the sop of gender dominance ensures the co-operation of men who are themselves the victims of domination: no matter what their status, they are granted the assurance of still being superior to women.[2] The German men, meanwhile, embrace the Hitlerian creed, which includes the words: 'And I believe in pride, in courage, in violence, in brutality, in bloodshed, in ruthlessness, and all other soldierly and heroic virtues.' If this is satire, it is also an accurate representation of Nazi ideology and only a slight exaggeration of a masculine gender identity considered normal in many parts of the world.

Burdekin focuses on two essential aspects of the masculine ideology depicted in *Swastika Night*: women's lack of control over their own bodies and over their offspring. To these correspond the two fundamental institutions of the novel's Hitlerian society: men's right to rape and the law dictating Removal of the Man-Child from his mother's care at eighteen months, so that he may be raised by and among men.

Understanding that rape is in its essence an assault on female autonomy, Burdekin articulates the logic of rape within a male supremacist society. In a traditional sexually-polarised society, women challenge male supremacy by their right of rejection. The female's selection of a sexual partner, 'natural' in much of the animal world, becomes a perpetual affront to human males' vanity. By depriving women of this right men transform them into mere objects to be used solely according to men's wishes. Given the cult of masculinity, of course men could not permit women to continue to exercise this right of rejection. Hence the institutionalisation of rape as a routine practice, a constant reminder to women of their lack of importance and autonomy. Men's obligations are only to one another; thus women in *Swastika Night* are free from rape if and when they wear an armlet marking them as one man's possession – and, indeed, this is their sole 'freedom'. Power over women, not sexual pleasure, is the issue – for only boys are considered beautiful, desirable, lovable. The women, for their part, are indoctrinated from childhood with their own insignificance and their proper role in accepting men's will. The logic of the social rules in *Swastika Night* is unrelenting. Women must not know that more girl children are needed, that the disproportionate number of male births is a danger to the society: '… if the women once realised all this, what could stop them developing a small thin thread of self-respect? If a woman could rejoice publicly in the birth of a girl, Hitlerdom would start to crumble.' And, of course, neither men nor women have any true knowledge of the past, any historical memory prior to the advent of Hitlerism.

In *Proud Man* Burdekin criticises Adlous Huxley's *Brave New World* for its assumption that human beings would be the same even under totally different conditions. She herself does not make that mistake. Her women, in *Swastika Night*, have indeed become ignorant and fearful animals; their misery is their only recognisable human feature. Burdekin is also careful to show even her positive male characters as seriously flawed by their environment. There are no simple heroes in her book, but there are men struggling toward understanding and, with the help of knowledge, each is able to overcome his conditioning to some extent.

The novel's protagonist, the Englishman Alfred, is a figure destined, like his historical namesake, to contribute to his country's freedom. But Alfred is emphatically not a warrior. Burdekin had published a pacifist novel, *Quiet Ways*, in 1930, in which she attacked the very idea of manliness as dependent upon violence and military prowess. In *Proud Man* Burdekin defines a soldier as a 'killing male', and in *Swastika Night* she continues the attack on militarism through Alfred's opposition to the ideology of Nazism. He realises that violence, brutality and physical courage can never make 'a man', but only ageless boys. To be a man, in his view, requires a soul. Therefore, liberation from Hitlerism, in *Swastika Night*, cannot come through violence and brutality, the 'soldierly virtues'.

Victor Gollancz, the original publisher of *Swastika Night*, added a note to the novel when it was reissued in July 1940 as a Left Book Club selection (it was one of the very few works of fiction the Club ever distributed). Perhaps because the pacifist impulses at work in *Swastika Night* would not have met with much sympathy once the war against Hitler had started, Gollancz included in his comments the following words: 'While the author has not in the least changed his mind that the Nazi idea is evil, and that we must fight the Nazis on land, at sea, in the air and in ourselves, he has changed his mind about the Nazi *power* to make the *world* evil ...' This upbeat message, however much needed at the time, dilutes and misrepresents the tenor of *Swastika Night*, for the book's lasting contribution is precisely its transcendence of the specifics of Nazi ideology and its location of Nazism, and militarism in general, within the broader spectrum of the 'cult of masculinity'. Hitler did not invent the concepts of inequality and domination, whether racial or sexual. He merely carried them one logical step further, and Burdekin began her critique there.

Complementing the emphasis on the 'cult of masculinity' is Burdekin's analysis of women's complicity in their own subjugation. The German knight von Hess, although he possesses the secret manuscript that gives him some knowledge of the past, still believes in women's inherent inferiority. Analysing their acquiescence, he concludes: 'Women *are* nothing, except an incarnate desire to please men.' Von Hess is thus shown to reproduce, at the same time as he criticises, the views of von Wied, a scholar-knight who, centuries before, had proved that women were not human. The ideas attributed to von Wied in *Swastika Night* closely resemble those of the pre-fascist Viennese ideologue Otto Weininger whose 1903 book *Sex and Character* develops an extraordinary catalogue of purported female characteristics. Drawing on Plato and Aristotle, Weininger sees the male principle as active, as form, while the female is mere passive matter, a nothingness that needs to be shaped by man, hence woman's famous submissive 'nature'. Woman is negation, meaninglessness, and man therefore fears her, Weininger writes; she is possessed by her sexual organs and only comes in existence through sexual union with man. To Weininger, who considers sexuality immoral, woman thus keeps man from attaining his true moral existence. He concludes that fecundity is loathsome and that the education of mankind must be taken out of the hands of the mother. Equating women with Jews, Weininger contrasts them with men and Aryans, but though the Jews are the lowest of the low, he writes, in words echoed in the Hitlerian creed in *Swastika Night*, 'the woman of the highest standard is immeasurably beneath the man of the lowest standard'.

Just as the knight von Hess, in *Swastika Night*, rejects some of von Wied's theories, so Alfred is able to reject some of what von Hess tells him. Evolving his own explanation for women's acquiescence in their Reduction, Alfred decides that women's lack of development is the result of their crime in not valuing themselves: they believed the male sex was not just different, but better. Hence they accepted the patterns imposed on them by men. The world's values are masculine, he thinks, because there have been no women; that is, no true women not deformed by the demands of masculinity. Women's submission is not due to their nature, Alfred realises, but rather to the fact that women have never had two things that are available to men. One is sexual invulnerability; the other is pride in their sex, 'which is the humblest boy's birthright'. Women, Alfred concludes, need to rediscover their own 'soul-power'.

Burdekin sheds further light on the origins of women's acquiescence to their Reduction in the analogy developed within the novel between the political and the personal, the public and the private spheres. The Nazi Empire treats its subject people the way Nazi men treat women – as objects to be conquered and subjugated. In describing how the Empire governed, by inferiorising rather than assimilating the subject peoples, von Hess says: 'Exclusion is an excellent way of making men feel inferior.' Although *Swastika Night* only hints at the causes of the 'cult of masculinity', Burdekin addressed the issue more directly in her earlier novel, *Proud Man*. In this work, which makes profound criticism of conventional gender ideology, Burdekin traces the root cause of patriarchy back to the male need to redress the natural balance that gives women greater biological importance than men.

Like Karen Horney, whose essays on feminine psychology were available in English in the 1920s, Burdekin sees the male imposition on women of a devalued social identity as resulting from a fundamental fear and jealousy of women's procreative powers. This explains men's insistence on women's inferior artistic (and other) abilities, the narrator of *Proud Man* asserts. Indeed, men's pride is an uneasy one, 'not founded on a solid biological fact'. Hence also the more profound training in appropriate gender-role behaviour that boys undergo – based on an anxiety that they will not develop into proper 'men' without an enforced separation from women – in single-sex schools, clubs, sports, and, above all, the military. The charm of war, Burdekin writes, is due to its exclusion of females. In *Proud Man* Burdekin distinguishes between gender and sex (to use our terminology) and concludes that men and women must be transformed: 'They must stop being masculine and feminine, and become male and female. Masculinity and femininity are the artificial differences between men and women. Maleness and femaleness are the real differences ...'

In their tone and vocabulary, Burdekin's arguments in *Proud Man* have an extraordinarily contemporary ring – a ring perhaps less apparent in *Swastika Night* when we read it today since its overt political situation belongs to our past. Burdekin speaks of the phallus as the guarantor of civic power; but, unlike Karen Horney, she never attributes to it any actual superiority. It is the social significance of the phallus that counts. This psychology finds its fulfillment in the nightmare scenario of *Swastika Night*, in which phallic pride has become the organising principle of society. Burdekin strips bare the disguises of adult 'manliness' (a pejorative term in many of her writings) and shows us men forever affirming their masculinity, and women, reduced to female animals, ever embodying a reassuring contrast with that glorious masculinity. She thus politicises a comment made by a thwarted female character in H.G. Wells' novel *The Passionate Friends* (1913). Complaining of the sexual specialisation forced on women, this character writes:

'Womankind isn't human, it's reduced human.'

Burdekin's perspective resembles that of the American writer Charlotte Perkins Gilman who, in her feminist utopia *Herland* (1915), has her male narrator slowly develop the conviction that 'those "feminine" charms we are so fond of are not feminine at all, but mere reflected masculinity – developed to please us because they had to please us.' A similar observation also occurs in Virginia Woolf's *Room of One's Own* (1929). With bitter irony Woolf writes: 'Women have served all these centuries as looking-glasses possessing the magic and delicious power of reflecting the figure of man at twice its natural size. Without that power probably the earth would still be swamp and jungle. The glory of all our wars would be unknown.'

Although Burdekin, in her earlier works, was already attuned to the problems of gender ideology, Hitler's rise to power apparently helped crystallise in her mind the dangers of conventional notions of masculinity. To a feminist following events in Nazi Germany (and, before that, in Mussolini's Italy), the logic of fascist gender ideology must have stood out. Nazi statements about women were clear enough. In 1932, a year before the Nazis destroyed all branches of the women's movement, the Reichskomitee of Working Women made an appeal to Germany's working-class women. Published in *Die Rote Fahne* (The Red Flag), a German Communist newspaper, the appeal denounced Nazi brutality and called upon women to engage in anti-fascist action, saying: 'The Nazis demand the death sentence for abortion. They want to turn you into compliant birth-machines. You are to be servants and maids for men. Your human dignity is to be trampled underfoot.'[3] Winifred Holtby, in her 1934 book *Women and a Changing Civilization*, also warned her readers about the attack on reason implicit in the development of fascism in both Germany and England. She concluded: 'The enemies of reason are inevitably the opponents of "equal rights".'

Hitler's view of the proper role of women was originally set forth in *Mein Kampf* (1924): they were to reproduce the race. Elaborating on this in his 8 September 1934 speech before National Socialist women, Hitler argued that the 'natural' division of labour between men and women involved a harmonious complementarity between the greater world (male) and the smaller world (female). 'The program of our National Socialist women's movement contains only one point – and this is: the child.' Political life, Hitler argued, was 'unworthy' of women; hence Nazi policy excluded them from it.[4] Unlike Burdekin's scenario in *Swastika Night*, however, Nazi policy encouraged the health and well-being of racially desirable women. Promotion of motherhood took the form of a series of laws providing for maternity benefits and care as well as for marriage incentives – for those people who could produce 'hereditarily valuable' offspring for the nation.[5]

Burdekin's special insight was to join the various elements of Nazi policy into one ideological whole. She saw that it is but a small step from the male apotheosis of women as mothers to their degradation to mere breeding animals. In both cases women are reduced to a biological function out of which is constructed an entire social identity. And she linked this reduction to the routine practices of patriarchal society. Joseph Goebbels, Nazi propaganda minister, had articulated the gender ideology of Nazi Germany in his speech on 11 February 1934: 'The National Socialist movement is in its nature a masculine movement ... While man must give to life the great lines and forms, it is the task of women out of her inner fullness and inner eagerness to fill these lines and forms with colour ...'[6]

A year after the publication of *Swastika Night*, Virginia Woolf, in *Three Guineas* (1938) also connected the tyranny of the fascist state with the tyranny of patriarchal society. Recent studies of fascism have further corroborated the connection. María-Antonietta Macciocchi, for example, in an article on female sexuality in fascist ideology argues that one cannot talk about fascism without at the same time talking about patriarchy. Her analysis locates the originality of fascism 'not in any capacity to generate a new ideology, but in its conjunctural transformation and recombination of what already exists'.[7]

A further aspect of *Swastika Night* of interest to contemporary readers is its resemblance to George Orwell's *Nineteen*

Eighty-Four. There is no direct evidence that Orwell was acquainted with *Swastika Night*, published twelve years before his novel; only the internal similarities suggest that Orwell, an inveterate borrower, borrowed also from Burdekin. As it happens, Victor Gollancz, publisher of *Swastika Night*, was also Orwell's first publisher, and Orwell's *Road to Wigan Pier* was itself a Left Book Club selection, in 1937, just as *Swastika Night* was in 1940.

Both *Nineteenth Eighty-Four* and *Swastika Night* depict totalitarian régimes in which individual thought has been all but eliminated and towards this end all information about the past, and even memory itself, have been destroyed – much more thoroughly in Burdekin's novel than in Orwell's. In both books the world is divided into distinct empires in perpetual and static competition. There is a similar hierarchy in each novel, and the most despised groups (proles; women) are regarded as brute animals. The hierarchical extremes alone are to some extent free of domination. The knights and the Christians are not subject to constant search in *Swastika Night* – the knights because of their important position, the Christians because they are Untouchable. Similarly, in *Nineteen Eighty-Four*, Inner Party members can turn off their telescreens, and the proles are not obliged to have them installed, for the proles simply do not matter. And, in keeping with the very concept of hierarchy, in both societies the upper echelons have material privileges denied to others.

Furthermore, in each novel there is a rebellious protagonist who is approached by a man in a position of power (O'Brien, the Inner Party member; von Hess, the knight). This powerful man becomes the mediator through whom the protagonist's tendency to rebel is initially channelled, and in each case he gives the protagonist a secret book and hence knowledge. In both novels, also, a photograph provides a key piece of evidence about the past. Winston Smith and Alfred each attempt to teach a lover/friend (Julia; Hermann) about the past by reading from the secret book, but meet with resistance or indifference. In both cases a curious detail occurs: Julia and Hermann sleep while the book is read aloud, a mark of their lack of both interest and intellectual development.

As in *Swastika Night*, in *Nineteen Eighty-Four* the secret opposition is called a Brotherhood. Despite the apolitical inclinations of Hermann and Julia, each is drawn into the protagonist's rebellion and ultimately destroyed by it. In both novels, too, there are official enemies to be hated: Goldstein in *Nineteen Eighty-Four*; the four arch-friends, enemies of Hitler, in *Swastika Night*; and the eternal mythical leaders, Big Brother and Hitler, to be adored. Finally, as if in enactment of the theories of Wilhelm Reich, in both novels a distortion of sexuality occurs: in *Nineteen Eighty-Four* by the prohibition of sex for pleasure; in *Swastika Night* by the degradation and Reduction of women which has made love and sexual attraction a prerogative of men. And in both novels sex is encouraged for the sake of procreation, but only with certain people.

Orwell gave names to phenomena that also appear in *Swastika Night*; indeed, the main contribution of *Nineteen Eighty-Four* to modern culture probably resides in these names: 'Newspeak' is Orwell's term for the reduction of language that is designed to inhibit thought. In *Swastika Night*, too, concepts and words have been lost. 'Marriage' and 'socialism' are such items, and the idea of women as proud and valuable human beings. 'Doublethink' is Orwell's term for the ability to hold contradictory thoughts in one's mind simultaneously without experiencing the contradiction, and by extension it refers to the ability to censor one's own thoughts and memories – as the women do in *Swastika Night* when they negate the evidence of their own senses in favour of the official ideology they have absorbed.

But Orwell cannot and does not provide a name for the key factor that explains the Party's preoccupation with domination, power, and violence: these are elements in the gender ideology that Burdekin labels the 'cult of masculinity'. By her ability to name this phenomenon and analyse its workings in the world, Burdekin gives her depiction of a totalitarian régime a critical dimension totally lacking in Orwell's novel. *Swastika Night* and *Nineteen Eighty-Four* are both primarily about *men* and their behaviour. Burdekin addresses this explicitly in her exposé of

the cult of masculinity. But Orwell, taking the male as the
model for the human species, seems to believe that he is
depicting innate characteristics of human beings. Thus the
despair one senses at the end of Orwell's novel and the hope
that still exists at the end of Burdekin's are linked to the degree
of awareness that each writer has of gender roles and power
politics as social constructs.[8] Orwell resolutely refuses,
throughout his works, to question a gender ideology that he
fully supports. Therefore, he can only, helplessly, attribute the
pursuit of power to 'human nature' itself. Burdekin, by
contrast, is able to see the preoccupation with power in the
context of a gender polarisation that can degenerate into the
world of *Swastika Night*, with its hypertrophied masculinity on
the one hand and its Reduction of women on the other. Tracing
the relationship between these two extremes, as well as their
continuity with the gender stereotypes of traditional 'civilised'
society, Burdekin makes a resounding critique of the dangers of
male supremacy.

Notes

1 See Andy Croft's important article 'Worlds Without End Foisted
  Upon the Future – Some Antecedents of *Nineteen Eighty-Four*' in
  Christopher Norris (ed.), *Inside the Myth: Orwell, Views from the Left*,
  London 1984, pp. 183-216. Croft considers *Swastika Night*
  'undoubtedly the most sophisticated and original of all the many
  anti-fascist dystopias of the late 1930s and 1940s'.
2 Deborah Kutenplon, 'The Connections: Militarism, Sex Roles and
  Christianity in *The Rebel Passion* and *Swastika Night*', unpublished
  paper (1984).
3 Susan Groag Bell and Karen M. Offen, *Women, the Family, and
  Freedom: The Debate in Documents*, Vol. II, 1880-1950, Stanford 1983,
  p. 383.
4 Ibid., pp. 377-8.
5 Jill Stephenson, *Women in Nazi Society*, New York 1975, pp. 41ff.
6 Cited in Clifford Kirkpatrick, *Germany: It's Women and Family Life*,
  Indianapolis 1938, p. 116.
7 Jane Caplan, 'Introduction to Female Sexuality in Fascist Ideology',
  Feminist Review, No. 1, p. 62.

8 For a more detailed discussion of *Swastika Night* and *Nineteen Eighty-Four*, see my 'Orwell's Despair, Burdekin's Hope: Gender and Power in Dystopia', *Women's Studies International Forum*, Vol. 7, No. 2, pp. 85-95, in which some of the comments in this introduction originally appear; and also my *Orwell Mystique: A Study of Male Ideology*, Amherst 1984, pp. 253-63.

Other works by Katharine Burdekin

Anna Colquhoun

The Reasonable Hope

The Burning Ring

Quiet Ways

The Children's Country (Kay Burdekin)

The Rebel Passion (Kay Burdekin)

The Devil, Poor Devil (Murray Constantine)

Proud Man (Murray Constantine)

Swastika Night (Murray Constantine)

Venus in Scorpio (Murray Constantine and Margaret Goldsmith)

CHAPTER ONE

THE Knight turned towards the Holy Hitler chapel which in the orientation of this church lay in the western arm of the Swastika, and with the customary loud impressive chords on the organ and a long roll on the sacred drums, the Creed began. Hermann was sitting in the Goebbels chapel in the northern arm, whence he could conveniently watch the handsome boy with the long fair silky hair, who had been singing the solos. He had to turn towards the west when the Knight turned. He could no longer see the boy except with a side-long glance, and though gazing at lovely youths in church was not even conventionally condemned, any position during the singing of the Creed except that of attention-eyes-front was sacrilegious. Hermann sang with the rest in a mighty and toneful roaring of male voices, but the words of the Creed made no impression on his ear or his brain. They were too familiar. He was not irreligious; the great yearly ceremony of the Quickening of the Blood, from which all but German Hitlerians were excluded, roused him to frenzy. But this, being only an ordinary monthly worship, was too homely and dull to excite any particular enthusiasm, especially if a man was annoyed about something else. Not once had he been able to catch the eye of the new solo singer, who with the face of a young Hero-Angel, so innocent, so smooth-skinned and rosy, combined a voice of unearthly purity and tone.

I believe, sang all the men and boys and the Knight in unison,

in God the Thunderer, who made this physical earth on which men march in their mortal bodies, and in His Heaven where all heroes are, and in His Son our Holy Adolf Hitler, the Only Man. Who was, not begotten, not born of a woman, but Exploded! (A terrific crash from the organ and the drums, and all right hands raised in the Salute acknowledged that tremendous miracle.)

From the Head of His Father, He the perfect, the untainted Man-Child, whom we, mortals and defiled in our birth and in our conception, must ever worship and praise. Heil Hitler.

Who in our need, in Germany's need, in the world's need ; for our sake, for Germany's sake, for the world's sake ; came down from the Mountain, the Holy Mountain, the German Mountain, the nameless one, to march before us as Man who is God, to lead us, to deliver us, in darkness then, in sin and chaos and impurity, ringed round by devils, by Lenin, by Stalin, by Roehm, by Karl Barth, the four arch-fiends, whose necks He set under His Holy Heel, grinding them into the dust. (With a savagery so familiar that it could hardly be called savagery all the male voices growled out the old words.)

Who, when our Salvation was accomplished, went into the Forest, the Holy Forest, the German Forest, the nameless one ; and was there reunited to His Father, God the Thunderer, so that we men, the mortals, the defiled at birth, could see His Face no more. (The music was minor, the voices piano and harmonised, with a sweet and telling effect after the long unison.)

And I believe that when all things are accomplished and the last heathen man is enlisted in His Holy Army, that Adolf Hitler our God will come again in martial glory to the sound of guns and aeroplanes, to the sound of the trumpets and drums.

And I believe in the Twin Arch-Heroes, Goering and Goebbels, who were found worthy even to be His Familiar Friends.

And I believe in pride, in courage, in violence, in brutality, in bloodshed, in ruthlessness, and all other soldierly and heroic virtues. Heil Hitler.

The Knight turned round again. Hermann turned round and sat down gratefully to resume his contemplation of the golden-haired chorister. He was a big boy to have still an unbroken voice. He must be above fourteen. But not a glint of golden down had yet appeared on his apple-cheeks. He had a wonderful voice. Good enough for a Munich church, yes, good enough for a church in the Holy City, where the Sacred Hangar was, and in it the Sacred Aeroplane towards which all the Swastika churches in Hitlerdom were oriented, so that the Hitler arm was in the direct line with the Aeroplane in Munich, even though thousands of miles lay between the Little Model in the Hitler chapel and the Thing Itself.

Hermann thought, " What's the boy doing here, then? On

a holiday, perhaps. He is not a Knight's son. Only a Nazi. I can make acquaintance with him without risk of a snub. Except that he is certain to be popular and rather spoilt."

The old Knight, after a few preliminary coughs (he was inclined to bronchitis), was now reading in his pleasant knightly German the fundamental immutable laws of Hitler Society. Hermann hardly listened. He knew them by heart, and had done since he was nine.

> As a woman is above a worm,
> So is a man above a woman.
> As a woman is above a worm,
> So is a worm above a Christian.

Here came the old boring warning about race defilement. " As if any man would ever *want* to," thought Hermann, listening with half an ear.

> So, my comrades, the lowest thing,
> The meanest, filthiest thing
> That crawls on the face of the earth
> Is a Christian woman.
> To touch her is the uttermost defilement
> For a German man.
> To speak to her only is a shame.
> They are all outcast, the man, the woman and the child.
> My sons, forget it not !
> On pain of death or torture
> Or being cut off from the blood. · Heil Hitler.

In his pleasant old husky voice the Knight delivered this very solemn warning, and went on to the other laws.

> As a man is above a woman,
> So is a Nazi above any foreign Hitlerian.
> As a Nazi is above a foreign Hitlerian,
> So is a Knight above a Nazi.
> As a Knight is above a Nazi,
> So is Der Fuehrer (whom may Hitler bless)
> Above all Knights,
> Even above the Inner Ring of Ten.
> And as Der Fuehrer is above all Knights,
> So is God, our Lord Hitler, above Der Fuehrer.

> *But of God the Thunderer and our Lord Hitler*
> *Neither is pre-eminent,*
> *Neither commands,*
> *Neither obeys.*
> *They are equal in this holy mystery.*
> *They are God.*
> *Heil Hitler.*

The Knight coughed, saluted the congregation, and lifting the sacred iron chain that no man not of knightly blood might move, he went up the Hitler arm and, turning sharp to the left, disappeared into the chapel. The worship was over.

The men and boys moved in an orderly drilled way out of the church. Hermann suddenly wished it was the custom to hurry and barge and jostle. That boy was going to get out long before he was. Then he'd have vanished, or be surrounded by other men. What hair! Down to his waist nearly. Hermann wanted to wind his hands in it and give a good tug, pulling the boy's head backwards. Not to hurt him much, just to make him mind.

Somebody near the door barked out an order:

"Come on, men. The church is wanted for the Women's Worship. Hurry. Don't dawdle there."

Hermann was very willing. He was not now in the least curious about the Women's Worship, when once every three months they were herded like cattle into the church, tiny girl-children, pregnant women, old crones, every female thing that could walk and stand, except a few who were left behind in the Women's Quarters to look after the infants in arms. The women were not allowed to go further into the church than the Goering and Goebbels arms; they were not allowed to enter even these less holy hero chapels; they had to stay jammed up in half the body of the Swastika, and they were not allowed to sit down. Even now two Nazis were busy clearing away the chairs the men had used. Women's rumps were even more defiling to holy places than their little feet, and they had to stand while the Knight exhorted them on humility, blind obedience and submission to men, reminding them of the Lord Hitler's supreme condescension in allowing them still to bear men's sons and have that amount of contact with the Holy Mystery of Maleness; while he threatened them with the most appalling penalties should they have any commerce with the male Untouchables, the Christian men, and with milder punishment should they, by word or weeping, or in any other way oppose that custom, that law so essential to Hitler Society, the Removal of the Man-child.

Hermann, when a light-hearted youth of thirteen, had once hidden in the church during a Women's Worship, impelled partly by curiosity, and partly by a wicked un-Nazi feeling of resentment at exclusion, even from something very low and contemptible. He would have been severely punished had he been caught; publicly shamed and beaten to unconsciousness. He was not caught, but the sinful act brought its own punishment. He was terrified. The mere sight of so many women all in a static herd and close by him—not just walking along the road from the Quarters to the church—with their small shaven ugly heads and ugly soft bulgy bodies dressed in feminine tight trousers and jackets—and oh, the pregnant women and the hideousness of them, and the skinny old crones with necks like moulting hens, and the loathsome little girls with running noses, and how they all cried! They wailed like puppies, like kittens, with thin shrill cries and sobs. Nothing human. Of course women have no souls and therefore are not human, but, Hermann thought afterwards, when his boyish terror had given way to a senseless boyish fury, they might *try* to sound like humans.

The small girls cried because they were frightened. They didn't like going to church. It was a quarterly agony which they forgot in the long weeks in between, and then it seized them again. They were terrified of the Knight, though that particular one was mild enough. He never bellowed and stormed at them as some Knights did in some churches. But he had such power over them—more than the Nazis to whom they must render such blind obedience. The Knight could order them to be beaten, to be killed. And then nearly always their mothers were crying at this quarterly worship, and that made the daughters worse. Perhaps one had just had her little boy taken away from her at the age of eighteen months, fetched by the Father in the usual ceremonious way (" Woman, where is my son? " " Here, Lord, here is your son, I, all unworthy, have borne——"), and where was he

A 2

now? his baby limbs in the hard hands of men, skilled men,
trained men, to wash him and feed him and tend him, and
bring him up to manhood. Of course women were not fit
to rear men-children, of course it was unseemly for a man to
be able to point to a woman and say " There is my mother "—
of course they must be taken away from us, and never see us
and forget us wholly. It's all as it should be, it is our Lord's
will, it is men's will, it is our will. But though a woman
might go through the whole ceremony of Removal dry-eyed
and not make a moan, and even utter the formal responses in
a steady voice, and though she might refrain from weeping
afterwards, yet, when she got into the church at the next
Women's Worship, she would be certain to break down. All
together, women fell into a sort of mass grief. One worked
on another, and a woman who had not suffered from a
Removal for several years would remember the old pain and
start a loud mourning like a recently bereaved animal. The
more the Knight told them not to, the harder would they weep.
Even the bellowers and stormers among the Knights could
not stop women crying at their worship. Nothing could stop
them, short of killing them all.

The Knight came out from the Hitler chapel and stood
watching the women and girls being driven in by a Nazi.
Already the sniffles were beginning; already some of the
younger children, at the mere sight of him, before he opened
his mouth, set up loud cries of terror. With perception
clouded by traditional fear, they could not see that his face
was benign and rather noble, with the possible cruelty of his
large hooked nose offset by a large calm forehead and sane
gentle eyes. They could not see that with this face and his
nearly white hair and beard he looked handsome rather than
martial in his sky-blue tunic with the silver swastikas on the
collar, in his black full breeches, with his Knight's cloak,
black lined with blue, shaking gracefully back from his
shoulders.

All the women in, the Nazi went out, banged the big
door behind him, and locked it according to the custom.
The crash of the door caused more loud yells. A woman
burst into deep low sobbing. The Knight remembered
a saying attributed to the Lord Hitler: " Germans, harden
your hearts. Harden your hearts against everything, but

above all against women's tears. A woman has no soul and therefore can have no sorrow. Her tears are a sham and a deceit."

The Knight pinched his lip under his moustache, looking at his congregation and thinking, "I think someone else must have said that. Poor cattle, there comes more and more for you to cry for."

For the Knight knew, what the women themselves did not know, that all over Germany, all over the Holy German Empire in this year of the Lord Hitler 720, more and more and more boys were being born. It had been a gradual loss of balance, of course, but now it was causing acute uneasiness. The end of all things was not accomplished. There were millions of Japanese heathens unconverted, and millions of the Japanese subject races who had not yet had much chance to see the light. And yet, if women were to stop reproducing themselves, how could Hitlerdom continue to exist? It seemed as if, after hundreds of years of the really whole-hearted subjection natural under a religion which was entirely male, the worship of a man who had no mother, the *Only Man*, the women had finally lost heart. They wouldn't be born now. There might be a physical reason. But no one could find out what it was. This particular old Knight, who knew a good deal, more than those of the Inner Ring, more than der Fuehrer himself—this old mild-faced German grey-beard, sunk in a depth of irreligious cynicism that since the death of his three sons was now known only to himself, looked at his women worshippers with a most unmanly un-German feeling of pity.

"It's all wrong," he thought. "There are things men can't do, not to go on for long in the same rigid way. Not for five hundred years without any change or relief. Poor cattle. Poor ugly feeble bodies. Nothing but boys. Women's only reason for existence, to bear boys and nurse them to eighteen months. But if women cease to exist *themselves*? The world will be rid of an intolerable ugliness."

For the Knight knew, what no other man knew, and what no woman ever dreamed of in the most fantastic efforts of her small and cloudy imagination, that women had once been as beautiful and desirable as boys, and that they had once been *loved*. What blasphemy, he thought, curling his lips a little. To love a woman, to the German mind, would be equal to loving a worm, or a Christian. Women like these. Hairless, with naked shaven scalps, the wretched ill-balance of their feminine forms outlined by their tight bifurcated clothes—that horrible meek bowed way they had of walking and standing, head low, stomach out, buttocks bulging behind—no grace, no beauty, no uprightness, all those were male qualities. If a woman dared to stand like a man she would be beaten.

"I wonder," thought the old Knight, "that we didn't make them walk on all fours all the time, and have each baby-girl's brain extracted at the age of six months. Well, they've beaten us. They've destroyed us by doing what we told them, and now unless the Thunderer can throw the whole mass of Germans out of his head we're coming to an inglorious end." With this blasphemy, a crowning one, the Knight finished his private meditation.

"Women, be quiet," he began, frowning at them as a matter of form. "Do not disturb the sacred air of this holy male place with your feminine squeakings and wailings. What have you to cry for? Are you not blessed above all female animals in being allowed to be the mothers of *men*?"

He paused. In dreary little scattered whispers came the formal response: "Yes, Lord. Yes, Lord. We are blessed." But a renewed burst of weeping followed as the women wondered where were the men they had borne. He is twelve now—he is twenty-five and Rudi twenty-one—if Hans is still alive he's seventy this summer, with a white beard like the Knight. But this last thought was in the mind of a very old and incredibly repulsive hag, far too old to cry.

The Knight went on with his homily. It was always of necessity much the same. There were so few things one could talk to women about. They had hardly more understanding than a really intelligent dog, and, besides, nearly everything was too sacred for them to hear. Anything that had to do with men's lives was banned, and naturally it was impossible to read to them, out of the Hitler Bible, the stories of the heroic deeds of the Lord and His friends. Such matters, even at long distance and second-hand, were far too holy to be spoken of into unclean ears. The most important thing was to get it firmly fixed in the heads of the

younger women that they must not mind being raped.
Naturally the Knight did not call it this, there was no such
crime as rape except in connection with children under age.
And this, as the Knight knew, was less, far less for the sake
of the little girls than for the sake of the race. Very young
girls if just adolescent might bear puny babies as the result
of rape. Over sixteen, women's bodies were well-grown and
womanly, that danger was past, and as rape implies will and
choice and a spirit of rejection on the part of women, there
could be no such crime.

" It is not for you to say, ' I shall have this man or that
man,' " he told them, " or ' I am not ready ' or ' It is not
convenient ', or to put any womanish whim in opposition to a
man's will. It is for a man to say, if he wishes, ' This is my
woman till I am tired of her.' If then another man wants
her, still she is not to oppose him; he is a man; for a woman
to oppose any man (except a Christian) on any point is
blasphemous and most supremely wicked."

The Knight coughed, and made a pause, an impressive
one, to allow this to sink in.

" She may tell the man who temporarily owns her about
what has happened, and there her responsibility ends. The
rest is Men's Business, not on any account to be meddled with
by females. And for you girls," he rolled his mild eye towards
the sixteen- and seventeen-year-olds, " be submissive and
humble and rejoice to do man's will, for whatever you may
think in your empty brains at moments, it is *always* your will
too, and be fruitful and bear strong daughters."

The women instantly stopped crying, except three or four
who were not even half listening. They all gaped at him.
The shock of being told to bear strong daughters was equal to
a half-stunning blow on each little shaven bristly head.
They couldn't believe their ears. The Knight couldn't
believe his, either. He had been used for so many years to
thinking one thing and saying another; his whole life was such
a complicated pattern of secrecy and deceit, that he could not
credit himself with at last making such a crashing mistake.
It was true that it was vital women should bear more daughters,
true that every German of the literate knightly class had nightmare dreams of the extinction of the sacred race, but it was a
truth that most not be spoken freely, above all not spoken to

the women themselves. All they knew was that in their
particular Women's Quarters was born a remarkable number
of young males, but not that the condition was general. If
they once knew that the *Knights*, and even der Fuehrer, wanted
girl-children to be born in large quantities; that every fresh
statistical paper with its terribly disproportionate male births
caused groanings and anxieties and endless secret conferences
—if the women once realised all this, what could stop them
developing a small thin thread of self-respect? If a woman
could rejoice publicly in the birth of a girl, Hitlerdom would
start to crumble. Some did, he knew, rejoice secretly, for
the girls at least could not be taken away from them, but
these were only the more shrinking, the more cowardly, the
more animal-motherly kind of women. For, even where all
were shrinking, cowardly and animal, yet some managed to
shrink more than others and fail even in the little unnatural
and human feeling allowed them, the leave to be so passionately proud of a male child, that not even the pain of losing
him outweighed it. But whatever women might think and
feel in private, in public there was no rejoicing whatever at the
birth of a female. It was a disgraceful event, a calamitous
accident which might of course happen to any woman but did
not happen to the best women, and as for a woman who had
nothing but daughters, she was only one half step higher than
that lifelong hopeless useless burden on Hitler Society, the
woman who bore no children at all. " Yet actually," thought
the Knight, pinching his moustache and stroking his nearly
white beard, and looking mildly down at his stunned flock,
" a woman who had ten daughters and wasted no time whatever on sons would be, at this juncture, a howling success."
Meanwhile he had made a howling error. " It's age," he
thought; " I'm losing grip. One can walk on ledges at
twenty, where one would fall over at seventy." But he was in
no hurry to cover up his error with words. He knew silence
is alarming to women. So he was silent, looking at them,
and they went on gaping. But at last they began to shuffle
uncomfortably.

" Something is troubling you? " he asked them, as politely
as if they had been men, or even Knights. His courteous
manner terrified them. They shrank away from him like a
wind-blown field of corn.

" No, Lord, no," they whispered. One, a little bolder, or possibly more hysterically frightened than the rest, gasped out, " Lord, we thought you said——"

" What did you think I said? " asked the Knight, still in that very polite way.

All but one woman knew then that they had misheard. They had actually thought, with appalling and yet quite typical feminine stupidity, that he had told them to bear strong daughters. It was all a dreadful blasphemous mistake. He had, of course, said " Sons ". " *Sohnen.*" The word was like the deep tolling of an enormous bell. The Knight was thinking it hard, vigorously, like the man pulling on the bell-rope. The women felt so deeply guilty that they even blushed, all but one. They recommenced crying. All was as it had been before. The Knight coughed, and resumed his discourse. But afterwards, when he had thankfully dismissed them, and signalled with a little bell for the Nazi outside to unlock the door and let them out and drive them back to their cage, there was a certain amount of astonishingly bright chatter.

" Shut up," said the Nazi gruffly. This waiting on the Women's Worship was a tedious and humiliating duty. He kicked at one or two of them as if they had been tiresome puppies, not savagely, just irritably. The women scuttled out of his way and were quiet for a moment, but presently they began again : " How *could* we have thought—did you? I did, but of course it wasn't—*I* didn't, I don't know what you're talking about—but I did *think* he said—yes, well—oh, how could anyone *think* such a thing? "

But old Marta, hobbling very slowly on two sticks, said, " He told you you were to bear strong daughters."

Perhaps she was so old she was no longer a woman at all, and therefore out of reach of all womanly feelings of shame and humility. She was not free, but perhaps by mere age had passed out of reach of psychic subjection. She was not a man, no, but not a woman either, something more like an old incredibly ugly tree. Not human, but not female. At any rate the Knight's hypnotism had rebounded from her. But all the other women despised her. Ugly as they were they could see she was uglier. A revolting dirty old woman, speaking an awful toothless German—she *said* she had had sons—a hundred years ago—but no one knew.

" He never said that—*never*. We only thought it. He said
we were to have *sons*. Of course. Sons. *Sons*. Marta, do
you hear? "

" I'm not deaf," said Marta. It was a fact, she had every
unpleasant attribute of old age except deafness—and senility.
" He said you were to bear daughters—*strong* daughters."

" It's a lie. Why *should* he say such a thing? "

" I don't know. It doesn't matter. That was what he
said."

They jeered at her and left her to hobble along by herself,
quite convinced and completely uninterested : as convinced
of the Knight's words as she was that the hard thing that
occasionally poked her in the back was the herding Nazi's
thick cane, and as uninterested as she was in his stick or in
him or in anything in the world except food (of which she got
very little) and the faint memory of Hans, her first child. The
Knight would have found himself in a certain amount of
sympathy with her, had he been in psychic contact. Marta's
cynicism was as deep, no, far deeper than his own, though
arrived at in an entirely different way.

CHAPTER TWO

HERMANN got out of the church at last, but the golden-haired
singing-boy was gone. Plenty of men were loitering ; the
women were being formed up at the Women's Gate of the
enclosure which surrounded the church ; there were numerous
lads and youths hanging about, but that particular one was
nowhere to be seen. Hermann started to walk very quickly
down the path which led to the Men's Gate, for already groups
of men and youths were crossing the big village parade-
ground outside the church enclosure, when he saw something
that made him wholly forget his purpose. A man, with his
hands in his breeches pockets, was standing on (right on with
both feet) the beautiful level clipped lawn which filled the
church enclosure. The man was idly gazing at the huddle of
women being pushed into some sort of order by their shepherd.

He was brown-haired and not very large. Hermann's heart bounded with a shock of joy. Brown curly hair, brown beard, grey eyes, standing on the grass, hands in pockets, quiet, aloof—it must be he!

" Alfred! " he cried.

The Englishman, for such was this nonchalant person who stood so firmly where he was not supposed to set his boots, turned round. He smiled in a very pleased way, and yet his greeting was undemonstrative. He did not even withdraw his hands from his pockets.

" Hullo, Hermann! " he said. " Is this your village, then? What luck! "

" Ja, ja! " said Hermann, longing to throw his arms round the older man's shoulders, but restrained, as he always had been, by something reserved in Alfred's manner, or in his character. Hermann never knew which it was.

" Well, well," said Alfred, at last holding out his hand. " Heil Hitler, Hermann."

Hermann hastily saluted and grasped the hand. He did not notice that Alfred had failed to salute. It would not have upset him if he had noticed. Englishmen were funny, informal, queer people altogether. And yet Hermann's two years in England when he had done his military training with the permanent army of occupation had been the happiest of his short life. At least, after he had met Alfred, a man of thirty then, a ground mechanic in one of the huge aerodromes on Salisbury Plain. Alfred was an interesting person to have for a friend. He was a technician and therefore had been allowed to learn to read. Hermann could not read, as when his military training should be finished he was going back to the land-work in Germany that had been his boyhood's labour. He never thought this extraordinary, that an Englishman should be able to read and that he, a Nazi, should be illiterate. It was part of the general plan, the Holy Plan of life in the German Empire. There were not enough Germans of suitable abilities to supply technicians for the whole Empire; some of the subject races must be taught to read. And they had nothing much to read but their technical books and the Hitler Bible. News was always broadcast. One didn't miss anything by not being able to read. But it was Alfred's type of mind that made him interesting to

Hermann, the contented rustic. Alfred was urban, quick-witted, a machine-man skilled and rejoicing in his skill; Hermann was slow-brained and bucolic, half-skilled, strong and rejoicing in his strength. In the army he had often pined for the land, and it was the more surprising that for Alfred's sake he had so often pined for the army in Germany.

"How's the farm-work going?" Alfred asked, when Hermann had done shaking his hand. "You look bigger than ever, mein Junker."

"*Get off the grass there !*" roared a harsh voice.

Hermann leaped, and Alfred walked.

"Bigger than ever," repeated Alfred, looking up at his young friend. "A fine German. You like the land as well as you did as a lad?"

"Oh, yes, yes," said Hermann slowly in English. "I like *that*. Do come on. Let's get away from all these people."

"You there!" said the bull's bellower, now on top of them. "What's your name? No, not you, Hermann. What's *your* name?"

"Alfred, E.W. 10762, English technician on pilgrimage to the Holy Places in Germany," said Alfred, holding himself a little more stiffly before this Nazi in authority, but still in a far from soldierly manner.

"Ach, Englander," said the Nazi, nodding in a sort of disgusted comprehension. "Let's see your pass, then," he added, in a milder manner.

Alfred showed it.

"All right. Remember now you're in Germany that when it says 'Keep off the Grass', that *exactly* is what it means. The grass round our churches wasn't put there for herds of Englishmen to gallop over. Verstehen?"

"Ja, Herr Unter-offizier."

"Heil Hitler!" said the Nazi, and saluted.

This time Alfred saluted in return.

"Let me see, you must be twenty-five now, Hermann," he went on as if there had been no interruption.

Hermann did not answer. So many memories were half painfully filling his mind—Alfred was so exactly the same—his curly short hair which would not grow even to touch his shoulders, his quiet level grey eyes, his nonchalant manner—all things Hermann had never really expected to see again, though they had sometimes joked about Alfred coming on pilgrimage—and there had never been any German to take Alfred's place. Hermann frowned savagely and bit his lip. Alfred glanced at him and took his arm.

"All you Germans are so emotional," he murmured.

And Hermann, who had just heard the Knight declaim the Laws of Society, which put him, Hermann, as far above Alfred as a man is above a woman, muttered in broken German, "I never thought I should—see you again. It's only now I realise how lonely I've been—since."

"Let's go for a walk," suggested Alfred. "Or have you got to go back to work? I'd forgotten the name of your village and your number, and couldn't remember anything but the district, Hohenlinden. But I should have dug you up somewhere."

"I needn't go back till this evening," said Hermann, recovering himself. "Have you got any food with you?"

"Yes, in my sack. I left it by the wall over there."

"Is there enough for me, too? You ought to have taken your sack into the porch."

They were talking now as they used to, each in his own language, understanding, but not straining themselves to form foreign words.

"What, in *Germany*?" asked Alfred, raising his eyebrows. "Common thieves in a German church enclosure?"

"Ach, boys, you know. It's there all right."

"But, Hermann, are you very hungry? Shall we go back to your farm and get some more for you? Your government, though paternal, and I've nothing to complain of, doesn't allow for luxuries, or more than one man's food."

"If *you* don't mind, ' nearly nowt ' is enough for me," said Hermann, laughing delightedly as he put the sack on his own broad shoulders. "Do you remember the man you called the Tyke? Everything was nearly nowt. And why was he called the Tyke? What is Tyke? I've forgotten everything."

"A generic name for Yorkshiremen. Well now, Hermann, don't tell me you've forgotten *my* generic name. I shall be upset."

"Ach, nein, nein!" cried Hermann. "Du bist der Moonraecher!"

"That's right, the man who rakes der Mond out of die

Pond. But why? But why, I don't know. That's one of the things I'd *like* to know. Those old names. Hermann, let's go and bathe. It's very hot."

" We'll go in the woods. I know a lovely pool. I've been there sometimes at night, Alfred, and if any Wiltshire men had been there they'd have set to raking as fast as we do in the Knight's garden when he's in a hurry for something to be sown and has given us no notice. It's all open, the pool. The moon shines right in. But I was always by myself. Alfred, are you really glad to see me? " Hermann said uncertainly, a little wistfully.

" Very glad," said Alfred seriously. But still Hermann felt something reserved in Alfred's manner, and on their walk to the woods he was silent and withdrawn.

" A queer people," the young German thought, after he had given up trying to make Alfred talk. " No one really understands them, and yet plenty of Germans like them." He knew that of all the numerous foreign stations where the Knights had to put in administrative and religious service, the English ones were the most generally popular. A Knight was only supposed to be absent from Germany for seven years. After that he governed a German district for two or three years, then he might be sent abroad again. There were plenty of Knights who having served once in England would pull all possible wires to get sent there again. This Anglophile feeling was not encouraged, but nothing seemed to damp it down. Of course some Germans hated the English, and never forgot that to them belonged the disgrace of being the last rebels against the might and holiness of the German Empire. There had been, a hundred years before, an English, Scottish and Welsh rebellion, a hopeless affair, sporadic and unorganised and very easily crushed by the Knights and the army of occupation. After it, by order from Berlin, one-tenth of the male population had been coldly executed. The permanent army of occupation had been enlarged (though the former one had proved amply big enough to deal with men who had no artillery and no aeroplanes) and the number of Knights had been increased, giving each Knight a smaller district. Since then there had been no trouble. But the English had remained just as queer as ever, sloppy and casual and yet likeable. He had once overheard a Knight say that they were fundamentally irreligious, and that that was what was the matter. They were conventional enough in their treatment of women and Christians; their women (and probably their Christians) were exactly like any others. But —Hermann suddenly caught himself wishing that Alfred was a German. Not because he would or might then be able to see more of him. His emotions had received a clarification owing to the shock of suddenly meeting his friend, and he now knew what he certainly never had *known* before, that he admired Alfred more than any other man in the world. " I look up to him," he thought uncomfortably, " as if he were a Knight. I do. I can't help it. I ought to be able to help it. Because he's not even a Nazi, not even my equal, only an Englishman. So I'm as high above him as a man's above a woman. That is absurd. Yes, yes, it is utterly absurd. *It's not true !* " At this first wholly conscious break in his racial-superiority feeling Hermann was shocked and at the same time excited. There was a thrill in the mental acceptance of what he had always felt, that Alfred was not only older and more experienced than himself, but a higher type of man. That his Englishness made no difference. Of course, Hermann thought, trying to excuse his treachery to Germany, Alfred is a *special* Englishman. They're not all like him. But he knew this was no excuse at all. You couldn't admit exceptions in the divine doctrine of race and class superiority. It must be in the Holy Blood. The blood of Germans or of Knights. If *all* Knights, all the numerous descendants of the original three thousand Teutonic Knights consecrated by Hitler, were not superior by *birth*—if there could be exceptions among Nazis, raising one here, one there, to a level with the Knights, why then a Knight *as* a Knight might not be superior at all. And he must be, *all* must be, or Society would crack. Hermann had pondered so deeply and with such painful unaccustomed logic that he felt a whirling in his head. He turned to watch Alfred walking, grave and aloof, at his side. They never could walk in step. Alfred was so much shorter. Sometimes Hermann would deliberately shorten his stride for a little way until it got too tiring, but Alfred would never try to lengthen his by a quarter of an inch. He didn't mind being out of step. It was a typical English untidiness. Hermann was overcome by a wave

of emotion in which love, irritation, fear and a wild sort of
spiritual excitement all mingled. He felt as if anything might
happen at any moment. He had forgotten the interesting
chorister as if he had never existed. And Alfred, apparently,
had forgotten him.

"Alfred!" Hermann suddenly yelled in his ear, "if you
don't take some notice of me I'll knock you down!"

Alfred started slightly.

"Ja, Herr Nazi," he said disagreeably.

Hermann turned and left him, making away back down the
path along which they had come. Alfred ran after him,
grinning, and caught him by the arm.

"Come, come," he said, "I will talk presently. Don't be
angry. But you are a Nazi, you know."

"It's the way you say things," grumbled Hermann, still
flushed with anger. But he allowed himself to be turned
round.

"Germans shouting at me always has some kind of bad
effect," said Alfred apologetically. "Either my leg muscles
go wrong and won't act or I let things drop."

"And what happens when an Englishman shouts at you?"
asked Hermann.

"I blow him away. Hermann, have you any sons?"

This was such an unexpected question that Hermann gaped.
Then he said, "No."

"I have three now," Alfred said. "I had two when you
were in England. Now I have another. But they're
very young. One's older. One is seventeen. Why
haven't you got any? Have you had bad luck and had
girls?"

"No. I can't stick women."

"But as you are a Nazi, if you haven't had any children
at all by the time you're thirty you'll be punished. It's only
the subject races who are allowed to omit begetting children
if they like."

"I've got five years yet."

"But you ought to have come round to a normal attitude
towards women at twenty-five. Don't leave it too long,
Hermann. You may find yourself in difficulties."

"I can't stand them!" said Hermann violently. "Oh,
for Hitler's sake don't let's talk about women!"

" All right. But I'm glad I'm a normal man. I've got a use for my sons. Women are neither here nor there."

"They're too much there," said Hermann, misunderstanding the English idiom.

" Oh, well, never mind," said Alfred, and he fell silent again.

But when they had bathed and frugally fed, and were lying in delicious ease in the shade of a huge tree listening to the sound of water falling, Alfred suddenly said, " Hermann, I am going to destroy your Empire."

Hermann chuckled sleepily. A stupid thoroughly English joke in Alfred's quiet rather deep voice was better than anything really funny from anyone else.

" How? "

" The way the acorn made this big oak."

" It was probably planted as a sapling. All this piece of the forest was planted."

" Well, like one of the oaks in the Holy Forest, the German Forest, the nameless one."

" Have you been there yet? "

" As far as I was allowed to go in, being only an Englishman. It's a lovely place. So hushed and silent. A man could think there."

" A man is supposed not to think, but to feel there. I suppose you'll be *thinking* when you see the Sacred Aeroplane. Or have you already been to Munich? "

" Not yet. Can't you get leave for a day and come with me? "

" I might. I'll try, anyhow. Our Knight, the Knight of Hohenlinden, is our own Knight."

" How do you mean? "

" He's our own family Knight, von Hess. He owns all the land and villages and towns for miles round and he lives in *our* village."

" Oh. That sounds hopeful for leave. Well, I shall still be thinking when I see the Aeroplane, partly technically no doubt, though I'm acquainted with the design of the thing from the Little Models, and as far as I can make out there's been no real change in aeroplanes at all. But I shall be thinking partly about the destruction of the German Empire. Of course I am only the acorn, you understand. The oak will grow out of me. I myself shall be dead."

Hermann grew faintly uneasy. He *must* be joking—and yet—" You'll be dead very soon if you blaspheme in public."

" You needn't wait for that. You can report my blasphemy."

Hermann rose on his elbow.

" Alfred—you—you aren't at all *serious*, are you? "

" Deadly."

Hermann knew it was so.

" But then you've gone mad."

" Well, have I? Look at me, Hermann. Am I mad? "

" No, you're not. But then—all this—why do you tell *me* about it? "

" You'd never betray me, surely? "

Hermann said earnestly, " I could, Alfred. You're making a mistake. I might kill myself afterwards, but I can see even you killed, for Germany."

" Well, that's very right and proper, but actually it doesn't matter. You can go and say I've said such and such, but even though I'm an Englishman you'd have to produce a wee bit of proof to have me killed. I should only perhaps have my pilgrimage cut short and be sent out of the country. I'm going to tell you all about it."

" But *why*? "

" The time has come for me to know how the thing strikes a decent ordinary lad of a Nazi. Do you, first of all, understand why an Englishman should want to destroy this Empire? "

" Not if he believes in Hitler. There's no reason at all."

" Perhaps some Englishmen don't believe in Hitler."

" *Alfred!* Don't you—you can't mean *you* don't believe Hitler is God? "

" Lots of us don't," said Alfred calmly.

" Then the Knight was right," muttered Hermann.

" What Knight? "

" Von Eckhardt. He said Englishmen were fundamentally irreligious. He didn't seem to mind."

." Perhaps he knew it didn't matter—from his point of view. Von Eckhardt was always more on the administrative than the religious side, wasn't he? Armed rebellion against Germany will always fail."

" I'm glad you realise that," said Hermann with some relief.

" Because," Alfred went on, " the Germans are the greatest exponents of violence the world has ever seen—except, of course, the Japanese. They are the greatest soldiers—except, of course, the Japanese."

" We're just as good as the Japanese! "

" Then why don't you go and eat them up and convert the last heathen by force? The peace between the German Empire and the Japanese Empire has deafened everyone for more than seventy years."

" We're still getting ready."

" Well, I won't tease you. I don't want to have to fight the Japanese myself, because I've got something better to do, and I hope if there is another war that Germany will win."

" You are loyal to a certain extent, then? "

" My calculations are based on German character, not Japanese character. I don't know what that is—though it's probably got the same rotten spot! "

" Rotten spot! "

" Rotten spot, I said. Now, Hermann, are you interested, or are you just going to be violent? If you want to fight me, say so; if you want to listen, be quiet."

" I *ought* to fight you. Beat you, rather. You can't *fight* me, you're too small. Oh, all right, go on."

" It seems to me it must have been like this," Alfred said, turning over on his back again. " After the Twenty Years War, when Germany finally came out on top of everyone, the beaten nations must have been all damned tired. They'd tried to meet force with force and had failed, and were ashamed of themselves and humiliated, but worst of all completely exhausted. So, as it is a much better thing to be beaten by God than by a company of men, however large and well armed, they all started to believe in Hitler, the divine representation of victorious force. It was suggestion working on exhaustion. Here and there, as the nations started to recover a little, there were rebellions, armed rebellions (or quarter-armed rebellions), always failures, but the nations went on being Hitlerians. They were rebelling against their Knights or the army of occupation (most of them), not against the

German *idea*. They were too tired still to do without religion, and they still wanted the appeasement of being beaten by God, not only by men."

" But you weren't *civilised* then," said Hermann. " You were only savage tribes, you and the French and the Russians and everyone. There is no shame in being beaten by civilised men."

" Well, there is a great darkness about our origins," Alfred admitted. " It's true we don't know quite what we were, say a hundred years before Hitler. But I believe we once had a great Empire ourselves."

" Nonsense. How could savages have had a great Empire? You didn't know how to build ships or anything."

" Why do so many of the Japanese subject races speak English? The Americans, the Canadians, the Australians, and some of your subject races too, the South Africans? "

" They were just English tribes, but all disconnected."

" I'm not sure of that, and I've got reasons for doubting other things you tell us, too. But never mind that. It's what *I* am now that matters, not what they were *then*. I am a man who knows that while armed rebellion against Germany must fail, there is another rebellion that *must succeed*."

" What?" asked Hermann breathlessly.

" The rebellion of disbelief. Your Empire is held together on the mind side of it by Hitlerism. If that goes, if people no longer believe Hitler is God, you have nothing left *but* armed force. And that can do nothing but kill people. You can't make them *re-believe* if they don't. And in the end, however many people you kill, so long as there are some to carry on, the scepticism will grow. And you can't ever kill all the unbelievers, because, though you can search a man's pockets or his house, you can't search his mind. You can never spot all the unbelievers. The scepticism will grow because it's a lively thing, full of growth, like an acorn. It will attack Germany in the end, Germans themselves will get sceptical about Hitler, and then your Empire will rot from within."

" It couldn't," said Hermann, under his breath.

" If Hitler is not God, there is no *reason* why Germany should rule Europe and Africa and part of Asia for ever. And if Hitler is God, why can't you beat the Japanese? "

" We shall. There's plenty of time."

" You've wasted your time. You had about five hundred years or so to beat the Japanese in, and all you've done is to have a series of completely indecisive wars. Air raids, and pinching bits of Russia away from each other and then losing them again. You've never looked like *really* beating the Japanese. And now you've hardly any time left at all. When I say no time, I mean you've only got about another seventy years. And you've had seventy years of peace."

" Well, and suppose your madman's dream was a reality, and the Empire did—did break up, would you like it any better to be ruled by the Japanese? "

" We shouldn't be. We don't believe the Japanese Emperor is God, you see. You can't rule men permanently except through an idea. *Men*, I say. You can rule boys— and perhaps Germans. Perhaps not. But as no German ever has been or ever can be a man it's difficult to say."

Hermann leaped to his feet, but, as Alfred did not, he didn't quite know what to do. Suddenly, beside himself with racial fury and a strange unacknowledged personal terror, he kicked Alfred savagely. Alfred then did get up, but slowly and calmly. His control was perfect.

" Come on then," he said, taking off his coat. " If violence it must be. If I don't go for your eyes, will you leave mine alone? "

Hermann, red and trembling, looked at Alfred's eyes and knew with despair and perplexity that the fight was off before it had started. The mere thought of gouging out Alfred's grey eyes made him sick, though he had watched without a tremor many a fight that had ended that way. And apart from eyes, he couldn't touch him, not even to give him a light flick. He had kicked him, but now he could do nothing more.

" Sit down again, Junker," Alfred said kindly.

" Why can't you leave me alone? " Hermann said thickly. He sat down, however.

" It's important," Alfred said. " Promise not to kick me again, or I shall have to sit the other way round. Two on the same place might lame me."

" Why do you say no German is a man? " asked Hermann, unable to attend to anything but the insult.

" They don't get a chance to be. It's the system. Look here, Hermann, what *is* a man? A being of pride, courage, violence, brutality, ruthlessness, *you* say. But all those are characteristics of a male animal in heat. A man must be something more, surely? "

" He's able to think, and control the violence and direct it."

" So can a woman. If a woman wants to beat her daughter and the girl's up a tree she doesn't run round and round roaring like a mad cow, she waits till the girl comes down for food. So there's nothing particularly manly in that."

" A man's able to die for an idea."

" So is a boy of twelve. Any German boy would go into the army at twelve and go to a war if he were allowed to. No, Hermann, you'll never get what a man is because you don't know. I mean the real difference there is that divides men from beasts, women and boys. A man is a mentally independent creature who thinks for himself and believes in himself, and who knows that no other creature that walks on the earth is superior to himself in anything *he can't alter*."

" What? I don't understand."

" It's difficult, I know. But I mean I might meet an Englishman who was more independent and spiritually stronger than I was. Then I should say, ' There's a better man *now*.' And I'd make myself as good. But you see a Knight coming along and you say, ' That man's a better man *by blood*. He's superior, whatever I do, for ever and ever; I must salute him, now and always.' Another time you see an Englishman coming along, and you say, ' That man's inferior by blood, I must kick him.' " Alfred looked round with a grin.

" Anyone would have. And I didn't kick you for being an Englishman but for being insulting. And it's no good talking, for Blood is a Mystery, and a thing no non-German can understand. It's ours."

" Yes, and as long as Blood is a Mystery none of you will ever be men. You hide behind the Blood because you don't really like yourselves, and you don't like yourselves because you can't be men. If even some of you were men the rest would like themselves better. But it's a circle. If there's going to be Blood there'll be no men—never. And while you're still boys, you'll think that violence and brutality and physical courage make the whole of a man. You'll have no souls, only bodies. Only men have souls."

" Do you mean, Alfred——" Hermann spoke calmly because under Alfred's influence he really was trying to think, and he found he could not be shocked or angry and have anything left in his mind to think with. " Do you mean that you believe in *softness*? In gentleness and mercy and love and all those foul things? "

" Don't you believe in love, Hermann? "

" Oh, friendship," Hermann muttered, turning his eyes away from Alfred's quizzical glance. " Yes. That's different. But *gentleness*? "

" It must be right because Hitler said it was wrong," said Alfred promptly. " I reject the Creed entirely as I reject Hitler and the Hitler Book and Germany and the Empire."

" And God the Thunderer? "

" I reject the idea that God lives in Germany or likes Germans better than anyone else. God, God, oh, well, I don't know. I mean I don't know *always*. But *men-gods*, no. No man is any more the son of God than I am. If Hitler is God, so am I. But it's obviously more sensible to think neither of us is. More modest too."

" What do you think Hitler was, then? Or do you deny His existence altogether? "

" I expect he was a great German soldier and a very brave man. But he wasn't independent, because he had to hide behind Blood. He wasn't *a man*. Now if you read the Hitler Book carefully—oh, I forgot, you can't read. Well, there's very little of it that's Hitler's own sayings."

" How do you know? "

" I've had nothing much to read except technical books and the Hitler Book, and I'm fond of reading, so I've studied it very carefully with a mind unclouded by belief in it as divine. It's quite obvious that a lot of the teaching has been put in later. And even all the Blood stuff, you don't know whether that was Hitler himself or a lot of people. It's an unsatisfactory book. Something wrong somewhere. It leaves you empty."

" Because you're not a German, not even a Hitlerian."

" Maybe. I wish," said Alfred, with a sigh of immense

desire, " that I had some other books to compare it with.
There's so much darkness. So much mistiness. Nothing but
legends. England's packed with legends. I expect all the
subject countries are. It gives the people something to talk
about besides their work or their wages or the misdoings of
their Knight. There's a legend about a great English Leader
called Alfred, who had a huge statue in Winchester (you
remember Winchester? we went there once together); it
was as big as the hill behind, and he had a knife and a
shrapnel helmet, but he wasn't only a soldier, because he
wrote a book. Now if I had *that* to compare with Hitler's!
And a man called Alfred is to deliver England from the
Germans."

" So your dream is based on your name? "

" I'm not only going to deliver *England* from the Germans.
I'm going to deliver the world," said the junior Alfred with a
perfectly modest air.

" What about the Japanese? "

" Oh, —— the Japanese. When the German idea cracks
we can all get together and crack their idea. It's only the
same one a bit different, I feel sure. But don't you see, young
Hermann, I'm not so mad as I seem, nor so vain. I am the
repository, the place where a very old human idea is kept.
There must be some idea that's the opposite of the German
one, and it must be as old as the German idea. Do you see?
And so it's not *me* that is going to do all this, but the idea.
And if you kill me it'll go to other men."

" And where's it been these last seven hundred years? "

" It's been homeless perhaps, for want of a place. Or
resting. Or hibernating. But never, never dead. What is
seven hundred years? Why, one man can live through a
hundred. Seven hundred years is no time at all. History is
only just begun—again."

" What do you mean? " Hermann asked.

" I don't know," Alfred said. " I'm going to sleep. Wake
me up when we ought to be going somewhere or doing
something."

CHAPTER THREE

HERMANN did not go to sleep. He watched Alfred. The slow even rise and fall of his chest, an occasional flicker in his eyelids, the relaxed look of his strong rather small hands, all gave the young man an intense quiet pleasure. He did not think at first at all of what Alfred had been saying. It was so wonderful to have him there, the real bodily Alfred, instead of the weakening gradually blurring mind-image he had held through the last five years. But after a while, a long while, feeling gave place to thinking, and his thinking was no longer bound by the hard heavy grip Alfred's mind had on his, and on his whole personality. When Alfred was awake Hermann thought almost like an individual, though a very weak individual with a longing for personal dependency, but now Alfred was alseep with his heavy influence relaxed Hermann started to think like a Nazi. A dreadful idea took shape in his mind. Alfred was a self-confessed traitor, an infidel, a blasphemer, an enemy more vicious and inveterate than any Japanese. And more dangerous. If there really was in England a collection of men of the same way of thinking—of course they could never *do* anything—but things might happen—Hermann didn't know what—and then Alfred must be the head of this ridiculous but horrible mind-conspiracy against Germany, against Hitler—yes, there was no doubt he would be the Leader. For a few moments Hermann left off Nazi-thinking and went back to personal feeling. Oh, if only Alfred had been by some miracle born a German and of knightly class, how he, Hermann, would have adored to serve him, to be his slave, to set his body, his strong bones and willing hard muscles, between Knight Alfred and all harm—to die for him. . . . Hermann's phantasy faded in a heat of shame. Even to think of an Englishman being a Knight was a sin against the Blood. No, but Hermann's duty, his obvious German duty here and now, was to kill Alfred where he lay. To stop his brain, his mouth, his wicked treacherous heart with one swift stroke of his knife on which was inscribed *Blood and Honour*. Alfred's blood, steaming out over the old last year's oak leaves, puddling and soaking the sacred soil of

Germany, was the only thing that could save Hermann's
honour. If he betrayed him—but how betray a traitor?—
he might not be believed. Alfred's whole idea, unless heard
from his own lips, was too absurd. It was absurd, anyway,
but it had a dreadful *sound* of sense in Alfred's cool voice.
And in that same cool voice he would deny everything, and
simply state that this young Nazi was mad, and that his
insanity was patent in the extraordinary phantasies he had
managed to invent. And Alfred's record would be looked up
and found to be excellent. It must be because he had been
given a pilgrimage. No, that was no good, but if he *killed*
Alfred, then there was certainty. No German would hesitate
for a minute. No German would condemn him, knowing
all the facts. To stab a sleeping man, to stab one's own
friend, the man from whom Hermann had had nothing but
comfort and aid and kindness—but where the welfare of
Germany was concerned there was no friendship, no personal
love; no gratitude could exist in opposition. Had not that
lesson been driven into Hermann's childish mind ever since
he could understand speech? *Nothing is dishonourable, nothing
is forbidden, nothing is evil, if it is done for Germany and for Hitler's
sake.* Well then he must do it quickly before Alfred woke up.
Alfred's helplessness in sleep was inhibiting, but at any rate
he himself—his soul (but then he had no soul) was temporarily
absent. To kill Alfred awake—no, that would be impossible.
This he *might* do. But as Hermann drew the knife from the
sheath he knew he would fail in resolution. He could
take the knife out, he could read the holy German words on
it, he could remember his Oath taken at eighteen when he
entered the Army, he could watch the sun-splashes flickering
on the bright steel, he could imagine it dulled with blood,
his duty done, his oath fulfilled, his friend lying dead—but
he could not, he *could not* make his arm obey him to strike
downwards into Alfred's body. Personal love did still
exist, and Alfred even sleeping had still a stranglehold on
Hermann's will. So, he was a traitor, a bad German;
he was *soft*. Hermann put the knife away and sat in a
trance of shame.

Suddenly not far away a terrific clamour broke out: a
small boy screaming, madly, desperately, for help, another
boy laughing—"Noisy little devils," Hermann thought,

with half a mind to go and kick them for making such a row; a bit of hazing, he supposed—but then—*was* the hazed one a boy? There was something thin, a light shrill sound in the vigorous yells. It was a girl! Then they must be both Christian girls, for it was miles from any Women's Quarters. And why should one girl laugh and another scream? Was it possible that girls should bully each other as the noble sex did? Hermann was disgusted at the idea of Christians being so close to him, and had it not been for his deep repugnance, which amounted to a fear of women, he would have got up there and then to drive them off. Alfred slept on unmoved. The screams went on and on, there was a crashing of under-growth, the other girl, the older laughing one—Hermann jumped to his feet. *Was* that older one a girl? There was a queer timbre about the laugh and the occasional words, more like a boy whose voice is near breaking. A boy! Hermann hurled himself towards the sound with the impetuosity of a mad bull, and there in a little clearing he came upon the angel-faced golden-haired chorister making a determined attempt to rape a well-grown little girl of about twelve. The child had not reached the age of submission and was therefore within her rights in putting up a sturdy resistance. And as Hermann stood for an instant, watching them rolling and tumbling, clawing, kicking and biting, he caught sight of a large red cross on the breast of the little girl's jacket. So it was a Christian! Hermann's whole body filled with delicious thundering warming floods of rage. He loathed the boy for being even interested in girls—with his lovely face, his unmasculine immaturity—Hermann was physically jealous; he was shamed; he had not killed Alfred, but here was something at last that he could smash and tear and make bleed and utterly destroy. He reached the struggling young animals with two jumps and seizing the boy by his long yellow hair he pulled him off the girl with such force that his neck was nearly broken. He then picked him up and threw him with every ounce of strength in his body at the nearest tree trunk. The boy, perhaps unfortunately for himself, hit the tree with his shoulder, not with his head. The little Christian girl got up and ran away, clutching at her disordered garments. Her passage was almost noiseless; she vanished in the wood like a wild animal. The boy came staggering back towards

Hermann, not with any heroic intention of putting up a fight, but because he had not enough sense left to run away from him. He was used enough to rough treatment, but the wrench on his neck and the crash against the tree had been too much even for his hard young body. Hermann jumped at him again, and with his fists beat him into insensibility. He took special pleasure in spoiling his face. When the boy was lying unconscious at his feet he started to kick him, in the ribs, on the head, anywhere, and would most probably have left him, not unconscious, but dead, had not Alfred, who had at last awakened and come to the scene, intervened.

" Stop that, Hermann ! You'll kill him if you kick his head with those heavy boots. Well now, I thought I heard something."

Hermann had stopped on the word of command. He looked at Alfred. He was red-faced, sweating, wild-eyed, a grim sight. The boy was a grim sight too. His face was already so swollen as to be unrecognisable. Alfred picked up a lock of his hair.

" It's that boy who sang so well in church this morning. I know him by his hair. Hermann, you monster, you've pulled a lot of it out. He was such a pretty boy."

" He won't be again," Hermann growled, and spat on the ground.

Alfred was going over the body. " Not dead," he said. " Collar-bone broken, probably ribs, internal injuries perhaps. His skull doesn't seem to be *broken*.. He must have an iron head. What shall we do with him ? "

" Leave the —— lying till he rots ! " said Hermann viciously.

" What made you attack him ? "

" He was trying to rape a Christian girl. I wonder you didn't hear her scream."

" H'm. A Christian ? Well, of course it would be a Christian. I did hear something, but I think it was the boy moaning when I woke up. Well, let's get him back to the water and try chucking some on him."

" I won't touch him."

" Then I must take him myself."

Alfred arranged the boy's clothes decently and picked him up. But when he got him to the stream the cool water with which Alfred bathed his head did not bring him back to consciousness. He lay like a corpse except that he was warm, and still breathed.

" We shall have to carry him somewhere," said Alfred at last, looking up.

" To the lock-up in the village."

" Oh, don't be a fool. Whatever he did he'll have to go to hospital before he can be punished, or even tried. Come, get him on to my back if you won't help with the transport."

" I won't touch him," said Hermann again, with sullen obstinacy. " It's nothing to do with you. If I choose to leave him here it's my business. I tell you, he was trying to rape a Christian, and even if she'd been a German she was under age. It was quite a little girl."

" I suppose you aren't at all annoyed because the *boy* is under age? " asked Alfred sarcastically. " Because he's a pretty lad who ought only to be interested in *men*? "

" You can do what you like and go where you please, I'm going home! " Hermann said furiously. " Heil Hitler to you and good-bye."

" Heil a donkey! " said Alfred, rather annoyed. " I don't see why even a Nazi should be such a stupid savage as you are just now."

Here the boy created a diversion by trying to sit up. He fell back with a stifled moan, and out of the corner of one hideously swollen eye looked at Hermann.

" Do you feel better? " Alfred asked in German.

The boy painfully turned the bit of eye he could see with to Alfred.

" Yes," he whispered.

" Can you stand? "

" I might."

They got him to his feet, and this time Hermann did help, impelled by a very sober glance from Alfred. The boy made no sound except a little grunting, though the process of getting up must have been torture.

" Can you walk? " Alfred asked him.

" My legs are all right," whispered the boy through his swollen lips. " I expect I can."

Alfred made a pad from the spare clothes in his sack to

go under the boy's arm where the collar-bone was broken, and strapped the elbow with his belt. The strapping pressed on the boy's broken ribs. He gasped, but said nothing.

" Now, march, my lad," Alfred said, taking him by the comparatively sound arm. " We've got about two miles to walk to the main road unless we meet a cart."

The boy stopped to be sick, and after the intense pain of the vomiting had to lie down again for a little while. Then he was helped up, and walked along fairly well, supported by Alfred. He said nothing. Occasionally small grunts and sighs escaped him.

" German boys are marvellously tough," Alfred said in English to Hermann.

" This one'll need it," said Hermann grimly. " He's not through yet."

" You've got no witness," Alfred observed. " Christians aren't allowed to give evidence against Nazis. Or even against Englishmen."

" You're a witness."

" Indeed I'm not. I don't know there was a girl there at all except from you."

" He'll confess all right. If he doesn't I'll give him another lamming later on."

" In violence, in brutality, in bloodshed, in ruthlessness, *and* in self-deceit," murmured Alfred. " You don't care if a child is raped. You don't really care if a Nazi has to do with a Christian. You beat this boy because you were jealous and angry. The boy is foul because he's been brought up to be so, but he has been at least honest. You're not even that."

" He's not brought up to defile himself with Christians."

" Christians," said Alfred, " are quite curiously decent people. I know some. *English* Christians."

" *What ?* " cried Hermann. " You know some ? "

" Yes. Wouldn't you like me to repeat that in German ? You'd have a witness then."

But the boy was not in a condition to take notice of what was said, even had the conversation been in a language he could understand. He took each step with agony, gritting together what remained of his teeth to prevent groans coming out of his mouth. He did not even find it odd that his aid on this *via dolorosa* should be the arm of a foreigner. He was in a nightmare of pain and shame, not shame for his cruelty and lust, but at being caught by a Nazi with a Christian. His life it seemed was finished, and yet only that morning he had been so happy singing (he adored singing) amid the admiring glances of men. Now all men would despise him, no one would love him any more, and his voice must very soon break, anyway. Meanwhile, set one foot somehow in front of the other, and don't groan. He managed two miles, in a condition in which a man of a less physically resolute race could hardly have moved a hundred yards, and then fainted. But now they were nearly out of the woods and the main road to the village was only a little way off. Alfred put the boy on his back and carried him to the road. They waited till a lorry came along.

" Where's he to go to? " asked the driver, looking at the mangled body with the usual brutal indifference to pain or bloody sights.

" The hospital or his own home," said Alfred.

" The lock-up," said Hermann. " Oh, dump him down anywhere in the village. We don't know where the little brute lives. He was in church there this morning and that's all I know about him."

" Sling him up on the sacks, then. I can't have him in front here, flopping all over the place."

The lorry was a small one-man affair with a tiny little driving-cab, and no place for a second man. Alfred and Hermann put the boy up on the hard full sacks, and the driver went on. After it had started Alfred let out a yell: "Stop! Stop!" But the driver either didn't hear or wouldn't stop.

" What's the matter? " Hermann asked, in sulky curiosity.

" Why, I ought to have gone with him."

" You're very tender of that boy," Hermann said suspiciously. " You saw him in church too, of course."

" Oh, shut up, Hermann. I'm sick of you. The lad's got my only jersey under his arm and my only belt round his elbow. When I get to the village he may have been sent on to a hospital in Munich or anywhere. I can't afford to lose clothes. *I'm* not a Knight owning land and factories and ships and private aeroplanes. *I* don't dress in blue silk and eat turkey every day. A jersey *is* a jersey to me."

" Oh, I suppose you think a Knight ought not to own land now? "

" I think a lot of things," said Alfred, walking very fast towards the village. " But I'm not going to talk about them now. Are you coming back to the village? Where do you live? "

" I work on the Knight's home farm. I've got a room by myself now over the cowshed. You can share it for to-night if you like."

The invitation was not gracefully given, but Alfred accepted it in a friendly way. They went on to the village in silence. When they got to the parade-ground they saw a small knot of men gathered in one corner. The lorry was not there, but all the men were looking at something on the ground.

" That's our boy probably," said Alfred. " Why don't they take him into a house? "

They went over to the group and found that it was indeed centred round the wounded boy. He was in a bad state, still faint or in a coma, and bleeding a little from the mouth.

" I thought so," Alfred muttered in English. " You've smashed him up inside somewhere. We oughtn't to have made him walk."

But he knew he couldn't suggest anything to this knot of Germans. They'd soon shut up the foreigner if he started taking charge. A Nazi official arrived presently, not hurrying exactly, but walking at a brisk pace. One of the other men had fetched him.

" Who's this lad? " he asked.

" No one knows. He's a stranger."

Someone said, " The Knight must know him if no one else does."

" Why? "

" Because he sang the solos in church this morning and the Knight arranges the music himself."

" It's a hospital case," said the Nazi official, who had experience of the results of brutal fights. " Fritz, go and telephone for the ambulance. How did he get like this? "

" I beat him," said Hermann.

" Why? "

" I'd prefer to make a deposition before the Knight's Marshal."

" Against him, this boy? "

" Yes."

" Oh, very well. But why you're such a bloody fool you can't see what a boy of that age can stand and what he can't —ach, Herr Marshal! "—this apologetically to a man who had been trying to attract his attention.

" Our highly born the Knight Friedrich von Hess desires you to tell me why this group is gathered here."

It was the Knight's Marshal, a Nazi of great importance in the district, who had happened to be passing across the parade-ground with his noble master. A little way off the Knight stood, too dignified to come nearer in case the group had something trivial as its centre. He stood leaning on his black staff of office with a graceful and somewhat bored air. His black cloak hung in soft folds from his shoulders; his head was bare, and his still thick silvery-gleaming hair lifted and fell a little in the gentle wind.

" Tell the noble one, please, that it's a boy hurt. We don't know who he is."

The Marshal carried back the message, and the Knight then approached. All the men were standing at attention. They saluted, and stood more stiffly than before, if that were possible.

" At ease," said the Knight absently. He looked down at the boy, not greatly interested at first, then with close scrutiny.

" Hitler! " he said. " What savage barbarian has done this? "

" I did, my lord," said Hermann, a note of hurt surprise in his voice.

" This is the very best soprano singer from the church of the Holy Teutonic Knights in Munich, and you've broken his chest by the look of it. Well, his voice would have cracked soon, I suppose. Have you sent for the ambulance, Adalbert? "

" Yes, sir. I've sent a man to telephone."

" He must have every care, though I don't suppose it'll be any good. He'll either die or his voice will break before he recovers. It was unfortunate he came here for his holiday. Hermann, fall out."

Hermann went a little way from the other men and stood again at attention. Alfred went with him.

" You were not ordered to fall out," said the Knight.

" No, my lord, but—— "

" Then go back."

Alfred had to go.

" Hermann, why did you beat that boy half to death? " the Knight asked.

" Sir, may I make a deposition before the Marshal? "

" Against the boy? "

" Yes, sir."

The Knight meditated.

" I think you had better come and make it before me," he said. " Who is that Englishman? "

" A man I knew when I was on military service in England, sir."

" Was he there when this whatever it is you've been doing took place? "

" Yes, sir. Partly."

" Then bring him to the Court-room with you, at once."

Hermann saluted and went back to Alfred.

" Come on," he said savagely.

" Where to? "

" We've got to go to the Court-room and *he* wants to hear the deposition."

" Naturally. If the boy recovers and hasn't lost his voice they'll try to hush it up. Chief singer at the H.T.K. in Munich! You have cracked a nightingale. I've heard them on the broadcasts in England. What a pity you aren't a musical German."

" He can't hush it up," said Hermann sulkily. " That boy will never sing there again however much he lives and his voice doesn't break. I'm glad."

" Is your Knight a religious or a musical Knight? "

" Of course he's religious. Oh, yes, he's very musical too. But he can't prevent me making any deposition. And when he hears what it is of course he won't want to," added Hermann defiantly.

" It'll be interesting to see. But I've been aware for a

long time that the one crack in your armoured tank blood-ethic, the only place you get any air through, is music."

Hermann used an impolite word meaning nonsense.

They waited in the Court-room for a little while, standing rigidly to attention, until the Knight came in and sat down in the big raised seat. He took a pen in his hand and put a piece of paper before him.

" The oath, Hermann."

Hermann swore on all sorts of sacred things and his honour as a German to speak the truth, then blurted out, " Sir, he was trying to rape a Christian girl of not more than thirteen."

The Knight's pen dropped from his hand. He picked it up again and said calmly, " Any witness besides you? "

" Well——" Hermann began, and looked at Alfred.

" Take the foreigner's oath," the Knight said.

Alfred began the oath in English, then stopped.

" I understand English. Go on."

The oath taken, the Knight asked, " Were you a witness of the attempted rape? "

" No, sir."

" Then what were you a witness of? "

" Hermann beating the boy, sir."

" Could you swear a rape had been attempted? "

" No, sir. It looked as if it might have been."

" Could you swear it was a Christian girl? "

" I never heard or saw the girl at all."

The Knight sighed gently.

" Well, Hermann, I will take your deposition, but if the boy does not admit it there is no proof."

" He can't deny it, sir," said Hermann sullenly.

" Are you certain it was a Christian girl? " the Knight asked sharply.

" It couldn't have been any other kind of girl, sir. It was at least three miles from any Women's Quarters."

" That does not make certainty. The younger girls do sometimes escape from the Women's Quarters and wander about until they are found and taken back. They get lost and wander for miles. And twelve or thirteen years old is just the right age. They are old enough then to be out of the direct personal control of their mothers and not old enough to

B 2

have much idea of their duties as women.   It might very well
have been a German girl."

" My lord, I saw her cross! " said Hermann with deep
indignation tempered in its expression by his respect for the
Knight.

" What were they doing—rolling, tumbling, fighting on the
ground? " asked the Knight, unmoved.

" They were on the ground."

" And you can swear you saw a cross, not a red handkerchief
in her jacket pocket or something of that kind? "

" I do swear it."

" It's a serious accusation," said the Knight.   " Almost the
gravest that one German can bring against another.   There
must be *absolute certainty*.   Do you still want to make a deposition against this boy? "

Hermann hesitated.   The will of the Knight was now set in
its full force against the young Nazi's.   He even began for the
first time to be a shade doubtful of what he *had* seen.   *Could* it
have been anything but a red cross on the child's jacket?
No, he was sure it was a cross.   But the Knight didn't want
the deposition made.   Everything in Hermann told him to
give up this impossible conflict and yield to the man who was
his born superior, his officer, and the lord of the land.   How
could a mere Hermann run counter to the known wishes of a
von Hess?   No vindictiveness or wish to justify oneself could
help now.   Such motives had faded away under the Knight's
steady gaze.   But something not in Hermann, but in Alfred,
who stood close beside him, almost touching his shoulder,
made him pull himself together on the very edge of surrender.
Alfred was telling him to stand firm and hold on to the
truth.

" Yes, my lord," said Hermann, very respectfully.   " I
will make the deposition."

Von Hess, a man of remarkable psychic sensitiveness, was
keenly interested in his defeat.   He felt no anger and not the
smallest twinge of humiliation, he was too sure of his own
standing, both public and personal, for that.   For a Nazi to set
his will against the known wishes of a Knight was shocking, but
this particular nobleman was incapable of being shocked,
owing to the secret and really shocking fact that he happened,
in face of his supposed religion and the whole plan of his

society, to be an individual. But how had that ordinary clod Hermann—perhaps not quite *ordinary*, the Knight had noticed one or two queer little things about him, a glumness, a permanent overcast look—but a clod, for all that—how had he managed to develop such a stubborn power of resistance? The Knight's gaze shifted quickly from Hermann to Alfred. The men's eyes met fair and square. Alfred knew he was doing what ought to be a very risky thing, comparable perhaps with trying to stare down a vicious bull, but he also was very sensitive. He didn't know why, but he had a strong feeling that the risk was not what it seemed to be. He offered the Knight a long cool stare which said, as plainly as if he had spoken aloud, " Hermann is right, you are wrong." The Knight understood. It was not really Hermann who was opposing him; it was this stocky Englishman. The clod was animated by a fiery and most resolute spirit emanating from the unholy flesh and bones of a foreigner.

" Here," thought he, electrically thrilled, " in the face of all probability, is a man. Or is it in face of? Is it not rather exactly what one would expect, if one hadn't been foolish? Men among the English, or among the French, or among the Russians, but not, no of course not, among the Germans. This is a most fascinating thing that has happened." He meditated on it in unbroken placid silence, his eyes still in harmonious contact with Alfred's. The mysterious flow, strengthening and ebbing and strengthening again, of two human spirits which are joined in sympathy, passed between him and the Englishman, excluding Hermann entirely, leaving him in a dark uneasiness. Alfred thought, " This old German knows something. Something that has nothing to do with Blood and Mystery and Knightliness. By God, this old German knows everything. Ah, lucky stars that shine on me !"

When the silence had lasted for what seemed to Hermann like an hour, he shuffled his feet on the floor. It was a most undisciplined thing to do, as he was still standing at attention, but he could not help it. His feet shuffled themselves; it was like a sneeze or a cough, involuntary and uncontrollable. The Knight turned his head.

" Stand at ease," he said.

Hermann relaxed. Alfred was relaxed already. Soldierly poses did not suit exciting mental adventures.

" Well now, the deposition," the Knight said. " Speak slowly, Hermann."

The Knight wrote down the accusation unhurriedly in his beautiful rather small hand, making the German letters meticulously as if he loved them. It was a work of craft, as clear and even as printing, yet individual and full of character.

" You are no good as a witness," he said to Alfred, when he had it all down. " You *know* nothing at all, except that Hermann beat the boy, which will not be in dispute."

He then wrote down that this deposition of Hermann Ericsohn, H.D.B.H. 7285, against Rudolf Wilhelmsohn —— (space left for the boy's official number, which the Knight did not know), had been made before him, Freidrich von Hess zu Hohenlinden, Knight of the Holy German Empire, day, year. Heil Hitler. He blotted the last sheet and laid down the pen. He folded the deposition and put it in his inside tunic pocket.

" Hermann, attention! Salute. Right about. Half left. March."

Hermann strode out, his boots clumping on the wooden floor. The Knight fastened up his tunic and gazed pleasantly at Alfred.

" I should like to know more about you, Alfred Alfredson, E.W. 10762, English technician, of Bulfort Aerodrome, Salisbury Plain, province of England." The Knight prided himself a little on his memory. Alfred had rattled off all these details when he took the foreigner's oath. The Knight had forgotten none. " First, what are you doing here? Pilgrimage, I suppose."

" Yes, sir. I have been graciously permitted by the Holy German authority in England to travel in Germany for the space of one month to see the Holy Places. Heil Hitler. My expenses are all paid. Shall I show the highly-born my pass? "

" No. How long have you been here? "

" In Germany, a fortnight. In this place, nearly twenty-four hours."

" Have you been to Munich yet? "

" No, sir."

" The Command in England must think well of you to allow you a pilgrimage of a month at your age."

" The highly-born is very gracious. ' I suppose they do."

The Knight thought, " And what a set of blind donkeys and outrageous idiots they must be. He may be the world's best technician, but he's an unsatisfactory subject or I'll swallow my ring."

" What kind of technician are you? "

" A ground mechanic for aeroplanes of any kind."

" You understand aeroplanes thoroughly? "

" Yes, sir. I believe I could make one that would get up if I had the tools and the time."

" Have you been up? "

" On test, sir, many times."

Alfred's eyes gleamed, literally. He had a trick of opening them much wider when any thought excited him, so that more light struck on the balls. The Knight saw this gleam and a dangerous look that went with it. " Naturally," he thought, " it must annoy *a man* past everything not to be allowed to acquire certain skills he knows he could acquire. And yet if we let the dangerous men learn to control the dangerous weapons of war where should we be? This fellow goes up on test, and he watches the pilot like a hawk, no smallest movement escapes him. I'd bet anything he thinks he can fly an aeroplane, and *knows* he can fly a gyroplane." A very fantastic idea was forming in the Knight's mind. He thought of his secret, of his three dead sons, and of his father, who had all shared it with him at different times. All dead. No one now. And this man thought he could fly an aeroplane, but he probably couldn't. Leave it to God—if the Thunderer strikes—then good. If not, if there is no God, or if God doesn't mind, or if God is with that old von Hess, then——

When the Knight spoke again his manner had changed. It was the manner of an old man to a younger one of his own class.

" I know Salisbury and Bulfort and all that part well," he said. " A long time ago I was the Knight of Southampton. I used often to go up to the Knights' Table in Salisbury, and sometimes to Bulfort. For some reason they had much better food, and they were very pleasant men, the Army Knights. The Army always seems to get the best food, do what one will."

Alfred said nothing, but he thought, " *I* wouldn't mind

dining in the Knights' Table at Southampton for a change.
I could do without Salisbury with an effort."

"And it was at Bulfort," the Knight went on, "that you
met that young labourer, Hermann?"

"Yes, sir."

"And you made friends with him?"

"Yes, sir."

"He was a most fortunate youth," murmured the Knight.

"Sir?" said Alfred, not quite sure if he had heard correctly.
He might have, but it was as well to make sure.

The Knight smiled.

"*I* know that it might be fortunate for a German youth to
make friends with a certain kind of Englishman. Other
people might see in it nothing but a condescension, caused by
lust or idle curiosity or some other rather trivial motive, on
the part of the German. But when I say he was a fortunate
youth, perhaps I ought to add that he may be of all German
youths the most deplorably unlucky. From one point of view,
yes. Alfred, why is Hermann always so gloomy? He works
on my own home farm, I am interested in the farm, I see him
often. He's a good worker, he likes his work, and yet he's
always overcast. Why is that?"

"I haven't seen him for five years, sir."

"You mean he could go on missing you for five years?"

"I don't know, sir. Perhaps in a vague way he could. He
was pleased to see me."

"I can understand that. And you are aware of nothing in
your friendship in England—nothing you told him, talked to
him about—that might affect him adversely, even for five
years?"

Alfred said very formally, "Most gracious highly-born,
how could anything that an Englishman could talk of affect a
Nazi adversely for five minutes?"

"Come, Alfred, there's no need for all this fencing, you
know really there is not. I give you my Knightly word of
honour——" The Knight stopped. Alfred was looking at
him in a strange way, almost pitying.

"Sir, where there is no liberty of judgment, there is no
honour. '*Nothing is dishonourable*.' If there is in a man's
mind *any* overriding idea, *any* faith, that can make all things
honourable, however cruel, however treacherous, however

untrue, in that man's soul there can be no honour. Your word as a Teutonic Knight is no good to me."

The Knight received this bitter stroke in silence, apparently unmoved. For an instant the old hot imperious blood leapt up, thundering in his ears, trying to drown with its clamour the small cold sound of this truth which he now for the first time heard from the lips of another man. *He* had always known it. But that he should hear it said! That the shame should be spoken aloud! And yet, what was he, Friedrich von Hess, for, if it were not to hold on to the truth? Hundreds of thousands of Knights, but only one von Hess. Literally now, only one. Suppose he did give way to the old savage desire to sweep away what *opposed*, what was alien, what dared to criticise; suppose he had Alfred beaten or tortured or murdered, the truth would still be where it was before, in his own mind. " If no one knows it at all," he thought, " if he is dead and I am dead, it will still be there. If there were no men at all, still certain things about men's behaviour would be *true*. ' Where there's no liberty of judgment there is no honour.' "

The Knight unclasped his hands. He laid them side by side on the desk before him and looked down at them. He took off his Knight's ring and put it on the desk. It lay between the two men like a great red shining eye.

" I give you my word as a man," he said.

Alfred was moved and embarrassed.

" O.K., sir," he said. " Well, I never talked to Hermann at all about anything *I* think. He was only a boy, anyway."

The Knight sighed, and put his ring on again. His finger felt cold and forlorn without it, and until he died he must wear it. Curious to think that that might be so soon.

" I think," Alfred suggested, " that Hermann is partly in trouble because he can't do with women. But that was nothing to do with me."

" It's not uncommon. Well, I have decided," said the Knight, getting up. " We'd better do it now."

" Do what, sir? " Alfred asked in astonishment.

" You think, don't you, that you can fly an aeroplane? "

" I'm sure I can," said Alfred stoutly, still quite at sea.

" Then you shall now take me up and fly over Munich and come back, and if we land safely I may have some more to say to you."

Alfred's first reaction was one of wild excitement and pleasure. To fly! To have the thing, the lovely sensitive thing, in his own mechanical control and under his own personal will! Dangerous? Horribly, really. Death in an hour or two, a few minutes, what did it matter? To fly ! To fly! Then he sobbered down a little, his eyes grew thoughtful.

" Would you tell me why, sir? " he said.

" I can't. I can tell you that I am to a small, but deplorable extent still superstitious. This is a superstitious fancy."

" We *may* be killed," Alfred reminded him.

" I think it more likely than not. But you will perhaps admit that though a Teutonic Knight has no honour, yet he is not likely to be panickily afraid of death."

" Of course. But why do you want to kill *me*? I'm longing for the chance to fly, it isn't that, and I'm not afraid. But why? "

" A dangerous man will be dead if you're killed."

" I see. And if you are? "

" Another, still more dangerous. But now I shall tell you no more. When we get to the hangar I shall send off the men on duty and say I'm going to fly the machine myself."

Alfred shivered with excitement.

" Suppose I turn us over before we get up? And we're just bumped or something and can't get out? They'll find me in the pilot's seat. An Englishman."

" We must take some risks."

" Is it a gyroplane? "

" No. A two-seater Hertz. Just a baby private plane."

Alfred whistled.

" Do you still think you can do it? "

" I'm sure I can. Only I mean I'd have been surer still about *landing* a gyroplane. Why is it that when gyroplanes are just as efficient and far safer, we always go on making so many of the old-fashioned planes? "

" There's no danger left anywhere in the Empire except in learning to fly old-fashioned planes or in flying them in bad weather. If there is no danger there are no brave men. We must have a hero's military funeral now and then. I shall get one. You, however, will not."

"I'll do without that," said Alfred, laughing delightedly. "Whatever your motives are, sir, I thank you very much. You don't know what it means to a man not to be ever allowed to fly when he spends his whole life with aeroplane engines."

"Those in power can always give curious and unexpected pleasures," said the Knight sardonically. "Now if I had you tortured for the open insult you offered me you'd feel aggrieved, but as I merely give you a good chance of being burnt to death you're very grateful. Now march."

On the walk to the hangar the Knight strode along in front, easy, graceful and very upright, while Alfred followed as suited his lowly status, ten yards behind. At the hangar the Knight's pilot on duty and two mechanics sprang to attention.

"I'm going to take the machine up myself," said von Hess, deigning no further explanation, though he had not piloted a machine for several years. "I may be back to-night, or I may not. All you men can go off duty. Dismiss."

They saluted and turned on their heels, walking smartly across the landing-ground.

"Who is going to start it for him?" a mechanic said.

"That fellow, I suppose."

"Who's he?"

"Don't know."

"Do you think the old Knight will be all right? He hasn't flown for ages."

"It's nothing to do with us. Obey orders, ask no questions. I hope he *will* be all right," added this correct Nazi anxiously. "He can get up, but is he in good enough form to come down again? I think in spite of what he said we'd better hang about near the ground. What d'you think, Willi?"

Willi nodded.

"Yes. He may find he doesn't like being up and come down at once and land all of a sprawl and we might be able to pull him out or something. We'll stay about for a bit."

Alfred meanwhile had run the machine out of the hangar. It was very light and easy to handle. The Knight got into the back seat.

" Shall I start it, sir ? "

" One minute. If we come down not too well but not too badly try to get us out of our seats."

" Yes, sir."

" And just get into your seat a second and see that these speaking-tubes are working all right. When we're up I'll give you the course and you can fly on the compass. It'll be easier for you than looking for landmarks, and you don't know the country. There, did you hear that ? I whispered it."

" Yes," Alfred whispered back down his tube.

He got out again, started the engine and tuned up. Everything was in perfect order, of course. A lovely thing, Alfred crooned, listening to the roar of the engine with an expert's perfectly trained ear. Not too new. Ah, you little beauty, you're mine, mine! Now then! He was not very much astonished that he got the aeroplane into the air without mishap. That was easy really. And yet when he stopped bumping and knew he was in the air he couldn't repress a bellow of triumph.

" Hoorah ! " he yelled. " We're up, sir ! "

" Go how you like," said the Knight's voice through the speaking-tube, " until you're well up. Then I'll give you the course. Remember this isn't Salisbury Plain. It's hilly country and you must be well above it."

Alfred rose farther and then started to bank. The little aeroplane was very sensitive.

" It's too easy ! " Alfred shouted. " Oh, its gorgeous ! It's heaven ! "

" Get more height as quick as you can," was the Knight's reply to these boyish exclamations. " It'd be silly to hit a mountain when you're enjoying yourself so much."

Alfred went on up, as fast as he could make the machine climb. He was intoxicated. He wanted to get about a mile above Germany and then lay the course straight for England, and fly till he got there, and then hide the aeroplane in some secret place. And what should he do with the Knight? Kill him, kill him! Kill every Knight and every Nazi that dared to stop a man flying! Kill them all !

"That'll do now," said the Knight's voice, cutting through the roar of the engine. "Get on your course." He gave the course and Alfred managed to come round and keep fairly well on it. "You're a natural pilot, Alfred. I've hardly felt a lurch."

"Yes," thought Alfred, "I am a natural pilot, and half your clod-fisted Nazis are most unnatural ones." And to his dismay it seemed only a minute or so later that the Knight told him to look down. There below them lay the Holy City of Munich, quiet and white in the afternoon sun. Alfred would have liked to drop a bomb on it, particularly and specially on the Sacred Aeroplane.

"Some day," he thought viciously. "Smash it all up *somehow*!"

"Now go back," the Knight ordered. "Come round in a wide sweep and I'll give you the course again."

Alfred shouted very loudly down his tube.

"*I'm not going back!*"

"Don't roar like that," the Knight said. "These tubes have amplifiers and it makes nothing but a buzz if you shout. Speak quietly. What did you say?"

"I'm not going back!" repeated Alfred in a quieter but extremely vicious tone.

But the only answer from his passenger was a faint cynical laugh. Alfred flew straight on, but the Knight said nothing more, and Alfred began to feel ashamed of his childishness. He hadn't the faintest idea where he was going or how much petrol there was in the machine.

"Can I go on a bit farther before we go back?" he asked soon.

"Who can stop you? But you've been up long enough for the first time. Far longer than a new Nazi pilot would be allowed. There's a nerve strain even if you don't feel it. You've got to land yet. You're doing well, but don't forget that."

Alfred started to come round. The Knight gave him the course, and again Alfred seemed to have hardly any time to enjoy himself before the Knight said, "Now look down. Can you see the landing-ground, over there to half left? Now spiral down to it and try not to get too far away. Land with your nose towards the hangar,

that's right for the wind. Now I'm not going to say another
word."

Alfred came down rather well, and had the plane in nice
position for landing, when he became aware of a group of men
running over the ground towards the hangar. He went up
again.

" Afraid? " asked the Knight.

" Those blasted fools! " said Alfred breathlessly.

" They'll get out of the way. Now do it this time no matter
where they are."

" But the idiots are standing *still* now! " cried Alfred in
agony. " If they'd only keep on *running*! "

" They're wondering what on earth I'm doing. Don't
worry about them. Pretend they're not there."

Alfred circled again, came down, flattened out and rushing
over the heads of the mechanics landed far beyond them.
Bump—hop! Bump—hop! Bump, bump, bump, safely
down—now nothing can happen but a tip-over—oh, Hitler,
the hangar! He had left himself too little room for the run
up. It seemed as if the hangar was rushing at him with
enormous speed and mouth wide open to devour him. He
switched off and tried to turn the plane; nothing happened,
he ran straight on into the hangar and fetched up with a
splintering crash against the further concrete wall. He hit
his head on something and was half dazed, but he was aware
of the Knight's voice a long way off speaking out of the
deafening thick silence, " Get out, man. Quick."

He scrambled out, surprised to find all his bones whole.
Gradually his head cleared. The aeroplane was much
battered about the engine and propeller, but there was very
little human damage. The Knight was standing on his feet
holding a handkerchief to his nose and a hand to his left
ribs.

" Are you all right, sir? " Alfred asked, feeling his own
head.

" A bruise or so. You weren't really going very fast."

" What ploughboy work! " muttered Alfred, in disgust with
himself. " I've smashed the lovely little thing up. What
ingratitude! I'm so sorry, sir; it was rotten. But I believe
I'd have done it all right if it hadn't been for having to miss
those blasted fools."

" You should have gone at them as I told you. Then you'd
have had plenty of room."

The mechanics now came tearing in to see what had
happened. Their relief at seeing the Knight on his feet
outside the aeroplane was very great. They looked at him
sheepishly, for all of them had disobeyed his orders to go off
duty, and tried to control their noisy panting. The Knight's
dignity was in some rather miraculous manner unimpaired
by his bleeding nose. He waved his disengaged hand at the
huddled aeroplane.

" I've smashed that machine up," he said coolly. " I
don't think you can do much with it here. You'd better
get another one sent down at once from the works. Telephone.
And by the way, am I forgetting things or did I tell you men
to go off duty? "

" Yes, highly-born, you did," they said, standing like a
little row of stone statues.

" Then what did you come back on to the ground
for? "

No one replied. Then Wilhelm, the pilot, an oldish man,
said, " My lord, we were wondering—we were afraid——"
He stuck, not liking to say that they all thought he might
make a mess of his landing, and possibly set the machine on
fire. The Knight looked at them over the top of his handkerchief until they couldn't help wishing that he had hit his
head just hard enough to be unaware of their disobedience,
then he swung round and walked out of the hangar, turning
his handkerchief to find an unreddened patch. In a few
steps he swung round again and called out sharply, " Alfred!
Have you a clean handkerchief? " Alfred jumped forward,
fumbling in his pockets. No, he hadn't one. There were
two in his sack, which was still in the lobby of the Court-
room.

" It doesn't matter," said the Knight. " It's stopping, I
think. Report to me to-morrow morning at ten o'clock at
my house."

" Yes, sir."

" Dismiss."

" Sir—may I say something? "

Von Hess took no notice of him but walked on about fifty
yards. Alfred followed a little doubtfully. He didn't know

whether the Knight was being genuinely official, or was only ignoring him because of the men in the hangar.

" Well, what is it? " The Knight had turned round and was waiting for him. No one could hear them now.

" Are you going to tell me to-morrow why you wanted me to take you for a flight? "

" Yes."

" Are you going to tell me anything else? "

" Yes."

" May I make a condition? "

" You can try."

" I want Hermann to hear it too."

" Why? "

" He has more right to hear it than I have. He must have more right."

" It isn't a question of rights, it is a question of mind and stability. Hermann hasn't much of either."

" I can make him stable."

" Can you? Can you make him hold his tongue until you say he can speak? If that time ever comes."

" Yes," said Alfred, as confidently as he had said he could fly.

" You don't know what you're letting him in for. Take him into a war, smash his limbs, pull his intestines out, blind him—he'd stand all that—but I don't know about this."

" I want him to believe something. He'd believe you."

The Knight thought for some time, drawing vague patterns on the grass with his long black stick.

" I agree," he said at last. " He shall be told. But truth is an intolerable burden even for a grown man. I shall be glad enough myself to throw it off."

" You're old, he's young. Some young German ought to take it from you."

" As you like, Alfred. It shall be as you wish. There may very well be physical danger in telling Hermann, but I expect you don't mind that."

" I've had to mind too many things in my life to mind anything *particularly*."

" Except not being allowed to fly? "

" Oh, well——" Alfred laughed. " I know that's rather childish really."

" When did you begin to mind things? "

" At sixteen I lost my faith."

" And you're now——? "

" Nearly thirty-six."

" Twenty years of seeking light in darkness and harmony in confusion. You get very tired of it sometimes, I expect."

" Yes."

" So that you'd like to die, just to be able to stop thinking? "

" Oh, occasionally one feels like that."

" Men are admirable sometimes.   Auf wiedersehen, Alfred."

Without a salute, or a Heil Hitler, and with a very pink nose and aching ribs, the old Knight took his way home.

CHAPTER FOUR

ALFRED limped back to the Court-house to collect his sack and stick. His head was aching and one knee was so severely bruised that he could only hobble, but he was gloriously happy. Now he had something that no one could ever take away from him, not if they tore him into little strips—he had flown. And there were other things too to make him content; at last some of the darkness was to be dispersed, some of his perplexities resolved; he was to *know* something instead of guessing, guessing until, strong and tenacious man though he was, he thought he must go mad. And yet, though he laughed at himself, with the intoxication of the air still upon him, he thought most of the flying.

At the Court-house the pious and blood-conscious Nazi on duty at the door was sullen and contemptuous of him.

" What do you want, Kerl? " he snapped, in mere average crossness as Alfred made to hobble past him into the entrance lobby.

" My sack and stick, please."

At the sound of Alfred's accent the Nazi's eyes brightened.

A dirty foreigner. Let him whistle for his sack and stick. The Nazi had only been on duty for half an hour; there were two hours yet to go before the Court-house would be locked for the night. He could while away a few minutes in pleasant conversation.

" And why did you leave your nice clean wholesome foreign lousy ——y sack and stick in our Court-house? "

Alfred was far too happy to take offence, even inwardly. Indeed he hardly heard what the Nazi said.

" The Knight told me to go with him at once."

" The Knight! " said the Nazi, aiming a swinging clout at Alfred's head. " 'The highly-born' from you, you scum."

Alfred ducked the blow with the neatness of incessant life-long practice. The sudden movement sent a sickening pain through his bruised knee. He winced a little and backed away from the Nazi, who laughed disagreeably.

" You yellow Britisher," he said. " Can't you stand up to a tap? All right, Lieblein, I won't hurt you, sweet little boy. I should have to go and wash my hands if I touched you, anyway."

" The highly-born called me to go with him at once, so I had to leave my sack and stick," Alfred explained again. " Please may I get them? "

" No."

" Could you let me have the stick? " asked Alfred, still politely. (He had flown, he was going to know things, what did this lout matter? As much as a rat or other unpleasant but individually powerless animal.) " I'm lame."

" Dear, dear, what a pity that is! I'm afraid you'll have to borrow the Knight's for the evening. I'm sure he'd be delighted to lend it to you."

Alfred burst out laughing, this amusing phantasy of the porter's was so near the truth. Probably old von Hess would lend him his staff if he could.

" *What's all this bloody row about?* " This interruption, an angry one, came from behind the Nazi, as the Knight's Marshal who had been busy inside the Court-room, came striding to the outer door. " This isn't a Boy's Nursery. Oh, it's you again! " he said as he saw Alfred. " What do you want? "

" My sack and stick, please, Herr Marshal. I had to leave them here because the highly-born the Knight wanted me to go with him at once."

" Then why the hell don't you get them without all this palaver? I'm perfectly aware you had to go with the Knight. I saw you come out of here."

Alfred said nothing more, but limped inside the entrance and collected his gear. He saluted the Marshal and grinned at the Nazi. " Heil Hitler! " he cried cheerfully. " Good night."

" Why didn't you let him get his things? " the Marshal asked severely.

" He's only a dirty foreigner, Herr Marshal," said the Nazi uneasily.

" Just because he's a foreigner you ought to have known that he couldn't have been in here at all without some serious reason. You be careful and let him alone. He's got some kind of business on with the Knight. You can't help having a face like a turnip-lantern, I dare say, but you can help opening it."

The Marshal banged back into the Court-room leaving the Nazi abashed.

Alfred found out the way to the Knight's home farm, which with his magnificent house was not far from the hangar and landing-ground. He wandered about the empty farmyard for a little till he found a man in the dairy. Alfred asked him the way to Hermann's room. This German was a cheerful person without any open contempt for foreigners. " Up over the cowshed," he said. " Through that door and you'll see some stairs. Supper will be in about three-quarters of an hour in the farmhouse dining-room. If you want to wash there's the pump."

" Can I have supper with you? " Alfred was surprised.

" Well, you're Hermann's English friend, aren't you? He said you'd be coming when the Knight had done with you. What did he want you for? "

" Oh, he talked about England. He used to be the Knight of a big port close to where I live. Oh, damn that boy! " Alfred had suddenly remembered that his jersey had gone careering off to some destination unknown to him, still under the sick boy's arm. Hermann would have no extra bedding, naturally, and the boards of the loft would be hard. However, it was not going to be cold. He stripped off his coat and shirt and had a refreshing swill under the pump. He combed his hair and beard and asked the friendly dairyman for a bit of rope or an old strap.

"My breeches won't stay up properly, and the boy's got my belt as well as my jersey."

"What boy?"

"You'd better ask Hermann about that. Thanks, that'll do fine. Will Hermann come up to the loft before supper?"

"There'll be a whistle for supper if he doesn't. Come straight into the house. It's all right, you know. You may be only an Englishman, but you're Hermann's friend on this farm. Be civil to the foreman, though. He's a small man with a very black beard."

Alfred thanked him. He went up to Hermann's room and lay down on the narrow hard pallet, relieved to rest his knee. Hermann had already made some preparation for his guest, as a pile of sacks was arranged in bed form in the least draughty corner of the loft, but Alfred thought there would be no harm in using the bed until his host came in. In spite of the aching of his knee he grew drowsy and presently was sound asleep.

He was roused by Hermann's laugh.

"What a fellow to sleep you are!" he said, looking down at his friend. Alfred blinked up at him.

"Is it supper time?"

"Nearly. I say, Kurt said you were very lame and couldn't walk without a stick. What's happened?"

"Oh, lots of things. But I think I'd better tell you afterwards. I'm glad you sleep out here by yourself and not in the house."

"I like it out here better," said Hermann. He had entirely recovered his temper, and his pleasure at finding Alfred in his own room, lying on his own bed, had given his face a temporary charming radiance. But now it clouded over into its usual dark unhappiness.

"That's the thing I like best. To be by myself and hear the cows underneath when they're in in the winter. They're out in the fields at night now. I should hate to sleep in the house. Have you got a headache?"

Alfred was feeling his head with his fingers and then shaking it as if he were rather doubtful about it.

" No, it's much better. But it was a fair crack."

" Have you been fighting? "

" I never fight unless I absolutely have to. There's the whistle, Hermann. Will it be a good supper? "

" Better than you've had many a time, I dare say. Potatoes, soup and bread, and as many apples as you like to eat. Of course you'd have done better still to have stayed and dined with the Knight."

" I could eat three Knights' Tables clean out," said Alfred, hitching up his borrowed strap. " They say that if a man sleeps a lot he doesn't need to eat so much, but I sleep all night and any time I'm at a loose end in the day as well, and I'm always hungry."

" It's soft to have all you want to eat always," said the young Nazi piously.

" Then the Knights must be jelly-fish."

" Ach, that's different. They *could* live hard if—if there was any occasion."

Alfred enjoyed his supper exceedingly. There was enough food, and good of its plain kind, and all the Germans were very pleasant to him, including the foreman, who was attracted by something in his stocky tough-looking figure and his darkish grey eyes. This man actually gave him and Hermann a little cheap cigar each to smoke after their supper. Hermann could not often afford to smoke, while Alfred's expenses on his pilgrimage were calculated to a pfennig, to keep him in good health, but to include no luxuries whatever. He had had no money saved. There was no incentive for Nazis or subject races to save money. They would be kept by the State when they were ill or too old to work, their sons were kept by the State, and women were kept by the State too, fairly well kept while immature and at child-bearing age. After that they were on a very narrow margin. Old Marta would have thought herself in the men's heaven if she could have eaten the meal Alfred had just finished. But Alfred had never worried about the ordinary day-to-day sufferings of women. He hardly realised they did suffer. It was natural and right that they should always have less food than men, and when they could bear no children why give them more than just what would keep them alive? They had no hard work to do. So his enjoyment was not spoiled by futile thoughts of others starving, and he accepted the cigar with delight as a fitting little coronet on a glorious day.

He and Hermann went off up to their loft to savour the smokes together, outside the company of those who could hardly help being envious. Smoking was neither forbidden nor encouraged in the Empire. The Holy One, the Hero-God, of course, had never smoked, nor eaten meat, nor had He drunk beer or wine. His colossal size (seven feet tall was He) and His phenomenal feats of strength owed nothing to the coarse rich food beloved of lesser Germans. But there was no absolute necessity to try to imitate Him in His way of life, in His complete asceticism (which included never even being in the contaminating presence of a woman), and most men smoked and drank beer and ate meat, when they could get them.

Hermann switched on the electric light, which was wired from the big system in the cowshed below. Alfred said, " The moon's up, Hermann. Let's open the door in the wall and have the light off. It's very warm still."

Hermann turned off the light and opened the door through which sacks would be pushed if the loft were used for its proper purpose. They pulled the bed up near the door and sat on it side by side. They lit their cigars and drew long, delicious breaths of smoke.

" I don't believe I *would* like to be a Knight," Alfred said. " I can't believe they can ever enjoy anything, having things all the time. I haven't had a smoke since I left England."

" Good, isn't it? " Hermann grunted. " But when they're done we shall wish we had another one each, and if one was a Knight then one could just go and get a smoke out of a box."

" Well, they're not done, only just begun, so let's not think of that."

They smoked in silence, looking out on the moonlit yard, with the big barn a jetty soft black, rising up on the other side. A cat picked its way across with dainty steps as though the yard had been full of puddles. The men were too peaceful even to hiss at it. Hermann was very curious about Alfred's doings after the Knight had sent him, Hermann, out of the Court-room, but he was quite willing to wait until Alfred was ready to tell him. And Alfred did wait, not wishing to spoil Hermann's pleasure, until the cigars were smoked to the last possible scrap, with the butts stuck on the ends of pins. They stamped the smouldering ends carefully out on the floor.

"Not a spark," Alfred said. "All gone. Quite dead. Now if I were a Knight, should I have another or shouldn't I? No, I shouldn't. I should know I could have one to-morrow morning. To-morrow morning!" he added, in a different tone.

"Is something going to happen?"

"It is. Some time to-morrow early you'll get a message to report to the Knight at his house at ten o'clock."

"About that bloody soprano singer?"

"No."

"Whatever can it be?" said Hermann uneasily. "How do you know? Do you know what it is?"

"Hermann, would you like there to be a war with the Japanese?"

"Hitler! Wouldn't I just? Is there going to be one? Hurrah!"

"There isn't. But this that's going to happen is going to be much worse than a war, at least for you. You've got to be braver than for that. Well, look here, I'll tell you something to show how strange and important it's going to be. I took the Knight up in his private aeroplane this afternoon. *I flew the plane.*"

"You flew the ——! But you're only an Englishman! *You* can't fly a plane. Oh, don't be funny, Alfred. I don't feel like it."

"It's true, Hermann. You must believe me or you'll have an unnecessarily bad shock, I flew to Munich and back with him, and came down all right, at least I would have, but for some fools in the way—there was miles of room really, but they made me nervous—but though I smashed the plane into the hangar wall coming in too fast, it was very funny really, just like a dog tearing into its kennel, but neither of us was hurt. At least I hurt my knee and head a bit and he made his nose bleed and bumped his side."

" Made his nose bleed! " said Hermann, dazed, catching at this one point in the incredible tale.

" Yes, yes. Aren't Knights' noses allowed to bleed if they bang them? But don't you see, *he* thought we might be killed."

" He's gone mad. The von Hess family—it isn't like others. You oughtn't to have taken him, Alfred. It was a wicked thing to do when he can't be—be himself."

" He's *not* mad," said Alfred very earnestly, then added with a chuckle, " not that I'd have minded. Do you think that I'd let the life of one batty Knight stand between me and a chance to fly? Never. But he's not mad. Well now, listen. To-morrow he's going to tell me *why* he wanted to have a good chance to be killed, to leave the whole thing (whatever it is) to the, to him, improbable good luck that I *could* fly a plane for the first time without a man on double controls with me. And he's going to tell you too."

" Why he wanted to be killed? "

" To have the chance of being killed."

Hermann shook his head hopelessly.

" I don't understand."

" Neither do I. But we shall understand to-morrow. I insisted that you should be told too."

" I don't want to be told anything! " cried Hermann in a panic. " The old man's mad and you took advantage of it to fly. It's all—all lunacy."

" Hermann, it is *not*. And you've got to be a man and stand up to something more than fights and farm-work. You're probably going to have hell, but don't run away from it, and I'll see you through. The Knight will help us too."

" I don't understand," said Hermann, almost in despair. " Why should we have to be told things and then helped? Why can't he let us alone? Why did you say *I* was to be told? "

" Do you want me to hear things from the Knight that you're left out of—like a boy of twelve who's left out of men's conversation? "

" Well, no; but—why not someone else? Oh, I mean—I don't know."

" Hermann, you love me, don't you? You trust me? "

" Yes," said Hermann in a low voice.

" In spite of my being an Englishman? "

" Yes."

" Then, if you can love and trust an Englishman, can you grasp the idea that there might be something important, some knowledge, some wisdom, that's for *all* of us, for all men alike? "

" Yes—I think I see—but not, Alfred "—Hermann's voice dropped to a whisper—" not if it's *against Germany*."

" The Knight is German."

" I know—oh, I know it can't be."

" I mean the Knight never could be against what is good in Germany. Indeed, Hermann, he's a very wonderful man, your family Knight. But shall we go to sleep now? It's getting late."

" Yes," Hermann said thankfully. " You're to have the bed."

" No, no. The sacks will do beautifully for me."

" Because of your knee, please, Alfred," Hermann pleaded. " Now you might just do that for me if I've got to be made wretched in some frightful way to-morrow."

" Oh, all right, lad. Have it your own way."

Hermann took off his boots, lay down on the sacks and turned his face to the wall. Soon, in spite of his fear and anxiety, he was fast asleep. Alfred, contrary to his custom, lay awake for some time.

And in his big house, on his comfortable bed, old von Hess also lay awake with a pain in his side and icy doubt shivering up and down his spine. Emotionalism gripped him, who thought he had done with it for ever long before, and would not be dispersed. His discarded childhood religion and ethic rose up like giants, and he himself, reduced to the dimensions of a child, cowered before them in impotence. Not for many hours could he nerve himself to do battle, and when he did there was no decisive result. When at last he went to sleep, exhausted, the illusion and the doubts were still there, but when he woke up in the healing daylight they had vanished.

In the morning he looked rather hollow-eyed, and the slightly swollen pink look of his fine aquiline nose gave him a dissipated air. But he was perfectly calm, and when Alfred and Hermann were ushered into his writing-room, Hermann knew that whatever he was, he was not insane. His grey eyes looked soberly over both men, and then at the Nazi servant who had brought them in.

" Henrich."

" My lord."

" No one is to disturb me, or to come any nearer this room than the door at the end of the passage. Stay there yourself till I send for you. You understand? *On no account* am I to be disturbed."

" My lord," the servant clicked his heels and saluted.

" Dismiss."

Heinrich went out. Hermann and Alfred were still at attention.

" At ease. No, I mean sit down, both of you."

Hermann gasped. Never before had he sat in the presence of this or any other Knight.

" Sit *down*, Hermann," said the Knight testily. " Do what I tell you, can't you? " His temporary irritation was the first sign he had given of any nervous strain.

Hermann hastily sat down on the chair next to Alfred's. The Knight was facing them, sitting behind a big desk, with his elbows on it and his hands lightly clasped. Hermann, painfully embarrassed by sitting before a Knight, fixed his eyes on the big ruby in the ring. Alfred watched the Knight's face with concentrated attention.

" I hardly know where to begin," he said, with a little cough. " Especially as neither of you will be able to understand all I'm going to tell you. Alfred may be able to understand about half, Hermann almost nothing. Perhaps I had better start with a personal explanation. Hermann, have you ever heard the expression in these parts, ' mad as a von Hess '? "

" Yes, highly-born, I—er—have heard it once or twice."

" My family is eccentric. It is not mad, none of them have ever been mad, though I really don't know why not, but they are eccentric, and for a good reason. Some of them," he added, " have committed suicide. Also for a good reason. A far better one than causes the very numerous other suicides among German men."

" Are there——" Alfred started, then stopped. " I'm sorry, sir."

" Yes, there are, Alfred. But I shall come to that in due course. Suicides, yes, more and more every year. Well, the reason for the von Hess eccentricity is a family curse of an unusual kind, a family curse of knowledge. It's the reason for the suicides among them. Weak men cannot bear knowledge." His eyes rested on Hermann, then passed to Alfred. " I think," he said, " that I will speak in English. Can you follow it well enough, Hermann? "

" Yes, sir."

" I want to make absolutely certain that Alfred understands everything I have to tell. I'm proud to say that most of the von Hess men have been strong. They were able to live with the curse and pass it on to their sons in due course. But though they have not let the knowledge kill them (except for a cowardly few) they have none of them passed it on to anyone else outside the family. I am the first to do so, because I am the last von Hess. Had I not been I should have evaded responsibility, like the others. But, as Hermann knows, my three sons were killed all together in an aeroplane crash many years ago, and by a curious fate none of them had at that time any male children themselves. I was not able to beget any more sons—the family in that crash came to an end. I could adopt a Knight's orphan, but I do not wish to. I never considered it seriously. It is unfair to inflict a curse on other men's blood. Besides, a family curse of this kind is a possession which happily or unhappily gives the von Hess Knights a different status from others of their order, and it was repugnant to me that another man's son should share it. Men are, fortunately, so foolish that they can be proud of a curse so long as it is a family one, and no von Hess throughout these generations and centuries has, though many of them must have been sorely tempted, destroyed the curse itself."

" Can Knights' families really maintain themselves from father to son for hundreds and hundreds of years? " asked Alfred, as the Knight paused.

" They cannot. The ranks of the Knights are constantly being filled up with Nazi male infants, for whom no particular man claims paternity. But curb your shrewdness, Alfred. I shall come to things like that in time. The von Hess family, by some extraordinary luck, has never lacked male heirs. They have a crooked finger." The Knight raised his left hand. " It comes and goes."

Hermann was dazedly thinking, " With Nazi infants? Nazi infants, Nazi infants. It comes and goes."

" The first von Hess," said the Knight, " is supposed to have been a friend of Hitler's. But I'm not certain about that. There were two men of the same name. Rudolf von Hess is in the heroes' calendar, but *the* von Hess, the important one, lived about a hundred and fifty years after Hitler died."

(" *Died?* " thought Hermann. " *Died?* Men die. Oh, Holy Thunderer, if I could get away ! ")

" His name was Friedrich, like mine. Well, this von Hess left two things to the family. One he acquired. One he made. He acquired a photograph, and he made a book. I think that I had better show you the photograph first."

The Knight put his hand into a drawer in the desk and drew out a hard stiff sheet of something wrapped in thin paper. He laid it on the desk in front of him, resting his hands lightly upon it.

" This is not, of course, the original print. It has been reproduced many times, and the plate itself has been renewed from time to time by photographing a particularly clear good print. But I give both you men my word that as far as I know this is an accurate photographic representation of our Lord Hitler as he was in his lifetime. You have both seen innumerable statues and pictures ; you know, as well as you know your best friend's face, what his physical characteristics were. Colossal height, long thick golden hair, a great manly golden beard spreading over his chest, deep sea-blue eyes, the noble rugged brow—and all the rest. But this is he."

The Knight unwrapped the photograph and passed it to Alfred.

" Hold it by the edge," he said.

Hermann was so wildly excited he could hardly see. His eyes blurred over, he rubbed them with furious impatience and looked again. He stared and stared, panting like a man running. He saw a group of four figures, two a little behind, two in front. The central figure of the picture was smallish (the two behind were taller than he), he was dark, his eyes were brown or a deep hazel, his face was hairless as a woman's except for a small black growth on the upper lip. His hair was cropped short except for one lank piece a little longer which fell half over his forehead. He was dressed in uncomely tight trousers like a woman's instead of the full masculine breeches of all the statues and pictures, and his form was unheroic, even almost unmale. Where were the broad shoulders, the mighty chest, the lean stomach and slender waist and hips? This little man was almost fat. He had, oh horror! an unmistakable bulginess below the arch of the ribs. He had a paunch. He had also a charming smile. Looking almost level-eyed at the young stripling beside him, his face was radiant, its ignoble rather soft features all made pleasing through happiness. The boy who basked in the sunshine of the God's favour was looking, not at him, but straight at the camera. He, though immature, had more of the holy German physique than either the Lord Hitler or the two behind. He had great thick long plaits of hair so light that it must have been yellow falling forward over his shoulders and down over his chest, a noble open forehead, large blue or light grey eyes, a square jaw and a wide mouth open in a half smile, just showing big white strong front teeth. He was dressed rather like a Knight's son at his First Blood Communion at fourteen, but the pale robe of this centuries-dead boy came down to little below his knees. His carriage was upright and graceful without being stiff. He looked, to Hermann's staring, protruding eyes, more noble, more German, more manly, despite his youth, than the small dark soft-looking Lord Hitler.

Alfred, as might have been expected, recovered himself first.

" I don't see," he said, " that it's very important really that he doesn't look like what he's supposed to. Thousands of Germans are small and dark, and if they have too much to eat they get fat. That doesn't make him not a great man."

" He was a great man. But was he God? "

" I never thought so. Not after I was sixteen."

" But there's more in the picture than just his appearance," said the Knight. " Who do you think he has been talking to and is smiling at? "

" A handsome boy of about fourteen, a Knight's son, but how should I know who he is? Is that Rudolf von Hess? "

" No," said the Knight. " It's a girl."

" A *girl*! " cried Alfred, wholly incredulous. Hermann merely gasped.

" A girl of about fifteen or sixteen. A young woman. Look at her breasts."

What they had not before seen, being so certain that the figure almost touching the Lord Hitler's must be male, now became plain to them. Under the folds of the soft short robe were full round feminine breasts.

" A girl! " Alfred breathed softly. A girl as lovely as a boy, with a boy's hair and a boy's noble carriage, and a boy's direct and fearless gaze. He and Hermann gazed and gazed, wholly ignoring the other people in the photograph. Alfred grew pale and Hermann very red. The Knight watched the younger men with much sympathy. He was too old to care now, but many a time when his blood was warmer had he got out his secret photograph to look at the face of that lovely German girl.

Again Alfred recovered himself first. He took his eyes with difficulty away from the photograph and asked in a low, uncertain voice, " Is it a—a special girl? A Knight's woman—daughter, something like that? "

" It's an ordinary German girl, a Nazi's daughter. Only special perhaps in being so tall. You see, she's nearly as tall as he is."

" The girls, just any girls, were like that? "

" Yes. Dressed like that, with long hair, beautiful, by no means forbidden the presence of the Holy One. All that came afterwards, and it was not his fault."

" Then," Hermann spoke for the first time in thick German, " it is a lie to say he had nothing to do with women. It's a lie, a lie."

" In the sense that he avoided their presence completely, yes. In the sense that he was not born of a woman, yes. In the sense that he excluded them from the human race and its divisions, allowing them neither nationality nor class, yes.

But you must remember that when Friedrich von Hess lived Hitler was already a legend. The records of his personal life, if there were any, were lost or destroyed. It is certain that he never married, but whether he had intercourse with women in a sexual sense or not, we do not know."

" Married? " said Alfred.   " I'm sorry, sir, that's a German word I don't know."

" It's a lost word.   It occurs nowhere except in von Hess's book. Being married means living in a house with one woman and your children, and going on living continually with her until one of you dies. It sounds fantastic, doesn't it? that men ever *lived* with women. But they did."

" The women were different," said Alfred. " You can see that from this photograph."

" You can," agreed the Knight. " Many a time I, and probably every other von Hess, have gone out after looking at that picture and seen how different women are. Thank God we were all very practical men. There had to be sons. There were sons. But about marriage, Alfred, you may not know it, but the Christians in their communities don't live like we do, men and women separately. They live in *families*, that is the man, the woman, and their children, sons and daughters, all together. I don't know *how* they do it, because their women look just like ours."

" I know they do," said Alfred absently. " I found out about Christians years ago. It's part of their religion to live with the women."

" I think," said the Knight, " that you had better give me back the photograph, you are not attending."

" May we see it again before we go? " Alfred asked. Hermann said nothing. He released a long breath and followed the photograph avidly with his eyes until the Knight had wrapped it up and put it away.

" Yes, Alfred. But it's no good, you know. It only makes one sad and empty and full of discontent. Perhaps a quarter of the burden of the curse on my family results in knowing what women used to be. There are none like that now, not anywhere in the world. There could be none for hundreds of years, no matter what happened. It must take generations and generations to make a woman like that one in the photograph."

" But why have they let themselves go *down* so ? " Alfred asked.

" They acquiesced in the Reduction of Women, which was a deliberate thing deliberately planned by German men. Women will always be exactly what men want them to be. They have no will, no character, and no souls ; they are only a reflection of men.   So nothing that they are or can become is ever their fault or their virtue.   If men want them to be beautiful they will be beautiful.   If men want them to appear to have wills and characters they will develop something that looks like a will and a character though it is really only a sham.   If men want them to have an appearance of perfect freedom, even an appearance of masculine power, they will develop a simulacrum of those things.   But what men cannot do, never have been able to do, is to *stop* this blind submission and cause the women to ignore them and disobey them.   It's the tragedy of the human race."

" I can't see that, sir," said Alfred.   " It must be right for women to submit to men.   Anything else would be unnatural."

" It would be all right," said the Knight slowly, " if men were infallible : if they always caused the women to be what best suits the health and happiness of the race.   But they have made a mistake in their leadership.   Little local mistakes do not matter, but a mistake which includes the whole world— for the Japanese with their slavish imitativeness copied it from us—is an appalling and ghastly tragedy.   We Germans have made women be what they cannot with all their good will go on being—not for centuries on end—the lowest common denominator, a pure animal—and the race is coming to extinction.   The men are committing suicide, but the women, whose discouragement is entirely unconscious, are not being born."

Hermann was gazing with his mouth open, but Alfred sat thoughtful and very serious.   " Yes," he said.   " There are too many men.   I thought it was local.   But we don't kill ourselves like you do."

" It doesn't really matter whether you do or not.   Even in Germany there is not, by a long way, a woman for every man ; in England the balance is worse, that's all.   You will get no more children than we shall."

"I cannot think," said Alfred, after a pause, "why men should ever have wanted girls to be different from that girl in the photograph. They must have been all mad, the men."

"They had a reason. The girl in that picture, with her beauty which is like the beauty of a boy, has also the power of choice and rejection. You men think of yourselves as seeing her and having her. But she need not have you. I don't mean that she can resist you as a child can, but that the law, made by men, will protect her. She can reject any man even though he plead with her in a way that is quite outside our sense of manly dignity; she can reject every man throughout her life. She has the right to reject der Fuehrer, though probably she would not. But she has the *right* to refuse any or every man, and if any man infringes it he is a criminal. How would you like that, Alfred?"

"It's a new idea to me," Alfred confessed. "Couldn't they be beautiful and have no rejection right?"

"I don't think so. You could, of course, let women grow their hair and dress in clothes which display their intrinsically ill-balanced bodies to the very best advantage. But I think that the haunting loveliness of that German girl comes partly from her knowledge that she has the power of choice and rejection, and partly because she knows she can be *loved*. Men cannot love female animals, but they can and have loved women whom they have moulded to a more human and masculine pattern, just as we love our friends. Men in those days could love their women, could feel weary for their presence, even when they were old and far past child-bearing. It's incomprehensible, but it's true. And now I will expose one more lie, and then I will go back to von Hess. You, Hermann and Alfred, have both been taught that the Christians are a race of subhuman people, ranking even below women in general."

"I haven't believed it for ages," said Alfred. "They're queer, but not so different as all that."

"Well, they're not a race at all. They're the remnants of a pre-Hitler civilised religion. It was once the religion of all Europe, most of Russia, the Americas, and a part of Africa. Hitler in his youth was a Christian himself. They probably know very little about themselves now. I expect I know a great deal more than they do."

" Hitler a Christian! " muttered Hermann, over and over again. " Hitler a *Christian*! "

" They say," said Alfred, " that they are a people expiating a great crime. That they are segregated and spat upon because they once spat upon the race of Jesus Christ their Lord, and persecuted it, and that when their time's up Jesus is to come again and forgive them personally, and set them up above the Germans."

" And do they still know why the Christians originally persecuted the Jews, that's the race of Jesus? I wish I had had your advantages, Alfred. I have never been able to speak to a Christian."

" It's rather difficult even for me. They say that the Jews killed Jesus, but that he, this extraordinary fellow, said that they were to forgive the Jews because they didn't know what they were doing at the time. But they disobeyed Jesus, even though he was the Son of God, and gave it the Jews hot for a thousand years. So they have to be spat on for a thousand years, and then Jesus will come again."

" They have their times a little wrong. They persecuted and humiliated the Jews for nearly two thousand years, and then the Germans took on the persecution and made it racial, and after a time killed all the Jews off. That was after the Twenty Years' War. The people who wouldn't worship Hitler when he became a god were, I suppose, killed, all but a few, and those were segregated."

" But why weren't they killed? "

" I suppose it was considered better that there should be something for the subject races and the Nazis in Germany to look down on. It was a sensible idea."

" And are the Christians dying out too? "

" No. They're just about maintaining their numbers. Though their God, Jesus Christ, was born of a woman and not exploded, like Hitler, their women had to share in the Reduction, but they have advantages over ours."

" The women have no souls," Alfred said, " they live with the men, but only as a dog might live with a man. They are not to be included in the Jesus heaven, and they take no part in their religious ceremonies. But they are different from other women. They're a lot livelier."

" That is because they're in constant contact with the

men. And also because they don't have to give up their boys.
The boys and men give them some of their strength and vitality.
What exactly do they think will happen when Jesus Christ
comes again? "

" The Sin will be forgiven, the women will disappear, the
Christians who are then alive will live for ever, the other
dead ones will come out of their graves quite whole and
handsome, the Germans and Japanese and all other infidels
will be judged and thrown into a lake of fire, and the
justified Christians will live for ever in complete and utter
happiness with Jesus. There shall be neither male nor
female, nor any more sin of any kind. That's what they tell
me. But they may have a lot of secrets they won't tell to an
Englishman ! "

" The religion has become very debased and impure,
but that would be inevitable. Women had a very high
place in the old Christian theology. Theoretically, their
soul-value was equal to the men's. Practically, of course,
it was not. They were not allowed to be priests. But
they were told by men that they had souls which Jesus loved,
so they developed the simulacrum of a soul and a sham
conscience. But when the Reduction of Women started
the Christian men acquiesced in it, probably because there
always had been in the heart of the religion a hatred of the
beauty of women and a horror of the sexual power beautiful
women with the right of choice and rejection have over men.
And when the women were reduced to the condition of speaking animals, they probably found it impossible to go on
believing they had souls."

" Supposing they had not acquiesced," Alfred said, " the
Christian women would still be beautiful like that Nazi's
daughter. That would have been all right."

The Knight laughed grimly.

" Then they would all have been killed, however inconvenient. You cannot imagine that *that* would ever have been
allowed."

The Knight put his hand again under the desk and this
time drew forth a huge book of deep yellow colour. As he
opened it the leaves made a peculiar thick crackling sound,
unlike the rustling of paper.

" Come round here a minute, Alfred. Look over my

shoulder. Hermann, come too if you like, but you can't appreciate the beauty of this. You see," he said to Alfred, " this is written all by hand in the smallest possible German letters, but still as legible as print, every letter being perfectly formed and perfectly spaced. It is written on specially prepared thin parchment sheets. Von Hess says in his introduction that it took him over two years to prepare the book itself. And when he started to write it he had to do it all from memory. Not one book of reference did he have."

" But why? "

" Because they were all being burnt. Destroyed."

" Ha ! " said Alfred, striking one fist into the other palm. " Then there *was* some history? It wasn't all darkness and savagery? I knew it! I knew there *must* be something more than Hitler and Christians and Legends."

Alfred went back to his chair lightly, like a triumphant man. Hermann stumbled back to his like a drunkard.

" There was history," said the Knight. " Listen to what he says: ' *I, Friedrich von Hess, Teutonic Knight of the Holy German Empire, of the Inner Ten, dedicate this book to my eldest son, Arnold von Hess, to him and to his heirs for ever. Keep it inviolate, guard it as you would your honour, for though what I have put down here is but the smallest fragment of the truth of history, yet I swear that, to my poor knowledge, it is all true.*'

" He thought, you see," said the Knight, closing the book, " that the time might come when men would again seek passionately for truth, and that this, his little hand-written terribly fragmentary history, might be a faint will-o'-the-wisp light in the darkness. A glow-worm light, he says in one place. He is always in despair—' Here my memory fails me,' or ' Here I have alas no further knowledge.' He was patient and thorough, a good German worker, but he was no scholar. Simply a man who had read a good many books to amuse himself. And yet, when the final battle for Truth was joined, all the scholars among the Knights fled away, leaving this one of no particular ability alone among devils. Yet *there* is a Book, a real book, the only one in the world."

" No, no," said Alfred excitedly. " There may be others. It's only a question of finding the people that keep them. There may be some English ones."

" There can't be, Alfred. The only men free from the threat of instant search are the Knights. Von Hess only managed to write his book secretly because, though disgraced, he was a Knight of the Inner Ten. We have only managed to keep it secret because we are Knights. Some other family of Knights *may* have a book like this, but I do not think so. I'll tell you why presently. But now you understand, Alfred, why I have shown you this book and this photograph. Because when I die, as I have no heirs, all my possessions will revert to the State, that is, to the Knights. The book would be found and destroyed. It is proof against time, against a long time, at any rate. Not against fire."

" It must never be burned," Alfred said. A shiver ran through him. " Never."

" Well," said the Knight, " I think I am going to give it to you. Will you protect it as far as you are able? "

" I'll die ten deaths," swore Alfred. " Even painful ones."

Chapter Five

" You must not think," the Knight went on, " that this von Hess, my ancestor, was a bad German, or one who had any quarrel with Germany's destiny to rule over the whole globe. Its destiny to power far greater than the published dreams of the hero Rosenberg was proved to be right and the will of God by the accomplished fact. The Germans had proved themselves fitted to conquer and rule by conquering Europe, Russia as far as the Ural Mountains, Africa, Arabia, and Persia, by consolidating their conquests, and by ruling with such realistic and sensible severity that rebellion became as hopeful as a fight between a child of three and an armed man."

" *Armed* rebellion," Alfred amended.

" Oh, I know there is a rebellion of the spirit. So did von Hess, so did the other Germans of that date. Von Hess believed, too, that this tremendously powerful German Empire

in the centre of the world would be able, in time, to attack
and crush the Japanese Empire, which at that time was still
growing. And that then the full destiny of Germany would be
accomplished. That has not happened. The Japanese rule
over Asia, Australia, and the Americas, but they cannot crush
us, neither can we crush them. The peace between Japan
and Germany is permanent. The Knights know this, the
Nazis do not."

Hermann groaned and hid his face in his hands. Then he
looked up imploringly at the Knight.

" Not even that left, sir? A chance to die for Germany? "

" A chance to die for Germany, perhaps. For the German
Empire, no. There can't be any more wars."

"But why? " asked Alfred. " I've often wondered why
you didn't get on with it."

" Neither the Japanese nor ourselves can afford to lose a
single man of the ruling race, that's why. Their population
is beginning to decrease, like ours. We cannot send our
subject races into battle and stay out of it ourselves. It's
against our honour, against our religion, and besides it's the
fixed policy of both Empires never to allow the subject races
to obtain skill with the really dangerous weapons of war.
You are taught to be soldiers, riflemen, for the sake of the
discipline, but you are not allowed to handle artillery or tanks
or aeroplanes. *Every* German and *every* Japanese is wanted
in the armies of occupation and the ordinary life of the fatherland country, and so there can be no more war between
us."

" Well, that's simple. And what are you going to do about
it, sir? "

" I don't know, and neither does anybody else. The *hope*
of war even is wearing very thin. A people which is conditioned for war from childhood, whose ethic is war and whose
religion is war, can live, though not very happily, on the hope
of war; but when that breaks down it must change its conditioning or perish, like animals which cannot fit themselves
to their environment. And neither we nor the Japanese can
change the conditioning without abandoning the religion and
the ethic. And policing unarmed subject countries with big
air fleets is not enough. No one thinks of it as remotely
approaching war. We have made ourselves too strong, far

too strong, and we're dying, both the huge Empires side by side, of our own strength."

"How would it be," suggested Alfred, "if you taught us all to use the artillery and tanks and aeroplanes and ships and submarines, and gave us tons and millions of tons of war material and we had a General Rebellion?"

"It wouldn't do. You might win. And even if you didn't, the Japanese *might* take the opportunity to attack us."

"They could do the same thing with their subject races."

"We should never trust them to keep their word. Neither would they trust us. But now we have got far away from von Hess. He was not troubled by these considerations. The German population was rapidly growing and he had no terrors about its destiny. The power of Germany was unshakable from without, and the Social Order within was fixed for all time in the Three Ranks—der Fuehrer, the Knights, and the Nazis. But in the midst of all this power and glory and pride there was, so von Hess says, a spiritual uneasiness. The Germans were not yet quite happy. Old ideas, pre-Hitlerian ideas, were still in the world, even though they could reach none by individual expression. The subject races were sullen and secretly contemptuous, still always dreaming, however futilely, of freedom. The shadows of old Empires——"

"Ha!" cried Alfred, springing up. "There *were* old Empires, then? You and the Japanese weren't the only ones? It's all lies, lies!"

"The Assyrian, the Babylonian, the Persian, the Egyptian, the Greek, the Roman, the Spanish and the British. In colonial possessions——"

Alfred interrupted him. "*The British!* And you tell us all those English-speaking races were just disconnected savage tribes! As if anyone but an idiot could ever believe it. You liars! You *fools!*"

The Knight rose to his feet also, and looked at Alfred with controlled but passionate condemnation. "You're proud of having had an Empire, are you? Proud of being an Englishman for *that* reason? Look at that poor clod Hermann there— he daren't face anything, believe anything, he hardly dares to *hear* anything, he's a shrinking, shaking *coward*, not so much

because he believes in Hitler, not so much because he's a
German, but because he's got an Empire! You ought to be
ashamed of your race, Alfred, even though your Empire
vanished seven hundred years ago. It isn't long enough to
get rid of that taint."

" It's you who have taught us to admire Empire! "
Alfred flung at him. " The Holy Ones! The
Germans! "

The Knight sat down again. " No," he said quietly, " it
was *you* who taught *us*. Jealousy of the British Empire was
one of the motive forces of German imperialism, one of the
forces which made Germany grow from a collection of little
kingdoms to be ruler of a third of the world. A tremendous
bitter black jealousy, so says von Hess, though when he lived
the triumph had long come. Unshakable, impregnable
Empire has always been the dream of virile nations, and now
at last it's turned into a nightmare reality. A monster that is
killing us."

" I don't want ours back," said Alfred more calmly;
" only I always thought it was so, and I like to know the
truth."

" That is wholly admirable," said the Knight. " I wish
Hermann liked to hear it too."

Hermann muttered something inaudible, but the Knight
took no notice. " As I was saying, the shadows of these old
ideas and of these vast old Empires still hung over Germany,
reminding Germans that Empires rise, and *fall*, reminding them
also of their own small beginnings. It was not enough for
them to know that they *now* ruled a third of the world, that
in them rested the only true and holy civilisation; they
wanted to forget that there ever had been, in Europe, any
other civilisation at all. There was so much beauty *they* had
not made, so many books they had not written, so many
records of wars in which they had not fought, and so many
ideas of human behaviour which were anathema to them.
Socialism, for instance, was absolutely smashed, practically,
but the idea was still there, in men's minds. No, Alfred, I will
not stop to tell you what Socialism was. You can read it in
the book. But if *you* were a Socialist you would think the
Knights had no right to own all the land and factories and
ships and houses of the Empire, you would think the people

who actually do the work on the land or in the factories ought to own them."

" Then I am a Socialist. Were there many of them? "

" It was really what amounted to the religion of Russia, from the Polish border to Vladivostok, and there were lots of them in every other country. But Russia, after the most tremendous struggle in history (or so says von Hess), was finally beaten, by the combined attacks of Germany and Japan. The home of Socialism was shattered. But do let me get on with the important things. The Germans of that time were blown up with an insensate pride, a lunatic vanity, for which of course there was a great deal of excuse. But they were still afraid. In the heart of the pride lurked a fear, not of anything physical, but of Memory itself. This fear gradually grew into a kind of hysteria (von Hess says the Germans have always been inclined to hysteria), which at last reached its expression in the book of one man. This was a typical scholar-knight called von Wied, a bookish person, says von Hess, a complete nervous hysteric, who, though bloodthirsty, had owing to physical disability to content himself with floods of ink. Von Hess says that had he known what von Wied was doing he would have murdered him without the smallest compunction. This book of von Wied proved that Hitler was God, not born but exploded, that women were not part of the human race at all but a kind of ape, and that everything that had been said and done and thought before Hitler descended was the blackest error of subhuman savagery and therefore must be wiped out. The fear of Memory reached its height with him, and he gave us the logical and Teutonic remedy, destruction. All history, all psychology, all philosophy, all art except music, all medical knowledge except the purely anatomical and physical—every book and picture and statue that could remind Germans of old time must be destroyed. A huge gulf was to be made which no one could ever cross again. Christianity must go, all the enormous mass of Christian theology must be destroyed throughout the Empire, all the Christian Bibles must be routed out and burned, and even Hitler's own book, hallowed throughout Germany, could only continue to exist in part. There was Memory there, you see. Memory of what we call the Preliminary Attack."

" In which Hitler fought at the age of fourteen, the Glorious Boy," said Alfred.

" Yes. But he was much older than that. And Germany was beaten, absolutely defeated. Von Hess doesn't mind admitting that, but for von Wied that was part of the Memory he was afraid of. You are all taught that Hitler fought in that war at fourteen, and that he had subdued the whole Empire at thirty, after which he was Reunited. But it took much longer than that. Hitler had been dead for nearly a hundred years when the Empire had grown to its present size."

" Lies, lies," muttered Alfred. " Lies, lies, lies! "

" This man von Wied might be called the Father of Lies. The arch-liar. Not that there hadn't been lies before. Von Hess admits that there was tampering with historical facts even in Hitler's lifetime. And he says, very justly, I think, that there is not the whole width of the Empire between the falsification of history and its destruction. Von Hess was all for telling the whole truth about the history of Germany and the history of the rest of the world. For, says he, surely, apart from any question of right and wrong, the truth is sufficiently glorious? But von Wied thought not, and he was willing to have his own great work destroyed so long as it was accompanied to the pyre by the other records of mankind."

" Didn't they even keep his? " asked Alfred in some astonishment.

" No. But I think some of it is incorporated in the Hitler Bible. Why, how can you keep a book which proves a man is God, or that advocates the destruction of records of other civilisations? It simply proves those things *were* there, and that Hitler was not always divine. There was plenty of Memory in von Wied's book. He screamed and snarled and foamed at it, so says von Hess, but it was still there. Not dead yet. Well, this book exactly caught the feeling of the nation at the time."

" In spite of the part about the women? "

" *Because* of the part about the women. I don't mean only because of that, but von Wied's theories about women were wildly popular with a large section of the men. You see, the lunatic vanity of the Germans was concentrated really in the males among them. The women hadn't beaten the world and made the Empire. They had only borne the children, and that was no more than any English woman or Russian woman could do. And these proud soldiers, the great-grandsons of the men who really made the Empire, were beginning to feel very strongly that it was beneath the dignity of a German man to have to risk rejection by a mere woman, to have to allow women to wound him in his most sensitive part, his vanity, without the remedy of a duel. They wanted *all* women to be at their will like the women of a conquered nation. So in reality the Reduction of Women was not started by von Wied. It had begun already. Rapes were extraordinarily common compared with what they had been even fifty years before, and the sentences for rape were getting lighter and lighter. Von Wied's theory was that the rejection-right of women was an insult to Manhood, that family life was an insult to Manhood, and that it was the wickedest possible folly to allow an animal (for women were nothing more than that) to have complete control over human beings at their tenderest and most impressionable period, their infancy. He said that the boys must be taken away at the very dawn of consciousness and before memory came to endure. At a year old, *he* said. We now give the women six months longer than that. He also held the theory that the beauty of women was an insult to Manhood, as giving them (some of them) an enormous and disgusting sexual power over men. He said, though, that this beauty was not real (for he would allow women no redeeming qualities whatever) but a sham made by long hair and a mysterious half-revealing half-concealing form of dress. He advocated shaven heads for women and a kind of dress that could conceal nothing and have nothing mysterious or graceful about it. They must dress all in one colour, a dirty-brown (as they do now), and must be, after the age of sixteen, completely submissive, not only to the father of their children, but to any and every man, for such was the will of the Lord Hitler, through his humble mouthpiece Rupprecht von Wied. He said there must be no love, only lust or a desire to beget sons, and that a sexual preference for one woman over another, except in so far as one might be stronger and healthier, was a weakness and wholly unmanly. The whole pattern of women's lives was to be changed and made to fit in with the

new German Manhood, the first civilised manhood of the
world."

" And what did the women do? " Alfred asked.

" What they always do. Once they were convinced that
men really wanted them to be animals and ugly and completely submissive and give up their boy children for ever
at the age of one year they threw themselves into the new
pattern with a conscious enthusiasm that knew no bounds.
They shaved their heads till they bled, they rejoiced in their
hideous uniforms as a young Knight might rejoice in his
Robe of Ceremony, they pulled out their front teeth until
they were forbidden for reasons of health, and they gave up
their baby sons with the same heroism with which they had
been used to give their grown sons to war."

" They don't do that now," Alfred said, frowning.

" They cannot be enthusiastic about anything *now*," said
the Knight. " It is not a new way of pleasing men, it is just
part of their lives. *They* thought, those poor little typically
feminine idiots, that if they did all that men told them to do
cheerfully and willingly, that men would somehow, in the
face of all logic, love them still *more*. They could not see
that they were helping to kill love. What woman now would
ever dream that a man could love her as he loves his friends?
But *those* women, aware of a growing irritation with them
among men, passionately hoped to soothe and please them by
their sacrifice of beauty and their right of choice and rejection,
and their acceptance of animal status. Women *are* nothing,
except an incarnate desire to please men; why should they
fail in their nature that time more than any other? "

Alfred shook his head.

" There's something wrong somewhere," he said slowly.
" I don't know what it is yet. I'll have to think it out. Go
on, sir. But I see I shall have to think about women seriously.
I never knew they were important before."

" As long as we can't all be exploded, they certainly are.
They're not important *in themselves*, of course. But I must
go back a bit. When von Hess read this terrific farrago of lies
and catastrophic nonsense and realised what a tremendous
hold it almost immediately obtained over the ordinary
Germans he was uneasy. When serious discussions of the
book started among the Knights, he was frightened. When

the subject was put down for debate at the Council of the Inner Ten, he was appalled. For he knew Germany *could do it*. Could destroy all records of the truth. With German patience and German thoroughness they could, once they had made up their minds to do it, rout out and burn every book in the Empire, even if it took them a hundred years. Well, he always opposed the idea, at every Knights' discussion, and for some time several of the Inner Ten were with him, and der Fuehrer as well. But meanwhile the enthusiasm for von Wied in the country at large was getting quite hysterical. More and more people every day were shrieking and screaming for Memory to be destroyed and their dark inside panic to be allayed. There were even whispers that von Wied ought to be der Fuehrer, seeing that he was the first man who recognised openly what everybody knew inside themselves, that Hitler was divine, and that the world, the real human world, was born in His Explosion. So the Inner Knights one by one went over to the von Wied party, and at last der Fuehrer went too. Von Hess was desperate. On such a serious matter there must be unanimity among the Inner Knights, but he knew that if he opposed too long he would be murdered. Yet he made one last effort to save Truth. He was above himself, he says. He argued, he pleaded, he raged, he says he even wept. He went on talking almost for a whole night. But he made no impression. The whole weight of Germany was against him. Inside the Council Hall there were the nine Knights and der Fuehrer, with grim set faces, listening to him still courteously, but quite immovable; outside there was the rest of Germany, Knights, Nazis, and women, all fallen into a hysteria of rage and fear and desire to destroy as universal and as potent as if some physical enemy had invaded the very soil of Holy Germany. And above this storm, riding it like God on a whirlwind, was the little mean figure of von Wied, a small dark cripple (so says von Hess) without manhood, stability, or even physical courage. Von Wied outside, being hailed as the Prophet, the Apostle, the Deliverer, the Voice of Hitler, even the Voice of God. Von Hess inside, defeated. The Knights rose at last and shouted him down, and der Fuehrer closed the Council, adjourning it to the next evening. Von Hess saluted and went out. He got into his car and drove home here, not actually to this house, his castle was up on the hill there, to the south of the landing-ground. It was summer, and beginning to get light. On the way he saw what he thought was a dead body lying by the side of the road. He stopped his driver and got out to investigate. It was the naked body of a woman, young, he thought, but the face was so mangled he could hardly tell. The eyes were torn out and the nostrils slit up. The hair had all been pulled out, leaving nothing but a ghastly red skull-cap of blood. The body was covered with innumerable stabs and cuts that looked as if they had been made with a pen-knife. The nipples had been cut off. Von Hess was no more squeamish than a good German ought to be, but he says he felt a little sick. However, that might have been fatigue after the effort of the night. He hoped that this untidy corpse was the work of some solitary sex maniac, but his hope was very faint. Next day he learned that it was the body of a girl who had laughed at a band of the new " von Wied Women ", a pretty young girl who didn't mind Hitler being God but couldn't see why women should be ugly. That was the temper of Germany in hysteria. If the women were like that, how would the men bear opposition in their blown-up pride of conquest? But von Hess was hardly conscious of physical danger. He was too despairing. He says, ' I cannot waste this precious parchment in describing my sensations. I was in the blackest despair known to man, for I couldn't think what to do.'

" When the morning was far advanced a Knight brought him a message from der Fuehrer in Munich, warning him, without any threats, that he must at once cease his opposition to the von Wied plan. But still he didn't know what to do, except go on opposing and be quietly murdered. Not till he was almost in the Council Hall that evening did his idea come to him. He says, ' I never have been anything but a rather stupid man. My brain is slow, the Knights elected me to the Inner Ten, I think, for reasons of character.' But once he had his idea he was not slow. He made instantaneous and humble submission before the Knights and der Fuehrer; he said that he had been mad before not to see the beauty and holiness and truly German simplicity and strength of the von Wied plan. He acknowledged Hitler as God. He begged that his own collection of books (a fairish library, he says) might have the honour of being burnt at once for Hitler's sake. None of the Knights believed in this sudden conversion. They thought he was afraid for his skin. They were astonished and disgusted even though they were relieved at the collapse of the opposition. And here I think we may know that there *have* been men of honour in Germany, Alfred, for this Knight, my ancestor, bore this imputation of cowardice all the rest of his life for the sake of Truth. He even refused to challenge a Knight, a personal friend of von Wied's, who a little later accused him almost openly of having given way to save himself. He wanted them to think him a coward. He also at this Council prayed der Fuehrer formally to be excused from further attendance at Council on the score of age and ill-health. A Knight cannot resign from the Inner Ten, but he can, if der Fuehrer allows it, be permanently excused from attendance. Von Hess says, ' I was not young, nearly sixty, but as healthy as a youth. However, der Fuehrer granted my plea.' They also promptly accepted his offer of his books, and because he had not succeeded quite in averting suspicion, because they did not quite think him only a coward, a small party of ordinary Knights was sent straight back with him to his castle to see the books put all in one room, and the doors and windows sealed. But before he left the Council Hall for the last time, he agreed to the adoption of the von Wied plan, and it was passed unanimously. He had to stay for the discussion of ways and means that followed, but he sat like a man ashamed, with his head down, taking no part unless he had to vote. At last he could go home with his escort of Knights, and it was then that one of them, the friend of von Wied, insulted him. He swallowed it like a little boy who has been over-bragging and daren't make his boast good. He knew from the contemptuous look in the eyes of the other men that his disgrace was complete. It would not be made public among the Knights, owing to the peculiar circumstances, but it would get round. He would be known as ' von Hess the Coward '. He would be let alone. He left home and went to England, where he bought a large sheep farm on Romney Marsh in Kent. Do you know it, Alfred? "

" No, sir. What did he go to England for? "

" It's a good place for sheep, and he wanted to be out of Germany. He let it be known that he was going to experiment with sheep-breeding. That was natural enough, he had always been a bit of an agricultural expert. What he wanted to do actually was to learn to make parchment. He didn't dare to buy it, though it was used for certain things, Knights' Commissions, and so on. Before he left Germany he saw his sons, Arnold, Kaspar, Friedrich, and Waldemar, and told them that he was in private disgrace with der Fuehrer, but that he had done nothing of which he himself was ashamed. He did not tell them what had happened, but he laid on them his strictest command that none of them should fight duels on his behalf, no matter what they heard. They all swore to obey him. If all his sons were killed, you see, there would be no one he could trust with his book. He also instructed Arnold (a good lad, he says, not very intelligent) to buy for him secretly a book on the technique of parchment-making, and a supply of some special kind of ink. He thought Arnold was just intelligent enough to do this without making a mistake. When he had them he was to bring them to his father in England. When von Hess had the book on parchment-making he settled down to breed sheep and kill some of them and make the leaves of his book out of their skins. In Romney Marsh. It's a queer flat green place, Alfred, below the level of the sea, misty and damp, but curiously beautiful. Von Hess wastes two whole lines of writing on his precious parchment saying it was beautiful and that its beauty made him sometimes happy. I know it is. I went there to look. It's a very great contrast to this part of Germany. He lived there for two years making parchment leaves, with much hard work and many deplorable failures. Nearly all his labourers and servants were English, he had but one Nazi lad, a faithful lout, one gathers, who had gone with him from Germany. This youth helped him with the making of the parchment. He didn't know what it was for, but the Knight had told him to hold his tongue and not brag about. He would, von Hess says, have had it torn out rather than say anything. As for the Englishmen, they took no notice. They worked for him, very lazily, so he says, Alfred, but in good enough temper and without inquisitiveness. No one came to see him, except his sons. His wife (that's the woman he permanently lived with) was dead, long before all this trouble. No Knight on duty in England or travelling there ever came to his sheep-farm in Romney Marsh. He says, wasting more precious sheepskin, ' I was so lonely that I began to understand about God. Not Hitler, not the god of the Germans, but about God, whatever God is, but I never could hold the understanding together. It came and went like the best part of the sunsets.' "

" Oh," said Alfred. " Oh, there is something *there*. Yes, like the best part of the sunsets. And not to be able to hold it together. Sir, this von Hess, he knew something."

The Knight said, " Great men, in their loneliness, might touch one another. Even though one was German and one English. Well, when he had made what he thought would be enough parchment leaves for his very scanty knowledge he sold his sheep-farm and moved slowly up through England, buying a little paper here and a little there on which to make the notes for his book, but never getting enough at a time to cause any remark. The Nazi boy, Johann Leder, drove his car; he had no other retinue at all. He slept at common English hostels, but this caused no surprise among the Knights who became aware of his travels. It was only disgraced von Hess, the Coward; naturally he would not care to go to the Knights' houses and Tables. He went far into the north, to the Island of Skye in Scotland, and there he settled down in a tiny house, a mere hovel, to write his book. His German estates had not been sequestrated; he could have afforded to buy himself a castle, but he no longer wanted anything but a room, a table, his special ink and some food. He planned and re-planned, made notes in tiny writing with pencil on his little supply of ordinary paper, and cudgelled his memory until it sometimes threatened to fail him altogether, and he fell into fits of panic and despair. You see, he must be certain of everything he put down, it must be well arranged, and it must be concise. Yet he knew nothing of the making of books, and had never written anything in his life except one or two papers on agricultural matters and private letters. After two years of this kind of concentration and planning he thought he had pinned down everything he could remember about the history of human beings, and had it arranged so that totally ignorant men could understand it. So he started to write it down in the parchment book, very slowly, making each letter with the utmost care to save space and yet leave the writing legible.

And when he had written about half he found his eyesight
was failing."

" Oh," Alfred breathed. " Oh, sir."

" Yes. He did not dare to go anywhere to have his eyes
looked at. He had never worn spectacles, and the doctor,
when he knew who this Knight was, might wonder why
sheep-farming and hiding his shame in the Highlands of
Scotland should affect his eyes so badly. Arnold bought
spectacles in Germany and brought his father a selection, in
fact for several years when any of his sons came to visit him
they brought various powers of lenses for him to try. But
they none of them knew what he was doing, for when they
were there he locked his room and did nothing. He says he
thinks Johann Leder knew, and indeed the lad must have
unless he was a half-wit, but he said nothing to anyone. So
with his spectacles von Hess got on again fairly well, but he
grew blinder and blinder, and could do less and less every
day. But his writing never grew less beautiful and clear:
by will-power, it seems, he kept it small and even and well-
formed. And in five years he had put down all the contents
of his notes, and his book was finished. There were just a
few leaves left at the end, but he says it was not his blindness
that prevented him filling them up, but that he had nothing
more to write that was certainly true. Then he sent for Arnold
and told him about the book. I often have imagined him,
perhaps on a fine summer evening—for the date at the end of
the book is June 6th (that is the month we now call Himmler)
—sitting there at the door perhaps of his little house, with his
spectacles on his nose and his eyes peering, hardly able to see
the expression in Arnold's eyes, and wholly unable to see the
beauty of Skye at sunset. I have been there; I fancied a
certain little house on the west side of the island was his. And
he would perhaps be still in his Knight's tunic, very shabby
and faded, with the golden swastikas on the collar that showed
he was of the Inner Ring. Or it might have been inside the
house by a fire in one of those incessant soaking mists that
make that climate so trying for nine months of the year. Well,
wet or fine, outside or in, he managed to make Arnold understand. Come here again, Alfred."

Alfred came round the desk and looked over the Knight's
shoulder. The old man opened the book a few leaves from

the end. Alfred saw a few lines in von Hess's craftsman's hand, then a space, and then some more German words in a writing which by comparison looked extremely coarse, weak and untidy.

" My father, Friedrich von Hess, Teutonic Knight of the Inner Ring of Ten, gave me this book on June 19th, 2130. Then being seventy years old and nearly blind, and having nothing else to live for, but, as he said, being filled with a perfect faith in the goodness and universality of God, he took his own life on the following day, June 20th, 2130. He told me to lead him up to a certain place in some rugged hills not far off, called the Scarts of the Coolins, and there I was to leave him for three hours. When I came back again my father was dead, having swallowed some poison which he must have had with him ever since he left Germany ten years before. There was a little scrap of paper beside him on which he sent greetings and love to Kaspar, Friedrich, and Waldemar, and to me, Arnold, he wrote, Be faithful and guard the book. So I here record my oath.

" I swear to be faithful and guard this book.
" Arnold von Hess, Knecht."

Under there was a list of names in various handwritings, preceded by the words *Und Ich*.

The Knight turned over the page and the names went on. The von Hess men were nearly all called after one of the old scribe's four sons. Alfred glanced down the list till he came to the last one, written in nearly as lovely a hand as the book itself.

Und Ich, Friedrich von Hess, Knecht.

" And do you swear to be faithful, Alfred? "
" Yes."

" Then take this pen, dip it in this special ink in this bottle here, and write your name under these."

" I'm not much good at writing, sir," Alfred said, ruefully. " I'll make a bad mess on the page."

" But you can write? "
" Oh, I *can*."
" You can copy the *Und Ich*."
" Ich bin nicht Ich," said Alfred. " I'm I."

Laboriously under the *Und Ich* he wrote a sprawling badly

formed " And I " in English script. Under the von Hess names he wrote " Alfred " and under *Knecht* he with toil and pain inscribed the word " Englishmun ".

" You might be an English *man*," said the Knight. " Give me the pen." Deftly he corrected Alfred's faulty spelling. " I suppose you never have any occasion to write? " he asked.

" Not often. There's nothing to write about. About all I ever write is ' Passed ' on a ticket for an engine."

" Don't you have to indent for stores, tools and so on? "

" The Nazi ground foreman does that. I'm the first man on that list without a surname. It looks odd, doesn't it? Just ' Alfred '."

" You could have put Alfred Alfredson."

" That's nothing. Those aren't surnames like von Hess. You are Friedrich Kasparsohn von Hess."

The ink was dry and the Knight closed the book.

" That Nazi, that Johann Leder, *he* had a surname. How did he have one? Hermann hasn't any more than me."

" I'll tell you to-morrow," said the Knight. He seemed tired. " How you lost your surnames, and anything I know about myself. I know you'll be bursting with questions. But now you must go, and though the book is yours now, Alfred, you can't have it yet. I must think of ways and means."

" Sir, how could you risk yourself in an aeroplane when you knew that if you were killed that book would be destroyed? "

" I am still a German, and a Knight. It is not so easy always to see where one's real duty lies. But I admit it was a superstitious weakness, going up with you. Hermann! "

Hermann jumped like a man suddenly wakened out of deep sleep. He sprang to attention.

" You are to go to the end of the passage, open the door and wait outside with Heinrich till Alfred comes. You are not to speak to Heinrich. Salute. Right about. March."

Hermann strode stiffly out and shut the door.

" Alfred, tell him from me he can work on the farm or not as he likes to-day. Keep with him. Look after him. He may try to kill himself, or you. Be careful and take this."

This was a small revolver the Knight drew from the desk.

" I'd better not, sir," Alfred said. " If they found it, or if I had to use it, there'd be a hell of a fuss. An ordinary fight doesn't matter."

" But he has a knife and you have nothing. You understand, Alfred, you simply must *not* be killed. Hermann has no control except under discipline. Why, ten Hermanns, a hundred of them, wouldn't pay for *you*."

" He won't kill me," said Alfred. " And he won't kill himself. I'll look after him. While I'm here," he added, rather uneasily. " I've only got another fortnight."

" You see, he *ought not* to have been told."

" No, he ought not. I'm sorry, sir. But perhaps I can get him out of his daze."

" There's a lot to be thought about," said the Knight, " so Heil Hitler, Alfred. You can come at—well, we'll say six o'clock to-morrow evening."

" Sir——" said Alfred rather dubiously.

" What? "

" Is it all right for an Englishman and a Nazi farm-worker to go on coming to see you? *Once* perhaps for a Knight's wigging."

" It's quite all right," said von Hess, with a tired smile. " The reputation of my family is fortunately so peculiar that I can do almost anything. Auf wiedersehen."

Alfred saluted and went.

Outside the passage door he found Hermann and Heinrich standing like two wooden figures one on each side, gazing into space, apparently unaware of each other. Alfred glanced from one to another and thought either would do well enough for models of the legendary Hitler. Both were young, huge and blond. He wondered if Heinrich's manly mien concealed a weakness, a strong desire for personal dependency, as did Hermann's. You never could tell to look at Hermann. If he had a soft chin, his fine golden beard hid it. " I dare say it's a good thing," thought Alfred. " If I can make him think only of me now, perhaps he'll be all right. Poor lad! I was wrong to let him be told. He's not even a quarter of a man."

These thoughts took no more time than a slight hesitation, when he had closed the door.

" Come on, Hermann," he said, nudging his arm. " The highly-born wishes us to potter off. March."

Hermann marched, with a jerk. He walked with Alfred in silence until they were out of the Knight's grounds and in the road that led to the farm.

" Where are you going? " he asked in a dull voice.

" Well, anywhere you like. The Knight says you can work or not, as you like. What ought you to be doing? "

" Hoeing."

" Then, if you want to work, give me a hoe, tell me which end I use, and I'll be with you."

" Did he say I didn't have to work? "

" He did."

" He said I was a coward."

" Oh, he didn't mean that. He was only ticking me off for being glad we once had an Empire."

" Is that all true? "

" What? "

" All he said? "

" Nobody could ever know. But by the way the tale came to him, I should say, *yes*. If a German was really set on telling the truth, I can't help thinking that as far as his knowledge went, he would tell it, and nothing else."

Hermann stopped walking down the farm road and turned round to face Alfred. No one was in sight.

" He did think I was a coward," Hermann said. " And so do you. You think I can't stand anything. So does he. But neither of you realise that it's worse for me than for you. He's used to it. You're glad, because you're an Englishman. I'm nothing, only a common Nazi." Hermann's voice broke. He coughed and recovered himself. " But you're both of you wrong."

" I was damned wrong," said Alfred. " I'm sorry, Hermann. I really thought you couldn't stand it. To have your God and your belief in the infallibility of Germany taken from you at one stroke. Why, of course, I couldn't stand it, if I had a belief in the infallibility of Englishmen, and if I had a personal English God. I've got all wrong over you. I never realised what it would be like."

" Did the Knight? "

" He didn't want you to be told. But no, he *doesn't* realise,

Hermann. The biggest influence in his life is old von Hess. And was *he* really a German? Yes, he was the Germanest kind of German; can you imagine any other kind of man being so single-minded, so devoted, so careless of *himself*, so patient, so strong? And yet all that Blood-stuff didn't seem to mean much. ' The goodness and universality of God ', that's what he thought at the end. He thought Germany ought to rule the world, and he thought the truth ought to prevail. He was a grand man. By God, Hermann, he believed in Germany more than you do."

" You talk so much," said Hermann, " you muddle me. What I want to tell you is that I *can* stand this, that I'm not really a coward, whatever 'you and the Knight think—but, Alfred, you can't leave me here."

" Where ? "

" In Germany. You say—*he* says that Germany is wrong—all that. Well, then, if I stay here I'll kill myself. What else could I do ? "

" You could go on hoeing."

A *cri de cœur*, wholly without pride, came from Hermann's bearded lips. " Alfred, if any man I trust will tell me what to do, I'll do it. You or the Knight. I don't care which."

Alfred took his arm. " Hermann, young fellow, you've been thinking too long. Let's get some hoes."

But he was thinking, " Ought any man to be like Hermann ? Would there have been men like Hermann when that girl in the photograph was alive ? Is he perhaps not so much childish but rather like a *woman*, when women were different ? But he's not going to kill anyone, and that's a good thing, anyway. How does one hoe ? "

Hermann went to the toolhouse at the farm to get two hoes, and then to the kitchen to receive his hedge-meal. The cook gave him a portion for Alfred, when Hermann suggested it, without demur. Their long session with the Knight had raised their status on the farm to privileged men. Either the Knight was ferociously displeased with them, in which case some sympathy was due, even to the Englishman, or else he held them in some special kind of favour. The cook showed his interest and curiosity by hints, but Hermann made no response and the man had to go back to his kitchen unsatisfied.

" It's all about that chorister, I suppose," he thought.
" Perhaps the Knight has heard he's dead."

In the field they found other men working, toiling up the
long rows between the roots.

" You draw the hoe *so*, Alfred.   Get in the next row to me
and don't try to go too fast.   It's hard work."

" These are mangold wurzels," said Alfred, chopping at
the leaves of one of them idly with his hoe.   " But they're
rotten little plants."

" Well, don't cut all its leaves off to improve it.   They
won't really grow in this part of Germany.   They don't
get enough damp.   It's one of the Knight's everlasting
experiments with a special manure.   And he thinks a lot of
hoeing will make up for no rain at the proper time."

" He's an agriculturalist too then, like the old man? "

" He's a very bad one," said Hermann, almost smiling.
" He does the most fantastic things.   Don't *dig* so.   Just
draw it along through the surface of the ground."

" Heilige Nacht! " muttered Alfred presently, referring to
the Night of Hitler's final disappearance in the Holy Forest.
" What a hog's job this is ! "

His knee hurt him, sweat poured off him and his back ached
ferociously.   Hermann, without any appearance of effort at
all, drew fast ahead of him.   But Alfred was ashamed to give
in.   He toiled along as fast as he could go, trying to catch
Hermann up.   He got farther and farther behind, for Hermann when he was in the swing of his work gradually quickened his pace.   " The fellow is just a turbine-driven hoeing
machine," Alfred thought, stopping for an instant to wipe
sweat out of his eyes.   " I hope there's something to drink in
the hedge."

Fortunately for him it was near dinner-time when they had
arrived in the field.   Before he was quite cooked a welcome
shout called them to the hedge.   Alfred undid his back,
which seemed to have permanently shortened itself into a
hoop, picked up his coat, and staggered towards the group of
hoers.   He was received with friendly jeers.

" It's all very well," he said, collapsing into the shade.
" I'm not used to it.   If you men tried to repair an engine
you'd look just the same mugs."

" That's a skilled job," said one.   " Anyone, even an

Englishman, ought to be able to draw a little hoe through the ground."

"The holy soil of Germany is too thick for me, I'm afraid. Sausage! You Nazis do live high. Do all farm workers get as good food as you? Is there some water?"

"There's some beer. Pass him some, Hermann. The poor little fellow's faint."

Alfred drank gratefully. The beer was thin, but there was plenty of it and it was not sour.

"Our food depends partly on whatever Knight we work for," explained a labourer. "Of course there are lots of things we don't have except on feast days. Butter—things like that. But ours is a very good Knight. The von Hesses are mad, but never mean. It's desperate the old man has no son."

Hermann sat next to Alfred in the hedge, munching slowly. He did not speak or listen to what the other men were saying. Once he turned to look at Alfred, a strange stupid lost look, vague and yet despairing, like a woman who had just had to surrender her baby son.

"It's *all right*," Alfred murmured in English. "The Knight will look after us. He'll tell us what to do. You go on with your hoeing and don't try to think."

Hermann nodded.

"If I hoed for a year or so," Alfred asked, "should I be able to go as fast as Hermann?"

"Not likely. Seeing he's the strongest man on the farm."

"Then I shan't bother to learn. I'll do a very little more at about five o'clock, when it'll be cooler."

"Where are you going?" Hermann asked quickly.

"To sleep. And then just to the store to buy some cigarettes. You see, my hosts and all good chaps, if you keep me in sausage and beer and soup I can buy cigarettes for you. Your paternal and gracious government gives me two marks a day for expenses, besides my railway pass. What shall I get?"

"The little cigars are better value than the cigarettes. Ask for the red-seal packets. Do you get all your expenses money at once, in England?"

" I can draw on any Knight's Marshal up to a certain amount. He writes it off on the paper and gives me whatever I want."

" Then you *could* draw it all at once and have a huge feast in Hamburg or wherever you landed? "

" I could. But I should be slung out of Germany on my ear with an impaired reputation for piety. And I should have to go back to work. I'd rather stay the whole month and see all the Holy Places."

" Which have you liked best so far? "

" The Forest. And the Rhine."

" The Rhine isn't particularly holy. Only in the one place where He swam across it."

" It's beautiful," Alfred murmured sleepily. " Now don't clatter your hoes, you men, when you go back to work."

" He wants kicking, Hermann. Why don't you do it? "

" You do it," said Hermann. " But it's no good kicking him. He won't be any different afterwards. And he might not bring back your smokes."

" Why don't we just murder him and take his two marks or whatever he has, and buy the smokes ourselves? "

" Because it'd be better to torture him, and make him draw all the rest of the money from the Knight's Marshal, and then just kill him after that. They can't worry much if one odd Englishman never comes back again. Come, lads. Time."

Herman sat up and took off his coat. He pushed it under Alfred's head for a pillow.

" Odd Englishman is right," he said.

Alfred, sound asleep by this time, opened his mouth and snored.

" Are all Englishmen as lazy as he is? " someone asked Hermann, as they plodded back to their work.

" They don't just rush about looking for work, any of them. But when Alfred's on a job he's quick and clever. At his aerodrome they think a lot of him. He'd have been ground foreman five years ago if he'd been a Nazi."

Hermann went back to his lonely row. The rhythmical

hard work soothed him; he managed to reduce himself,
very nearly, to an automatic collection of expertly working
muscles. A peace, the peace of emptiness, came to his mind.
But for all his physical absorption he was aware of it when
Alfred, two hours later, woke up and moved off across the
field.

He waved to Hermann, who made an answering gesture
with his hoe. He hoped Alfred would come over to talk to
him, but he did not. He went to the gate and vanished.
Alfred was feeling as strong as ten men. All his life he had
been more refreshed, not only physically, by sleep than by
food or drink or love or lust or triumphs of skill. He never
understood it, but however despairing and bewildered he
had been by his almost life-long struggle to *think* light into
the darkness of human origins, when he woke after a sleep
he always felt renewed to battle, with his gloominess and
dejection and fear of madness gone. It was as if something
inside himself, not his brain, went on thinking, much better
than he could; and though it could not tell him anything
definite, yet he always had the feeling of being a little farther
on than when he lay down. He would go to sleep sometimes
on thoughts of suicide and eternal rest from this bitter conflict, all the worse because it was like a battle with wind and
mist; but he would wake up determined to live till the last
possible minute of his appointed time. "For," he thought,
in these giant moods, "if I go on thinking long enough and
hard enough, I *must* understand." After his sound sweet
sleep in the hedge, the sounder and the sweeter for his wakeful
night and his furious unskilled exertion with the hoe, he knew
that the world really was a paradise. For no Valhalla or
Hero's Heaven or everlasting supernatural bliss of any kind
would he have changed this German landscape and himself
walking in it. He had been happy when he lay down,
owing to the light that had dawned with the Knight's tale;
and now when he woke up he felt that his secret mind, the
one that could never give him any direct message, but which
was always strong and hopeful, had taken its usual forward
leap.

"I shall understand *everything* now," he thought—" when
I get von Hess's book to read it will all be plain. The difficult
part, thinking by myself, is all done. And I was right.

D

There's no Blood. Men are men. Some are stronger than others, that's all. And this woman business. I must think about women. How does one do that? Do they think about themselves?" He made a serious effort to think unsexually and objectively about women, and he was, at least, successful in concentration. When he next realised his physical surroundings he had walked right through the village and was limping along the road towards the woods where he and Hermann had bathed the previous day. "It seems six weeks ago," Alfred thought, turning round again. "Damn my leg. I've walked it farther than it need have gone." But he soon forgot the discomfort again in the interest of his thoughts. Presently he stopped suddenly. He stared down at his stick. "God!" he said aloud, apparently to the stick. "What a weird idea! Has it a hole in it, some-where?"

But his idea had no holes, logically, it was merely quite fantastic and impossible. He began to walk towards the village again. "And it is quite likely right," he thought, "for when I first began to think that I was superior to nearly all the Germans I met I thought that was fantastic and im-possible too. Everything's fantastic if it's out of the lines you're brought up on. At first I must try it on the Knight. Now I mustn't go through the village again without buying the cigars. Red seal. And I ought to get back to Hermann. Six o'clock to-morrow! That'll be another six weeks. My life is lengthening rapidly."

Alfred began to sing a tune he had heard from a Scotsman, a haunting melancholy air which was unlike German music. It had come out of the tribal darkness of old time. "*Row bonny boat, like a bird on the wing, over the sea to Skye.*"

The tune had two parts and there never seemed any reason why one should stop singing it, except that the words came to an end. One part of the air slid into the next and the end of the next slid back into the beginning. The Scotsman used to play it on a wooden whistle, over and over again, until he had sunk himself into a dark Celtic gloom that always left him more cheerful next day. He had a very good whistle, and though he never admitted it, Alfred was almost sure it was a Christian-made whistle. Its tone was so sweet. Perhaps von Hess heard that tune when he was in Skye all those years. How the poor brave truth-defender must have missed the German music! Miles from a public wireless set and unable to have one of his own, unless Arnold brought him one and kept him supplied with valves and things. There'd be no power anyway. But of course he was very rich, he could keep on ordering new ones from England whenever he wanted one. There could be nothing suspicious about the disgraced Knight having a wireless. But perhaps he didn't care to hear anything of the outside world, not even the music. Alfred was not a musical man; he could not sing well, or play a wooden whistle, not even a Christian one, which, in the Scotsman's hands, seemed almost to play itself. But he was very fond of music and at times deeply affected by it. It was hard sometimes not to have a genuine inferiority feeling when he heard a Bach chorale or cantata perfectly rendered by the Nazi choir in the great barracks church in Salisbury. The Germans had such astonishing musical ability. Why, any four bumpkins among them could sing you into happiness or despair, according to your underlying mood, with a simple little part song. And the composers themselves. Bach, Brahms, Beethoven—when one heard them, yes, it *did* seem for a little while as if the Germans had some natural born superiority. For music was important, Alfred was sure of that. Bach was great in a way no man of action was great. " If they'd said *he* was God," Alfred thought, " maybe I'd be a believer yet." A sudden pleasing notion struck him. Perhaps he was *not* German! Perhaps he was long pre-Hitler and belonged to some other lost civilisation. Perhaps he was *English* ! But then he shook his head. There was no particular reason to suppose that the great composers were not German, when the Germans were so obviously an intensely musical nation. " Wagner," thought he, " is as German as the Sacred Aeroplane. But Bach— well, no, but he is above being anything really. He must be, he probably *is*, a kind of peak civilisation in general. The Nazis themselves are inclined to get much more excited over Wagner. Perhaps he really is since von Wied's time, as one's told. An expression of panic somehow, hysteria, all that violence and brutality and holy virtues. But I don't believe anything they say any more. German simply means

man-who-is-afraid-of-the-truth. Except for von Hess. Perhaps at one time they were all like von Hess. Then *there*
was a nation fitted for rule. But directly they started to rule
they went rotten. Then power is rotting, and the more power
the more rot. But I have power over Hermann, and dozens
and dozens of other men, and I'm not rotten. It is *physical*
power that's rotting. It all comes back to that. The rebellion must be unarmed, and the power behind the rebellion
must be spiritual, out of the soul. The same place where
Bach got his music from. From God, perhaps. What is
God? 'A perfect faith in the goodness and universality of
God. The understanding comes and goes like the best part
of the sunset.' Fancy worshipping that little soft dark fat
smiling thing, when they might worship Bach or von Hess.
But of course they don't know about von Hess. And they
don't know Hitler was a little soft dark fat smiling thing, and
he must have been a great man, anyway. Perhaps it's as
sensible as worshipping any other man. Now, cigars, cigars,
think of cigars, or those poor bloody holy Germans will have
no smokes to-night."

CHAPTER SIX

PUNCTUALLY at six on the following evening Alfred and
Hermann presented themselves before the Knight. Von Hess
issued the same orders as before to Heinrich, and after
the door had closed behind the servant he bade Alfred and
Hermann sit down. But neither of them did so. Hermann
started to speak, hesitated and stopped. Alfred helped
him.

" He has something he wants to say to you, sir."

" Well, get on with it, Hermann."

" My lord," said Hermann, looking not at the Knight but
straight in front of him, " if you would graciously allow me I
would rather do my work on the farm and not hear any more
about the book of your thrice noble ancestor. I am not,
please, a coward, but I do not understand very much when you

and Alfred are talking. I would rather hear things from Alfred. So I beg, highly-born, that I may be excused."

"Of course you may," said the Knight, secretly relieved, but courteously concealing it. "I know it's all very difficult, and if you don't want to hear any more, why, it's best you shouldn't."

"I am not afraid to hear things, sir. Only I do not understand very well, and would rather do my proper work."

"Then dismiss. Oh, Hermann, how are those mangolds looking?"

"Poorly, sir. About half the size of Wiltshire ones at the same stage of growth."

"They'll be better after the hoeing," said the Knight, hopefully. "Dismiss."

Hermann saluted, turned stiffly and went out. Alfred sat down in response to a word from the Knight.

"How is Hermann, Alfred?"

"Collapsed."

"He seems all right."

"Oh, I don't mean physically. He works like a dynamo. But he didn't behave at all as we thought he would. He was violent enough when he still believed in Hitler and I didn't, but now you've knocked all his props away. He's collapsed completely into personal dependency on you and me. He's our dog now, not Germany's dog. Hermann has a very weak soul, a baby soul. But he asked me to tell you that though he considers you his father, God and Authority all rolled into one, or words to that effect, he cannot stay in Germany when I go. He says he must kill himself then. He couldn't carry on."

"Even if I tell him he's not to kill himself?"

"I still think he might. It's a great worry. If I overstay my pilgrimage leave they'll drag me back in handcuffs, and I shall be a marked man. Unless you could apply for me to be your private ground mechanic, or something like that."

"I don't want to do that. You're an army mechanic and a good one. All sorts of questions would be asked. Besides, I want that book to be out of Germany before I die. I don't know when that will be. I'm old, and I get bronchitis in the winters. No, you must go back at the proper time, Alfred. I suppose what Hermann really means is that he can't now live without *you*."

" Well, he can't *talk* to you, sir. You're too high above him. He'd be completely alone really."

" He's always been unhappy, ever since he went to England. Even when he still had all his props. I've never seen such a worker as Hermann. The farm has been his only real hold on life the last five years. Well, I'll think of something before you go. Some way to get him to England. Back to the army, perhaps. No, that won't do. There'd be a rain of questions over that. This Empire is so damned well run no one can do anything quietly."

" He *said*," Alfred suggested dubiously, " though whether he really means it only you could tell, probably, that he would submit himself to Permanent Exile rather than stay in Germany without me."

" Oh," said the Knight. " He said that, did he? H'm."

Permanent Exile was a terrible punishment to which death was at any rate theoretically preferred. Few Nazis, given the choice, would have been so lacking in pride as to say they would choose the Exile. It was a sentence given usually only for the very gravest crimes of sedition against der Fuehrer, or religion, or Germany. No single Knight could deliver the sentence, it must be pronounced by a Knights' Court. It meant that the culprit lost his German status entirely and for ever, that his Blood was proved to be now infected and unworthy; he was expelled permanently from the Holy Land, and thereafter was treated as if he belonged to an inferior and conquered race. Alfred had never seen any of those poor outcasts, and it was a subject on which no German would dwell, talking to an Englishman.

" He has to knock a piece off the Sacred Aeroplane, or something awful, hasn't he? " asked Alfred.

" As a matter of fact they'd kill anyone who did that, in case he became wholly reckless in despair and boasted about it. It is usually for treason of some sort though. There's only one private crime that can be punished by Permanent Exile."

" What is it? Murdering a Knight? "

" No. Bringing a *malicious* false accusation against a

German of having intercourse with a Christian woman. It is considered the worst thing one German can do to another, far worse than beating him up or killing him. A mistaken false accusation would be severely punished, for the accuser ought to have been certain before he brought it, but a malicious one is a very serious crime. If Hermann really will go through with it——" The Knight paused, frowning. " I don't believe he'd face it."

" But anyway, will accusing only a boy do ? "

" The Knights' Court would consider it worse to accuse a boy. A young clean creature in the first dawn of his German manhood. Trying to taint him for life with false filth."

" But what about the boy ? I'm perfectly certain it was not a malicious false accusation, even though Hermann *may* have been mistaken. And I don't believe he was."

" The boy is dead. He died yesterday of internal bleeding."

" The poor silly little lout," said Alfred regretfully. " We oughtn't to have made him walk. Only he seemed to get along all right."

" This can hardly be a gentle or humanitarian age," observed the Knight. " The people in Munich are much annoyed that the boy's dead, but really only because he might have sung for six months or so longer. But though the boy, whatever his character, could hardly have let Hermann go into Permanent Exile if his evidence could save him, we needn't worry about his evidence because it can't be given. Hermann must make another deposition to the effect that he is overcome with remorse at the boy's death, that there was no girl there at all (because if there *was* a girl, there is a very strong presumption that it must have been a Christian) and that he brought the accusation in a fury of anger because he was attracted to the lad, and he rejected Hermann's advances with scorn. I dare say there *was* a bit of personal feeling in it. Hermann didn't give the lad just an ordinary hiding."

" No," agreed Alfred. " He had a tremendous access of violence and brutality and soldierly virtue. He'd have kicked the lad to death in the wood if I hadn't stopped him."

" It doesn't matter," said the Knight callously. " As far as

the boy is concerned his life wouldn't have been much good
to him. Hermann would have stuck to it as tight as wax
that it *was* a Christian, and the boy would almost certainly
have confessed. And then he'd have been officially done
for."

" What, exiled? "

" No. As he was only fourteen he'd have been severely
beaten when he was well enough to stand it. But he'd have
had a mark against him for life. But about Hermann, his
two depositions will go up to the Knights' Court. I shall go
to give evidence about the taking of them; Hermann will
confess again by word of mouth, and he'll undoubtedly be
given Permanent Exile. That is, if he has the nerve to go
through with it, and if he really wants to do it. It seems a
curiously roundabout and dirty way to get an innocent man
out of the country, but, as I said before, this Empire is too well
run. The Authority knows where everyone is, and only
Knights and Christians can move about as they like."

" Or pilgrims, for a little while. Sir, I have thought of
something about the women. You say they are discouraged
and won't reproduce themselves."

" I can't say that as a fact. There may be some obscure
physical reason as to why girls are not being born in the
proper quantity. As von Hess says, research into sex biology
was not encouraged even in his time."

" Oh, why? "

" They were afraid the biologists might prove for certain
that it is the male who determines the sex of the child, and
then no one can ever blame a woman for not having sons.
That would be highly inconvenient. Also they were afraid
that it might be established that the female, being the more
complicated and developed physical machine, takes more
vitality in her conception and gestation. That the female is
physically the better sex and that with tired parents more boys
are likely to be born."

" Is there any human evidence to support that? "

" As a rule more boys are born in times of scarcity, sieges,
long blockades, and war, when parents are certainly under
the influence of nerve-strain and fatigue and under-nourish-
ment. The official explanation was that Nature is worried
by the destruction of males and leaps in and restores the

balance. I don't think it at all likely that Nature does things as quickly as all that or as conveniently, and Nature does not mind, either, a shortage of males. One male can fertilise hundreds of females. A shortage of females is the only *naturally* serious thing."

" And that's what's happening now? Without the parents being fatigued or severely under-nourished or under nerve-strain? "

" Yes."

" And you know that women are unhappy, somehow? "

" I know *that*. You would know it too if you were a Knight. They can carry on all right till they get all together at their Worship, and then their deep grief expresses itself in the most miserable caterwauling."

" But if a woman is of herself nothing but an animal, just a collection of wombs and breasts and livers and lights, *why* should they be unhappy now, when they are at last required to be nothing but animals? "

" A cow bellows when her calf is taken from her."

" For a few days. Then she forgets. But your older women then, they are quite happy? They never cry? "

" They always cry, except one incredibly old and filthy thing called Marta."

" Why should the older ones cry if they're only animals? Or why should the young girls cry? "

" What are you getting at, Alfred? I think myself that women have some terribly deep discouragement. I don't deny it."

" But you don't see that that *proves* they must be something else besides animals and an innate desire to please men, like a good bitch with her master. They *are* animals and they *are* pleasing men, or the pattern would be changed. So they are, according to you, being themselves for the first time in history, perhaps. But actually they are discouraged. Why? "

" I don't know," said the Knight. " All of us want to know."

" It's as plain as a swastika that women *are* something more than animals and a reflection of men's wishes."

" But, Alfred, think of them. Even think of the German girl of long ago. She was beautiful, certainly, but just as adaptable and pliant. Women have *always* followed the pattern set, so how can they ever have had anything in themselves? "

" When I was a young boy I was brought up to believe that I was different in some deep unalterable way from all Germans, and that because I was different I was inferior. When I grew up I realised this was not so, and then I thought all that Blood business was religious nonsense, that all men are equal in a way, though some, both individuals and races, have special *abilities*. The Germans have musical ability, for instance. And martial ability. However, I naturally discussed that with no one, and Germans kept on telling me I was inferior. And suddenly one day when I was working in the shop with a very decent but fearfully blood-conscious Nazi I realised if he was *right* in this great difference, then I was not only equal to him, but, of course, superior."

" But why, Alfred? I've no doubt you were, but why of course, *if* he was right about the Blood? "

" Because if there's any real difference, the thing you are yourself is the best thing. A man doesn't want to be an elephant or a rabbit. The elephant if it could think wouldn't want to be a rabbit or a man. It wants to be *itself*, because itself is the very best thing there is in the world. In a way, it is the world, it is all life. The life you are yourself is all life. If you look with envy or longing or inferiority-feeling at any other kind of life, you have lost your life, lost your Self. So if a German *is* a different kind of life, a really different kind, he feels superior, but *so do I*. An *acceptance* on my part of fundamental inferiority is a sin not only against my manhood but against life itself. Do you know the type of Englishman who is always trying to be taken for a German and will hardly speak his own language? "

" Yes."

" You despise them a good deal more than an ordinary fellow who never pretends? "

" Yes, I certainly do."

" And so do most Germans, even those without your knowledge. The Germans consciously want us to accept our inferiority, *unconsciously* they despise us for doing it. For unconsciously they are in touch with life and know it is a crime against life. Well, the reason why women have never been able to develop whatever it is *they are*, besides their animal body, is because they have committed the crime against life. They see another form of life, *undoubtedly* different from their own, nothing half so vague as Blood, but differing in sex, and they say ' *that* form is better than our form '. And for that reason men have always unconsciously despised them, while consciously urging them to accept their inferiority. And just as those futile Englishmen are neither English nor German, but only half-baked cowards and idiots, so women are neither men nor women, but a sort of mess."

" But, Alfred, Alfred, you *cannot* mean that women ought to think of themselves as superior to *us*? It's a lunatic thought."

" It's a logical thought," said Alfred. " You mustn't think of women as they are now, it is very muddling. You must think of the argument. Everything that is something must want to be itself before every other form of life. Women are something—female, they must want to be that, they must think it the most superior, the highest possible form of human life. But of course we must not think it too. Otherwise the crime is committed again, and *we* shall be a mess. Women must be proud of having daughters, we must be proud of having sons. Could a woman, ever in the world, have been as proud of having ten daughters and no son as a man could be of having ten sons and no daughters? "

" No ! " gasped the Knight. " Of course not. As far as I know."

" Then the crime was committed in the real tribal darkness before history began, and there you are," said Alfred, satisfied.

" Where are we? " demanded the Knight.

" There's the explanation why women always live according to an imposed pattern, because they are not women at all, and never have been. They are not *themselves*. Nothing can be, unless it *knows* it is superior to everything else. No man could believe God was She. No *woman* could believe God was He. It would be making God inferior."

" But apart from God, how could women ever think themselves superior, whatever they turned into, when they cannot be soldiers? At least they can be, they have been, as you'll read in von Hess's book, but only a few particularly gifted by

Nature. There must always be force of some kind, to uphold
any kind of law. Women cannot apply force."

" The human values of this world are masculine. There
are no feminine values because there are no women. Nobody
could tell what we should admire or what we should do, or
how we should behave if there were women instead of half-
women. It is an unimaginable state of things."

" Your whole argument is fantastic."

" The argument is as sound and solid as a new block of
cylinders. The ideas raised by it seem fantastic. But you
cannot pick a hole in the argument. Now *I* was thinking
about how it was to be put right, and the crime stopped.
There are two things women have never had which men have
had, of a developing and encouraging nature. One is sexual
invulnerability and the other is pride in their sex, which is the
humblest boy's birthright. And yet, until they can get back
those two things, which they lost when they committed their
crime and accepted men's idea of their inferiority, they can
never develop their little remaining spark of self-hood and
life. We know it is still *there*, or they wouldn't be unhappy
now."

" Of course they can never get complete and certain sexual
invulnerability," said the Knight. " No matter what sort of
laws you make. Laws can always be *broken*."

" I don't mean anything about laws. I mean a personal
invulnerability. Wild animals, female animals, have it.
They have a mating season, and at other times they keep the
males away. They don't want them and they don't have to
suffer them. But I don't mean that women can go back to
that. I mean a soul-power which would come from being
themselves, from being women. Men would never *want* to
force them. It would be unthinkable, impossible."

" Nothing is or ever has been unthinkable or impossible to
men. Von Hess says so."

" Nothing is unthinkable to men who are born of mess.
Lots of evil things might be unthinkable to the sons of men
and women."

" And what is your remedy, my dear Alfred? " asked the
Knight sarcastically.

" The remedy, in theory, is as simple as the argument.
The highest possible masculine pattern of living should be

imposed on women, and when they have come up again to a little understanding, it should be explained to them the crime they at one time committed; that men do not really admire them for it, that inside themselves they hate them for it, and that they may, *must*, now consider themselves superior and bring their daughters up accordingly. Could women possibly be taught to read, before they are themselves, I mean? There's no imaginable limit to what they might be or do afterwards."

The Knight laughed, a little hysterically.

"Alfred, you are really the most fantastic thinker. You don't even know that women could read—read, write, make books, music, pictures, houses (all inferior to men's, of course), be lawyers, doctors, governors, soldiers, fly aeroplanes——"

"*Did* they, by God!" Alfred was amazed and instantly jealous. "And you won't let us! Well!"

"All that, and yet you're saying the only remedy for all sin (as far as I can make out) is that women should think themselves superior to *us*."

"To all other forms of life as well," said Alfred soothingly.

"Certainly you have reached your conclusion by logic. Why, the women who could do all those things never thought themselves *superior*. They were aiming at equality only, the modest little things."

Alfred sighed.

"You will think about women and not about the argument. *Of course* they never thought themselves superior then. They were not *being* themselves. They were living an imposed masculine pattern just as ours do now. They were no more *women* than ours, they were only in a better position to become so, if any man had had the common sense to see what the real trouble was, and tell them about it."

"They didn't know there was any trouble."

"Well, *you do*. You told me that the pliancy of woman is the tragedy of the human race, and when I tell you what causes it you cannot see it or take in the argument at all. You won't look at it impersonally, and that probably has been always the trouble with Germans. But let's leave the women now. We can't *do* anything about it. Do you think there are any books in the Japanese Empire?"

" No," said the Knight. " I won't leave it for a minute.
Supposing what women are is just an inferior sort of man,
and that they *were* being themselves when they were moulded
to the most masculine pattern and could imitate men fairly
well, as they did in Socialist Russia, what becomes of your
argument then? The Russian women certainly weren't
unproductive of girls.'"

" When women are being what they are *really* the pattern
will never change. They won't allow men to change the
pattern. And yet you say yourself that women never mind
the pattern being changed, however much it's to their own
disadvantage. Were women ever doctors and lawyers and
writers and things in Germany? "

" Yes."

" And what happened? "

" Hitler discouraged them. But, mind, he didn't want
them to be wholly illiterate and ugly and animal, and lose
their nationality and class and rejection-rights."

" No, but he wanted to change the pattern a little. And
what had the women to say about it? "

" They were wildly enthusiastic about him and everything he did."

" Then there's your answer. Why should women be
wildly enthusiastic about a man at all? It's an unnatural
crime to allow something totally different from yourself to
impose a pattern of living on you. Now it may astonish you,
but the average Nazi doesn't dislike me at all. I have lots
of friends, fellows I like and who like me, among the Nazis
in England. And that's because though I have to accept the
German pattern of living and belief outwardly, because I
belong to a conquered nation, inwardly I have thrown it off.
They realise, unconsciously, that I am really myself, different
(if there is any real difference between English and Germans)
and *therefore* superior feeling. And they *like it*. They despise the German-English consciously, *and* unconsciously.
They only despise *me* consciously, and half the time they've
forgotten all about it."

" They wouldn't like it much if you ran about saying
you were superior."

" No. Because then religion and tradition and all sorts of
conscious things would get in the way. Besides, it would take

a very long course of impersonal and objective thinking before any German could realise that he *could* still feel superior without making everybody else in the world feel inferior. Do you see what I mean?"

"I can understand your argument when you apply it to yourself and us. But, after all, we're all *men*."

"And therefore not so different. Probably without any right to *fundamental* superiority feeling among ourselves."

"But when you go on to women, I cannot follow you. Their depth of inferiority lies in the very fact that they *are* so different."

"Why does it?"

"Because their physique and their mental make-up prevent them doing anything worth while, doing it *well*, that is, except just their animal job of bearing children."

"And which sex has been setting the standard of what is worth while?"

"Well, the male sex," the Knight admitted.

"And how do you know what women will do when they have stopped being submissive and despising themselves and causing the tragedy of the human race?"

The Knight shook his head.

"Now we're back at the same place again. I will think about what you say, and try to understand it. But I am one of the men, I expect, who cannot be impersonal."

"Well, of course your thinking has been conditioned by von Hess. The only hope probably for impersonal thinking is having to think by yourself. *Any* kind of tradition must rot you up."

"And why haven't you thought about women before? They have always been there. I didn't make them, neither did von Hess."

"I never knew they were important. If you could have made me believe fleas were important I would think seriously and impersonally and as far as possible without prejudice of fleas. I should not say, immediately, oh well, *it's only a flea*. Low, low, base flea."

"But if someone seriously put it to you, a flea thinks itself superior to everything, and the whole of life——"

" It does ! " cried Alfred. " And God likes it to think like that ! Yes, whatever God is, He must want women to feel themselves superior, and fleas, and lice, and men. It's just a condition of healthy life. And now, do you think there are any books in the Japanese Empire? Old books, I mean. Oh, highly-born, let's leave the women. There's so much I want to know."

The Knight almost visibly dragged his mind away from the question of women, which as Alfred treated it was repugnant and absurd and yet somehow held an unholy fascination for him, and turned it on to the Japanese Empire, which suddenly, however huge and however potentially dangerous, seemed friendly by comparison.

" I don't think there are any pre-imperial records there either," he said. " We do not know, of course ; Asia and America are vast places, and the Japanese, however slavishly imitative they are, could probably never manage to be as thorough and as patient in destruction as our people. But von Hess has a speculative sentence about that point. He says : ' Either we shall at some time conquer the Japanese and thus have the whole world and its records under our control, or the Japanese, whose only mental characteristic as a nation is ape-like imitativeness, will copy us and destroy the records themselves in each country they conquer.' All I know is that the Japanese of the Samurai class believe themselves to be the originators of civilisation in Asia and America and Australasia, which is rather amusing, seeing even their pre-westernisation culture, what you might call their own native culture, was borrowed from the Chinese. The Japanese are quite incapable of originating anything at all, or creating anything except yellow-faced babies. Fortunately now even that low form of creation is failing them."

" You are a little prejudiced against them perhaps," Alfred suggested. " Have you met many Japanese ? "

" I was on duty for five years on the Eastern Frontier in Persia, and after the truce had become to all intents and purposes an absolutely permanent peace (until something different happens in one or other of the Empires) there was courteous if not exactly friendly contact between us and the Samurai. I applied for the duty on purpose to get in touch with the Japanese, and I found it duller than anything you like to imagine. They are an utterly boring people. They think of nothing, no *nothing*, except war-machines, their honour and the Emperor."

" But then how do they differ from most German Knights? Isn't it that when you see people you *can* criticise who have the same idea of life as you, you see not perhaps how bad the idea is but how dull it is?"

" I've always known it is a bad idea, and I have always been able to criticise the other Knights. And I do assure you that the Japanese are a great deal duller and more stupid than we are. We have the remnants of a great culture of *our own*; our music, for instance, is ours, it expresses something we have lost certainly, but which *was* German when it was alive. The Japanese have nothing but a few dirty rags all cut off other nations' clothes. If they were to conquer the world, culture could never start again, it would be a lost, permanently lost, human activity."

" Are the Japanese women the same as ours?"

" I never saw any. But the Japanese regard women in the same way as we do, *of course*, as beings without nationality. They copied von Wied's idea, and the women of Asia and America—women all over the Empire—are just the same— ugly, animal and wretched. If only some other nation had conquered the East—the Chinese, or the Siberian Russians, or the North Americans—things would have been very different."

" And if only some other nation than Germany had conquered Europe things would have been different, wouldn't they? Or is it perhaps the conquering itself that is wrong? It is hard to tell which comes first. Whether dull, stupid, soulless nations make the best conquerors, or whether conquest makes nations dull, stupid and soulless. What were the British like when they had an empire? Does von Hess say anything about that?"

" It wasn't a conquest empire really. It was made by restlessness. The English and Irish and Scotch and Welsh just roved about on the sea and took places before other Europeans got there, or places the others didn't want, and suppressed the practically unarmed native inhabitants and just stayed there. It was an empire ruled in the most sloppy way you can imagine; everyone did exactly as they pleased

without any reference to the British Government, and only the
dark races were treated with a certain amount of authority.
It was never strong in a military sense, and when it could no
longer be defended by a big and efficient navy (von Hess
allows you a certain talent for sea-fighting) it just fell to pieces.
The Japanese got most of it and we had the rest, the African
portions."

"And what does he say about the character of the people?
Were they dull, stupid and soulless? Or was a sloppy
Empire better than a military one?"

"He doesn't say. You see, he knew the Germans were
in their madness committing a great crime against humanity
in destroying the records, but he never attributed the madness
to militarism and conquest, thinking those bad things in
themselves. He blamed a flaw in the German character.
A tendency to moral cowardice, mad spiritual panic, he calls
it in one place. His few remarks on the English character
have reference to this weakness of Germans, for in what he
calls the Nordic population of the islands, that is among
the English and the lowland Scots, he finds an opposite
tendency. He thinks little of your ancestors as soldiers or
administrators, he says your general culture was nothing
to compare with the French, that your music was almost
non-existent, and that your only claim to great literature
rested on two poets, both inferior he *thinks* (he says ' *I*
think ') to the greatest Germans, and a magnificent trans-
lation of the Christian Bible. But he says, the English
have one claim to real greatness, which lies in a tough-
ness of moral fibre, an immovable attachment to what
they believe, often in the face of large majorities, to be
right, that von Hess finds admirable. He says, ' They are
sturdy heretics. The best of them are incapable of spiritual
panic, even the ordinary men among them are hard to move
to dubiously moral courses by spiritual pressure. If they
get a notion that a certain thing is right they will hold
to it with the utmost stubbornness. A Christian sect
called the Society of Friends gained influence far out of
proportion to their small numbers by their tenacious devotion to their principles, which included a refusal to bear
arms for any purpose whatsoever. When England was in
the gravest danger both in the 1914 war and the Final

European War a large proportion of these men still refused to fight, no matter what moral or physical pressure
was brought to bear on them, and what is more remarkable than that is that in the 1914 war there was in the
country at large even a certain amount of sympathy, not
with their pacifism, but with their moral attitude. A
genuine Friend (not a coward hiding under the shelter of
the sect) was right not to fight because he believed fighting
to be wrong. A man must do what he thinks right and
(Englishmen are inclined to add) I am the sole judge of
what that is.' Von Hess goes on, ' You cannot imagine
a similar strength of moral feeling among large numbers of
Germans, or that any of them could respect pacifist
principles in time of war; but that very tolerance of
sincerity in ideas which oneself finds loathsome shows a
reserve of spiritual power which I cannot help envying for
our people. In these English and Scotch heretics of all
ages and in the common men who could not withhold
from them all sympathy, England's real greatness lay. If
they can resist, not the physical destruction of their
records, for that will be impossible, but the Germanisation
of their character, and somehow, in face of all the decep-
tion they will suffer, remain themselves, there will be soul-
power in Europe after the passing of this dark evil time.'
There, Alfred. Have these heretics' qualities descended to
you? Have you resisted the Germanisation of your character?
I think many of the English have, most successfully. That's
one reason why the Knights always try to be sent
there."

" I don't think I have," said Alfred dubiously. " I
shouldn't be tough enough not to fight when the other
Englishmen were fighting. I don't really believe in fighting
at all, but I should have to go in with them. It's a new
idea to me that a man might refuse to fight with his own
people."

" You must remember it was a religious principle with them.
It can't be with you. Your childhood's religion was ours,
and now of course you have none."

" Well, it is vague. I react against bloodshed and violence
and cruelty because it's your religion, but I don't know
that I could let any man have even a chance to call me

a coward. Von Hess was a better Englishman than I am."

"He saw that he must be called a coward for the sake of truth."

"Well, I *could* do it, of course," Alfred said, after a pause. "Yes, if it was a question of protecting the book, I'd let my best friends think me a coward. Why couldn't he have collected just one or two more books, the Christian Bible, for instance, and left them with Arnold just the same?"

"He doesn't say. But I think it may have been very dangerous for *anyone* in Germany in the state it was in then to buy anything but technical books. I expect he didn't dare to risk it, not through Arnold, an agent or anyone. And his own were already sealed up. And those sort of books, just on cheap paper, wouldn't have lasted. He says he made his book to endure for thousands of years. Before you go I'll show you how to touch up the letters with a paint-brush if any of them show the smallest sign of fading."

"He might have sent Johann Leder to buy a Bible in some little quiet place in England, and then I should be able to read our claim to literary greatness."

"I know he would have got other books had it been possible. But if he had been found out, we shouldn't even have had *his* book."

"And how were all the things destroyed? Were there a great many books?"

"Millions. And records in stone and in paint and in architecture."

"However was it done? It must have taken twenty years."

"More likely fifty or a hundred, and it must have cost as much as a small war. I don't know how it was done."

"But doesn't he say?"

"It wasn't done then. Only starting to be done. He wastes no parchment talking about that."

"But *someone* must know. There must be records with der Fuehrer, or the Inner Ring."

"Alfred, you're being stupid. If you murder a Knight

you don't bury him in a Holy Field with a tombstone explaining how you killed him. You hide the body and hope
people will think he's been lost or fallen down a crevasse or
drowned himself. Those Germans wanted future generations,
Knights, Fuehrer and all, to be ignorant, wholly ignorant of
the *existence* of other civilisations."

" I see. But there must be legends. We've got legends
about all sorts of things."

" There are no legends about it in Germany. None
that I've ever heard, and I've collected legends since
I read the book at twenty-one. The Germans were
ashamed of it really. They deliberately forgot it as soon as
possible."

" I think in England it's got mixed up with our loss of
freedom," said Alfred. " I don't know anything in particular
about books being burned, certainly. We moonrakers say
that there was once a great building in Salisbury with a
pointed tower where the Holy Swastika Barracks Church
stands. But the Germans tell us we didn't know how to
build with mortar before they taught us, that we could only
put up primitive monuments like Stonehenge."

" The thing with the pointed tower was probably a great
Christian church. There were thousands of them, some very
beautiful, von Hess says."

" Why didn't they just keep them for Hitler churches,
then? "

" Because they were built in the form of the cross and were
packed with records in stone of past civilisation. But Stonehenge is much older than your Salisbury church."

" Does von Hess mention Stonehenge? " Alfred asked,
thrilled and surprised.

" He does, because it was famous in Europe. There is
nothing so good in Germany."

" How old is it? "

" He says it wasn't absolutely certain, but that it was pre-
Christian, pre-Roman, probably Druidic."

" And why didn't the Germans blow that up? "

" Because there's nothing civilised about it, and it served
to remind you of your tribal darkness."

" Well, it's a queer place," Alfred admitted. " I often go
there to think over things. All those great stones lying about,

and the two that are still upright with the thing across the top.
I'm glad they left Stonehenge."

" It's not *yours*," said the Knight.   " Your ancestors were
running about in Jutland or some such place when men were
worshipping at Stonehenge."

" It's mine *now*.   You've made it mine.   Your people
have always dinned it into me that that's *our* primitive savage
monument, and you can't take it away from me now.   I'm
glad you've got nothing like it in Germany.   How did von
Hess get that photograph of the girl? "

The Knight smiled.

" It's a curious reflection that every man who sees that photograph looks more at the girl (once they know it is a girl)
than at Hitler, even though *when* they see it they suppose
Hitler to be God."

" I   didn't   suppose   him   to   be.   Surely   you   didn't
either? "

" Of course I did, at twenty-one.   You can't teach children
dangerous secret heresies, because they can't be trusted not to
talk about them.   The von Hess boys are brought up like any
other Knight's sons, and at twenty-one, or when the father
thinks the youth has gained some stability of character, he
receives this severe shock."

" And of course the father is always an unbeliever? "

" Yes.   It makes a difficulty, a gap between father and son,
but the son comes to understand at last, and then they can
make friends.   There were few happier times in my life than
the years I spent making friends with my father first, and later
with my sons."

" Please," said Alfred, a little uncomfortably, as the
Knight did not go on.   " How did he get the photograph,
sir? "

" Oh, he'd always had it.   It was a much-cherished
possession of his family, one of the few unofficial pictures of
Hitler that were left.   They took great care of it and when von
Hess left Germany he took it with him.   He knew that all
photographs and pictures of Hitler would be gathered in,
and all the statues destroyed, if he was going to be God.
Even greatly idealised, as he was in the statues, he was still
not impressive enough and not German enough to be God.
The Thunderer would naturally have exploded him with a

much larger, blonder, nobler type of physique. Von Hess when he's writing about Hitler states that he has no doubt whatever that it is an authentic photograph of him, and he describes it exactly, so that there shall be no doubt he means *that* photograph. The placing of the figures, their clothes, the somewhat peculiar position of Hitler's hands, and a detailed description of all the faces. He says the girl is a member of the Hitler Mädchen, probably a sort of leader among them, and that the men behind are two of Hitler's bodyguard. Of course Arnold had it when he got the book, and they've been together ever since. Now it is yours."

" Ah," said Alfred, " that'll be grand."

" I wish you were an older man—no, I don't. But that girl is not important except to show what a shaky basis our religion has. How many lies there are that can be shown in just one picture."

" And as showing how von Wied changed the pattern for women. Didn't von Hess think that important? "

" Yes, he did. He found von Wied's ideas so disgusting and unmanly that he writes quite a long piece (he apologises for the length of it) about the history of women. Oh, I suppose she *is* important. But you'll only make yourself unhappy looking at her."

" I'd rather be unhappy. Are all the composers you say are German really German? "

" Beethoven, Bach, Brahms, Mozart, Wagner, Schumann, Meyerbeer, Gluck, Mendelssohn, Schubert, Handel, Haydn, Bruckner, Strauss—oh, scores; I couldn't give you offhand the whole list von Hess gives. All German or Austrian. When they wrote their music the Austrians did not call themselves Germans, but of course they always were. But there are some big things we play that I can't believe are German, and I believe it's Russian music. Von Hess mentions one great Russian composer called Tchaikowski, and several lesser ones. Then doubtless there is a good deal of French and Italian and Spanish music attributed to minor German composers. You often hear things that don't go at all with the other work of some particular man you're supposed to be studying."

" And no English music? "

" There *might* be," said the Knight doubtfully. " But

I doubt if much of it was good enough to last.   There's a most
interesting thing about the music, Alfred," he said, his eyes
brightening with enthusiasm for the subject : " those enormous
works we play of Wagner aren't supposed to be only played;
they're operas.   They're supposed to be acted and sung as well
as played."

" You mean like a Hitler miracle play with heroes? "

" Yes."

" Then why don't they do them? "

" Because the operas are jammed up with beautiful and
heroic and sexually attractive women.   Von Hess says he
knows the operas will have to vanish as themselves."

" I think that's rather silly.   They could have put lovely
heroic boys in the places of all the women and let the men love
the boys.   Men do love boys, nearly all of them, at one time
or another, in one way or another."

" The only unfortunate thing is that boys can't possibly
sing the music."

" Ah, that is rather a facer.   Could women really sing in
those days? "

" Judging by Wagner's music, in which you can trace all the
songs once you have the clue, the women had voices of enormous range and power.   I never can imagine what it sounded
like, however hard I try.   No boy could sing more than little
bits of the songs, even in the soprano parts.   I do not particularly care for Wagner's music, but I often wished I could slip
back in time and hear one of those operas performed.   They
must have been in their way magnificent."

" Why doesn't someone write an opera for men and boys,
with not such difficult soprano songs? "

The Knight sighed, and the light went out of his
eyes.

" No one can write anything now, not even a new march.
No one has written anything for hundreds of years, except the
most flagrant hash-ups and plagiarisms.   You can't cut all
culture off at the root and expect it to go on flowering at the
top.   Lots of us, most of us, love music.   Many of us are
excellent instrumentalists and quite a number of us can sing
in tune and with feeling.   But we can't *make* music.   We have
nothing to make it out of.   No one knows or ever did know, so
says von Hess, quite what will cause a vigorous culture, or how

the creative spirit in men works.   But he says, one culture seems
to grow out of another, one will go rotten, and another spring
up on its grave, with a bit of the old one in it, like manure you
see, and those wretched mangolds that won't grow, but they'd
have grown even less if I hadn't put something into the
ground first.   Now we have nothing in the ground.   We
didn't let the old cultures die, we killed them.   Now we
have nothing, except the memory, in our music, of our
own.   But we killed even part of our own, our literature—
that is all gone; we have nothing but the Hitler Bible and the
legends, and what *we* call the history of Germany.   We are
stagnant.   We're not exactly barbarians, we have technical
skill and knowledge, we are not afraid of Nature, we do not
starve.   But in the rich mental and emotional life men live
when they are *going somewhere*, aiming at something beyond
them, however foolish, we have no part.   We can create
nothing, we can invent nothing—we have no use for creation,
we do not need to invent.   We are Germans.   We are holy.
We are perfect, and we are dead."

" It's extraordinary it should all absolutely stop, like that,"
Alfred said.

" No more extraordinary than that my nose should bleed
when I hit it hard on a rigid steel-bar.   One thing follows
from another.   It's the same with all the other arts.   There
are men who can draw, men who can paint, men who can
carve in wood and stone.   And all they can do is to copy.
They have technique, they know about perspective and so
forth, but they can *make* nothing.   Statues and pictures of
Hitler and the heroes, all exactly alike, all weak and dull.   If
they draw a picture of a cat, well it is a cat.   If the man is
clever it is like a photograph of a cat, if he is not it's like a bad
photograph of a cat.   None of it is art, none of it is worth
doing.   I don't know what a real picture is like, but I do
know it must be very different.   No, there is no civilised
culture in the world now, only remnants of the old.   Our
music, the traditional tunes of the subject races, and all the
legends.   The real legends, not the Hitler ones."

" Tunes like this," Alfred said.   He whistled the Highland
air, the Skye tune.

" That's a Celtic lament," said the Knight.   " It has the
true Celtic melancholy.   The Scandinavian tunes are rather

similar. I think it comes from long dark winters, lack of sun.
It would sound better if you whistled it in tune, and in the
right key. It's a lovely melody."

" I may whistle out of tune, but that *is* the key. Why, I
can hear Angus at it now."

" It's the wrong key," said the Knight. He went to a
corner of the room and took a violin out of its case. He tuned
it and played some runs and arpeggios and chords with such
power and grace that Alfred sat open-mouthed with
admiration. Then he played the Skye tune as Alfred had
whistled it.

" You hear that? "

" Yes, that's right. It starts on that note."

" Then listen to this."

The Knight played it in a different key, lower down on
the violin.

" *That* is the key. Are you so deaf, you unmusical English
dog, that you can't hear the difference? And are you so
half-witted that you think that any music from the simplest
to the greatest can ever be played except in its own key, the
key that suits the form and thought of the composition?
Would you transpose the symphonies of Beethoven, and then
think they would sound just the same? Yes, you probably
would."

" The first key was the one Angus always played it in,"
said Alfred obstinately.

" And what did he play it on? "

" A whistle."

" Of course. And the key of the whistle was D flat. You
can make accidentals on those primitive home-made wooden
whistles by not wholly stopping up the holes, but owing to
their small range you cannot conveniently play anything
except in the key of the whistle itself. Had Angus sung it
or been able to play it on a violin he would, of course, have
put it in the right key. Now here is another Celtic tune,
either Irish or Scottish in origin. I heard it first from a
Japanese."

The Knight played a simple, sweet and very melancholy tune on the violin. First he played it in single notes
and then with a rich deep double stopping. Alfred was
entranced.

"Ach, you like that, do you?" asked the Knight sarcastically. "Ach, how English you are, Alfred! No one should play double stopping with Celtic melodies. They were not made for that, they are too sweet themselves. The harmony overloads them, and makes them sickly. It is just what you *would* like. Shall I play it again?"

"Yes, please," said Alfred, unabashed. "It's lovely."

The Knight played it again, with tremendous feeling, his cloak shaking gracefully back from the shoulder of his bow arm, his great nose bent down towards the violin, and his eyes rolling towards his appreciative audience. Afterwards he played an aria of Bach, a severe cold piece of music.

"Just to get the taste out of my ear," he explained, when he had finished.

"You play beautifully, sir," Alfred said. "Even an English dog can hear that."

"I used to play a little," said the Knight, with a sigh, putting the violin back in its case. "Not well, really. Now my fingers are getting stiff. If I really wanted to play something I should have to practise three hours a day for three months and at the end of that time they still would not be supple enough."

"Did you say you had that lovely tune from a Japanese?"

"Yes. But *he* didn't make it. The Japanese have no more real music in them than a tom-cat, and their singing sounds very much like cats. It is an American traditional tune, an old tune. He knew its name, but no words. It is called 'Shenandoah', and the Shenandoah is a river in North America. That Samurai was one of the very few who had a tiny spark of intelligence and taste."

"But if it is an American tune why should it be a Celtic tune?"

"Because there was a strong Celtic influence in America. I don't care what you say, Alfred, if the man who made that tune was not a Scotsman or an Irishman, or else under hypnotic Celtic influence, I would—I would break my violin. It *is* a Celtic tune. Now sing me or whistle me an English tune. I think I will have the violin out again to play it. I can hear it when you whistle, but it is not quite itself."

"No German but you has ever heard this tune," said Alfred. "It is a secret one."

Alfred whistled a tune, and the Knight played it through. He smiled.

"And what words do you sing to it? Secret rebellious words?"

"Yes. We sing:

> "*God send our warrior-king,*
> *God send our valiant king,*
> *God send our king.*
> *Send him victorious,*
> *War-worn but glorious*
> *Long to rule over us,*
> *God send him soon.*

> "*Thy choicest arms in store*
> *On us be pleased to pour*
> *On churl and thegn,*
> *Scatter the enemy!*
> *Death to all Germany!*
> *England will yet be free*
> *In that great reign.*"

"What!" cried the Knight. "Do you mean all you good English Hitlerians sing that song?"

"No. It's a heathen song. But all of us know it, and *some* of us sing it, sometimes. A great leader is to arise and arm us, you see. There are stores of arms taken from the Germans left over from the war if we knew where to find them. Parts of aeroplanes and tanks and things."

"They'd be a lot of use, after six hundred years and more, wouldn't they?"

"Oh, I know. It's all nonsense really."

"What do churl and thegn mean?"

"Nobody knows. They're the men who are to be armed, anyway."

"*Kerl*, of course," said the Knight. "Those must be very old Anglo-Saxon words meaning common fellow, *Kerl*, and officer. Like Nazis and Knights."

"And king means leader. Fuehrer. We have two words for leader, you've only one."

" On the contrary, king is a German word. It comes in von Hess. *Koenig.* A king was not in later history quite the same as a Fuehrer. It became a hereditary office. Der Fuehrer is chosen. Kings were born. When there were no more dynastic kings in Germany, and history had vanished, the word vanished too. But you've still got it because you are still fundamentally irreligious and disloyal. I'm glad. Only you'll never beat Germany and free yourselves by force of arms. You mustn't allow yourselves to be made stupid and violent by your secret song."

" We don't really. Only the English tune helps us to keep ourselves together—such of us as want to."

" But then it is not an English tune," said the Knight.

" It *is* an English tune! " said Alfred angrily. " It is a very old sacred English tune. I'll bet you it was sung all over the old empire to different words."

" It may have been, but for all that it is not an English tune. It is a German tune. I have heard it in Saxony. Besides, I should know it was German if I had not heard it in Saxony. It is a typical good, sound, rather dull German tune."

" You want to have everything, even our tunes now! You leave us nothing, nothing at all! I wonder you allow us to eat or to wear any clothes! "

" Alfred, do not get so heated. I shall have to play you some more double-stopping. And whatever you say, and if you kill me, you will never get me to admit that that tune is anything but German. Whistle me another English tune."

Alfred whistled another, a sad but sweet melody. The Knight played it, first in single notes and then with harmonies that brought tears to Alfred's eyes and made him forget the insult the Knight had offered to the sacred secret English tune.

" The double-stopping is all right for that melody," he said. " It is more sophisticated than the Highland air, not quite so *purely* sweet—yes, it is allowed to have double-stopping. It goes well. Ganz gut! "

He played it again. Alfred thanked him, bending his head down so that the Knight should not see his tears. He was ashamed of himself for being so deeply affected, and yet there was something about the old German's playing or about the tune itself——

"You are allowed to have that tune," said the Knight, laying the violin back in its case. "It is not Celtic, and not German. Certainly not Russian, 'nor is it at all like the French or Spanish folk-melodies. It has a quality of its own. What are the words?"

"It is a love-song from a man to a beautiful youth, and it starts, ' Drink to me only with thine eyes.' "

The Knight softly sang these words in a voice that had lost all tone but was true and clear.

"Ah, yes," he said. "Of course it is a love song. But it was never written for a boy. The words have got altered like your rebel song. It's an old song written in the time when women were beautiful, and men had to woo them, to court them, perhaps to be rejected. Ah, yes. Now if you think of that German girl in the photograph you can come to a faint understanding of the tune—not musically, it is very simple there, but emotionally. No tunes like that have been written since men gave up loving women. No tunes at all of any kind a quarter as good as that little English song. But, Alfred, you must go. I have wasted all our time in trifling matters and have explained nothing. I have to go to Munich to-night."

"In the aeroplane? The new one?"

"I'm going in my car. I'm being more careful now, taking no risks whatever. And have you had any supper?"

"No, sir."

"Then go to the kitchen and find out what Knights' personal servants get to eat. They live too high for an officially Spartan empire, but the Knights are not Spartans except voluntarily, and the food is always there, so naturally the servants eat it."

"What is Spartan?"

"Another warlike half-civilisation like ours. Now, be quiet, Alfred. Stand to attention. I am going to summon Heinrich to take you to the kitchen. Come to-morrow earlier, say at four. Bring Hermann with you. I must find out what he really wants to do. And think of some more tunes. But no, we have so little time. Only I must show you—ach, here is Heinrich!"

Chapter Seven

"Hermann," said von Hess, when this curious trio were together again upon the following day, " are you really willing, you an innocent man, or a comparatively innocent man (you killed that boy), to submit to Permanent Exile in order to go to England with Alfred? "

Hermann's face twisted like that of a man in severe pain, but not out of any unmanly feeling of pity for his youthful victim.

" My lord, I am willing," he said in a low voice.

" And are you sure you can put up with the examination, the confession, the Knights' Court sentence, the public degradation, and the journey through Germany? "

" I can put up with all that, sir. Please, highly-born, I am not a coward."

" You don't know what it'll be like. Have you ever seen a Nazi degraded and sent to Permanent Exile? "

" No, sir."

" Well, I have once. It's terrible. Even though I do not believe in the Blood, I found it terrible. And I cannot do anything for you, or give you countenance, or speak to you after the sentence is passed. I shall never be able to speak to you or see you any more after that."

Hermann's face twisted again.

" My lord, it will be my deep grief not to see you any more. I—I think I will not do it."

" Then will you be a good lad and do your work and behave yourself sensibly? "

" No, my lord. If I don't go I shall kill myself."

" But then you won't see me any more either, at least it's all very problematical."

" I think I had better go, sir," said Hermann.

" You must be certain. Once I've started this I can't possibly stop it. It'll roll over you like a tank. Do you think you can live in England without killing yourself? Because if you're going to do that anyway you might just as well die a good German in Germany and be buried here."

" I can live in England with Alfred. He says he can get me work in an English farm, under Englishmen. In Wiltshire somewhere not too far from Bulfort."

" And will you protect Alfred and my book that I've given him as far as you are able? "

Hermann held his head up higher, and drew a deep breath.

" With my heart's blood, my lord."

" Well then, as you can't go on being a Nazi and my man, you are Alfred's man, to serve him and protect him as you would me."

" I shall do that, my lord."

" Then now listen. I went to Munich last night on this business of the boy Rudolf, who died the day before yesterday. I have shown no one your deposition yet. You are officially under Knight's Marshal's arrest for beating the boy so severely that he died. But that would be an accidental killing and naturally nothing much would happen except that you would be flogged to teach you to be more careful in future and remember that boys of fourteen, however tough, are not men. If I make this deposition public "—the Knight touched his tunic pocket—" nothing would happen at all. To kill a boy in the commission of the disgusting crime of race defile-ment is not murder in any true German's eyes, any more than it is murder to kill a bluebottle. But to get you Per-manent Exile you must dictate another confession to me, that this first deposition is a malicious false accusation, and to make it plausible you'd better say you brought it out of sudden jealous hatred of Rudolf, because he wouldn't have anything to do with you."

" Yes, sir," said Hermann, in an expressionless voice.

The Knight paused.

" Hermann, there is a Knights' Court in a week. But I must give notice of the case to be brought. If you miss this one there will be no more for three months."

" I'll go before this one."

" But it means that you must come and make your second deposition to-night. It must be taken with the other to Munich to-morrow. And to-morrow you will have to go to jail in Munich."

" I will do that, sir."

"And you won't be able to go to England with Alfred. In Germany he must pretend to be as disgusted with you as anyone else. Besides, you'll be under guard till you're on the ship."

"Will they send me straight there after the degradation?"

"I believe they will."

"Then I shall be there about the same time as he is."

"You can go to my house even if you do get there first," Alfred said. "Thomas and Fred and young James will be there. Will he have any money, sir? Or will he have to walk from wherever he lands into Wiltshire?"

"He'll have any money I give him. I can't give him very much, of course. But they won't take it away from him. In England until he gets work he'll be entitled to an old woman's ration of food, which is half nothing, and of course if any English farm foreman cares to employ him the estate owner won't stop his wages. And, Hermann, you won't be allowed to look like an Englishman, or be able to pass for an Englishman as long as you don't speak."

"I know, sir. I shall have to wear a special red uniform and if I take it off I shall be beaten."

"Yes, you'll be a recognisable outcast. Every Nazi has the right to kick you, and every Englishman to scorn you. Are you sure you can stand it?"

"Yes, sir. When shall I come to give the highly-born my second deposition?"

"Oh. About five. But stay now if you like, Hermann."

"Sir, I would rather work on the farm to-day, if you please. We have not even to-day quite finished the mangolds."

"Oh, damn the mangolds. Oh, well, all right, you'd better go. You'll be happier working, I expect. I'll give you my last commands and advice to-night. Dismiss."

Hermann went out. The Knight looked very distressed, but he said nothing.

"Sir," Alfred ventured after a long silence, "will they let him choose his place of exile? What if they send him to Russia after all he'll have been through?"

"They let them choose any place in the Empire so long as

it is out of Germany. If an exile said he wanted to go to South Africa they'd send him there. The punishment is in the exile and being an outcast, they don't mind where a man goes to."

" A real one must feel bad about it."

" I'm afraid Hermann will for a bit, even though he loves you and he's not a real one. He ought not to have been told, Alfred."

" All Germans ought to be told."

" Yes, but not yet. The time is not come."

" How will it come? "

" I don't know how. There are two things that might happen. First, I do not think, the nation can stand another fifty years without war. Perhaps they can't even stand thirty. Then the deep wretchedness which comes from being unable to adapt to changed conditions, permanent peace in this case, will make them do *something*. They may turn upon the Knights and der Fuehrer, revive some of the old socialist feeling and believe that it is the Social Order only that is causing them misery. In that case there would be civil war, some Nazis being loyal to the Knights, and some Knights, a very few of them, siding with the discontented Nazis. But the subject races would probably not be content to let the Germans smash themselves up, but would raise idiotic rebellions; that would pull the Germans instantly together, and whatever they did about the Social Order Germany would turn and rend and smash the subject races again, and be glad to do it. But I don't believe any of that is so likely to happen as a gradual, or not so gradual, loss of faith. An uncertainty about the religion, the ethic, our whole philosophy. Because it *is* a stinking corpse, and its smell is coming through. It is a religion which must die directly there is no *possibility* of war, it is really only very useful and lively actually in time of war. Well, then, when this loss of faith is getting a real hold in Germany, when men in their extreme wretchedness are beginning to grope about for new ideas, for new thought, for a new ethic, that is the time the Evangelists of Truth must start their mission. They *may* come from all sorts of places, both within Germany and without, but I know one place from which, if we all have good luck, a message *will* come, and that is from England. Not in my lifetime, not probably

in yours, but some time. You must make the nucleus,
Alfred, with the help of my book and your own character,
and you must train the men. Train your sons—have you
sons?"

"Three."

"Good. Get three more. And train other men's sons.
Accept no weaklings into your truth society, and no stupid
men, not yet. Make sure of every man you have, and don't
try to have too many. And warn them, warn them, Alfred,
with all the soul-force you have, against violence. I don't
mean telling them just not to kick physically against the
German authority, I mean warn them against accepting
violence as a noble, manly thing. We Germans have done
that, we have brought force to its highest power, and we have
failed to make life good, or even, now, possible. So for God's
sake warn them against all our bodily soldierly virtues, and
make a new set of spiritual virtues, and preach them. Make
them understand von Hess. Officially and on the top he
still believed in force, in conquest, in physical domination of
man by man, but his virtue and his heroism were of the soul.
Remember that 'the choicest arms in store' for men are
spiritual honesty and courage. Sometimes," the Knight
went on, fixing his large grey eyes dreamily on Alfred's, "I
think that the past civilisations with all their unimaginable
complexity and richness—for von Hess says he cannot tell a
millionth part of their wonder—sometimes I think that
perhaps even they were only the childhood of the race; that
this gulf, this dreary blankness, is like the dullness that comes
on boys sometimes at adolescence, and that our manhood is
yet to be. That perhaps God allowed men to commit this
crime against truth through his handy instruments, the
Germans and the Japanese, to make a break between childhood
and manhood, to give us a rest, to enable us to overcome regret
for what cannot come again. If we knew the marvels of our
childhood we might want to get back into it again; so long
as we do not know, but only know that it was *there*, we can go
forward with good heart. It will be your business, and the
business of your descendants, to let these dull boys, these
stupid destructive adolescents, know that they are not perfect,
that they *have* had a brilliant childhood, and that they will,
if they can but proceed with their duty of growing up, pass

on to a maturity before which the childhood genius even will be like a candle in daylight. Have you any man to whom you could trust the guardianship of the book *now*? You must not leave it, like I did, to chance. You have no reason to do so. I was uncertain of my duty, you are not."

" I have a man," Alfred said.

" How old is he? "

" Seventeen."

" Too young," said the Knight, shaking his head.

" He's the best man to leave the book to I know. It's not that he's braver or stronger-minded or more trustworthy than lots of others of my friends, but he's the cleverest."

" Well, I hope he will be a great deal older before he actually has to take charge of it. It is your son, I suppose? "

" Yes, young Alfred."

The Knight smiled, remembering something.

" Has this valiant King-Fuehrer who is to deliver you all from Germany got a name, by any chance? "

" Why, yes. His name is to be Alfred. The same name as a great English king who lived some time before we were conquered."

" Conquered which time? "

" Ah, I don't know."

" But you do know you were conquered twice? That the Germans were not the first invaders, but the second? "

" We have a legend that we were conquered before, but that we ate up the conquerors. But the Scots say they had never been conquered at all."

" That is interesting. Yes, you were conquered, and von Hess mentions it because it had important results in Europe. About a thousand years before Hitler, the Normans, who were men of Scandinavian descent, settled in the north part of France, conquered the Anglo-Saxons and took England."

" And did we eat them up? It doesn't sound like it."

" In a way you did. They had to stop ruling England from France, they became English, and then tried for hundreds of years to rule France from England. That is as if the Knights of Southampton and London and all the English districts remained there all their lives and later on their descendants

raised an army of Nazis and Englishmen and Welsh and
Scotch and Irish, and attacked Germany."

"That wouldn't be such a bad scheme, just to go on with
until we can tell the truth."

"I'm afraid more than half of you is bloody-minded," said
the Knight, shaking his head. "As to the Scots never being
conquered before Germany did it, it seems likely enough.
Von Hess just says that at a certain date—I've forgotten it,
seventeen something—Scotland and England were united and
the British Isles were all under one king. It sounds more
like an arrangement, a marriage or something, than a war."

"Does he say anything about a king called Alfred?"

"Yes. He organised the Saxon law, and prevented
England from becoming Scandinavian."

"Ha!" said Alfred, grinning with pleasure. "There *was*
one, you see. And there *will* be one. Young Alfred's son,
perhaps. The messenger."

"It would be a good idea if I wrote to the Knight of London,
and told him to round up all the men in the province of
England who are called Alfred Alfredson, and who have named
their eldest son Alfred. I shall tell him he can safely shoot
them all for certain disloyalty."

"Oh, that wouldn't be fair, sir. Why, it's nearly as
common a name as Hermann."

"What, going on and on from father to eldest son? And
that reminds me, you asked me how you lost your surnames.
I think it is because the German Government wished the
common men, the Nazis and the subject races, to have as
little family feeling as possible. The Knights are allowed to
have family feeling; you see how dangerously strong it can be.
The von Hess men have never done anything about the book,
but none of them have destroyed it, as is their duty as good
Germans. But the Knights are aristocrats and must have
family pride. The Nazis are only allowed to have pride in
Germany; the Blood itself is to be their family, and so all
their surnames were proscribed, and there is only a limited
number of ordinary German first names they are allowed to
call their sons. No man can cock himself up with the
possession of a rare name. But all that was arranged long
ago. I do not really *know* about it. It's just part of the social
order *now*. Knights have surnames, Nazis don't."

" And what were *we* to take pride in ? "

" Oh, nothing. Your surnames must have been proscribed to prevent the Nazis being jealous. After all, every man in the Empire has a registration number, and what more can you want than that ? "

" Oh, I don't care. Alfred's good enough for me, and we call the young 'un Fred. But there's another thing that's been puzzling me a lot. If you wanted to Germanise us, why did you let us keep our own language and our own script? It's bound to hold Englishmen together if they have a different language and a rather different way of forming letters. It would have been easy to enforce the speaking of German in the Boys' Nurseries."

" We didn't want to Germanise you in any way except in making you accept our philosophy and your inferiority. If our blood and our language are sacred we cannot have every little Russian and Italian and English boy acquiring our language as a birth language. It is not fit for such as you to have by *right*, you must learn it for our convenience, that's all. There are two ways of running an Empire. One is to make the foreign subjects feel that they are far better off inside the Empire than out of it, to make them proud of it, to give them a really better civilisation than their own, and to allow them to attain full citizenship by good behaviour. That was the Roman way. There were thousands of men who proudly and gladly called themselves Roman who hadn't a drop of Roman blood in them. They had the legal right to do it, and shared in the privilege of the ruling race. The other way is to make the subject races think themselves fundamentally inferior, believing that they are being ruled by a sacred race of quite a different kind of man, and to deny them all equal citizenship for ever. That is our way. We could not dream of allowing any man to call himself German unless he is German by birth. We are the Blood. All you are the not-Blood. So you must speak your own languages and write your own script, and think, in English, how holy we are, how Hitler could never possibly have been anything but German, and how there can never be any other philosophy or way of life than ours. You are not even allowed to have equality within the religion. There are several ceremonies in our churches from which foreigners are excluded. Exclusion is an excellent way of making men feel inferior. Then again, within the religion which you're all supposed to believe in and quite a lot of you actually do, you are always laymen. You can never be priests——"

" But what is a priest? "

" A man who conducts the ceremonies of a religion."

" That's only a Knight."

" We had the sense not to have priests *and* Knights. That always leads to trouble. Church and State really *are* one in the German Empire, and der Fuehrer is the Pope."

" I don't understand."

" In the Christian religion the priests—that is, the men who conducted the ceremonies and might go into what corresponded to the Hitler chapels, the holy men—were usually a different set of men from those who did the administration and the governing and the fighting."

" What an amazing idea! But one set or other must have been paramount."

" Not at all times. The priests had spiritual power and the Government had temporal power. The nobles were often more afraid of the priests than the other way on."

" The priests were armed, then? "

" No. But they could curse people."

" What of that? Knights have often cursed me."

" They could exclude them from the benefit and blessing of God."

" Could they really? I don't believe it."

" Of course no man can ever exclude another man from God. The people *thought* they could, that's all."

" Then they ought to have killed the priests."

" But that in itself would have excluded them from God. The priests were sacrosanct, like der Fuehrer and the Inner Ring."

" But you say they weren't *Knights*, only priests, with no real power at all except cursing. Naturally a man's sacrosanct if you get flogged to death for hitting him in the face. If I could hit Knights in the face and have them do nothing to me but curse me, there are one or two in England I should slap—quite gently, of course."

" I'm afraid you're too irreligious to understand. The people, and even the nobles, could not approach God except through the Church, that is, the priests. Just as you can't approach a Knight except through the Knight's Marshal. And you couldn't approach der Fuehrer at all, in any possible way. And if you annoy the Knight's Marshal you won't get through even to a Knight, will you? Then this was the same : if the people or the nobles annoyed the priests seriously they were cut off from God."

" What would that matter when God was not cut off from them? Why, supposing der Fuehrer has heard of me and says, ' I want to see that interesting fellow Alfred who is going to take von Hess's book back to England,' none of you can keep *him* away from *me*. If you can, he's not Fuehrer at all, *you* are. If the priests could keep God away from men and say, ' You can go on blessing this chap, but you must now keep from benefiting that chap,' then He's not God. He's inferior to the priests. And while der Fuehrer is only a man and doesn't know me or a millionth of the people under his rule, God must know everybody and if they want to come to Him or not. Nobody could ever have believed such a crazy idea as that a man could keep God away from other men."

" God gave the priests the power to keep Him away from them."

" That's crazier still, because it would mean that God deliberately resigned and gave away His freedom of judgment to a lot of priests. Why, if those people believed all that they were in a way less civilised than you are. Dumber, anyway. When I was a little boy and still believed in Hitler I never thought any Knight or der Fuehrer himself could keep Hitler away from me. As far as me and Hitler went you could all have fallen into the sea. I used to pray, ' Please, Hitler, let me get into the Technical School,' without thinking I had to go and bother a Knight about it."

" Ours is not a supernatural religion, not in the same sense. There is no hell in it, and as the soldiers and priests are one, and ours is a warlike religion, you are ruled in a soldierly way, not in a priestly way."

" It'll be a merry day in England when you try to rule us in a priestly way," said Alfred, chuckling. " Knights' heads will be sold for a shilling for the teeth."

" And yet the Messengers will have to go more in a

priestly fashion than a soldierly, if they're to be any good."

" Ah, that's different. They're not going to go about pretending they can get between God and any man. They're going to tell the truth. There's nothing priestly about that. Who are the arch-devils? I suppose they're really no more devils than Hitler is God."

" Eh? " said the Knight. " Who do you mean? "

" The devils in the creed. Does von Hess say what they really were? "

" Oh, them. Well, Lenin and Stalin really were a bit like devils because they were Russian leaders, and the toughest fight Germany had, by a long way, was against Russia. Lenin, however, was dead long before Hitler came to power, and he never got anywhere near Stalin personally."

" He never flew to Moscow in the Sacred Aeroplane at the head of the air fleet? "

" Of course not. He was far too precious ever to be allowed to risk a finger-nail."

" Then he wasn't a hero? "

" I've no doubt at all that he was a brave man, because Germans would never follow a coward. But he wasn't allowed to *do* anything. It's only for purposes of divinity he's allowed to go into action."

" Then was Roehm as bad as he is made out in the Hitler Bible? The arch-traitor, the deceiver, the fiend who took on the form of one of the Hero-Friends? "

" I don't know why he's been picked out for Judas, because there were several men in it."

" Who's Judas? Several men in what? "

" Judas is in the Christian religion. The friend of Jesus who betrayed him. Roehm was a man who either did rebel against Hitler soon after he came to power, or did not rebel and was killed for some other reason. Several men were killed, and von Hess says the episode remains obscure. It may have been important at the time, but it certainly was not a full-dress rebellion. Roehm was a friend of Hitler's, and a man of considerable power before he did whatever it was he did wrong, but I really don't know why he and none of the other delinquents got into the Creed. They were

most of them important Nazis. As for Karl Barth, the fourth
one, I can find out nothing whatever about him. Von
Hess doesn't mention him. I think it possible that, seeing
two devils are Russians and one is a German traitor, Karl
Barth may represent the other enemy, Christianity. He also,
I think, must have been German, and naturally to Hitlerians
a German Christian would be more deadly than any other
kind."

" Being tougher? "

" Or more disgraceful."

" Karl Barth ought to be in the Hitler Bible. The other
three are mentioned in the Hero-Fights."

" Karl Barth is a mystery," said the Knight, sighing.
" One we can never clear up. He may have been an ordinary
man like Roehm, or a great leader such as Lenin and Stalin
undoubtedly were, or he may have been another such man as
von Hess, a man of soul. On the other hand, he may have
been a really evil fellow. I never say the Creed without
wondering about Karl Barth."

" I don't know how you can say it at all without laughing."

" It is absurd, and yet it is not absurd. That Creed has
held this huge Empire together for over six hundred years.
Nonsense of such endurance value almost ceases to be nonsense."

" That's dangerous thought. If it endured for a million
years it would still be nonsense, just as if no one believes in
truth ever it wouldn't stop it being truth. How do you
think I'm to get this book to England, sir? "

" I've thought of that. I am going to wrap it and seal
it and address it as from me, with my name written on it, to
the Knight of Gloucester. He's a friend of mine. If the
Nazi officials open your sack anywhere, either this side or the
other, they'll never dare to break a Knight's seal. And no
Knight would do it. It would be a discourtesy for which
I could challenge him. I shall write on the outside of the
package, ' By the bearer, Alfred, E.W. 10762,' then no one
will be officious enough to think they ought to take it away
from you and send it through the post. If they ask you
what's in it, you will tell a large fat round lie and say you don't
know. If they ask you why you, an Englishman, were

chosen to be Knight's messenger, you'll say that I took a fancy to you, which isn't quite such a lie."

" And what if some Nazi official remembers it and presently writes to the Knight of Gloucester to know if he ever got his huge important-looking parcel? "

" The Knight of Gloucester will then take it up, through your Knight's Marshal, with you. And you will simply say you're very sorry but it fell into the Avon, or the sea, or whatever you think best, but that anyway you've lost it. And that you hardly liked to write to the Knight of Gloucester to tell him so. Then the Knight of Gloucester will simply say to himself, ' Poor old von Hess is quite batty at last, to trust anything to a half-witted Englishman,' and he may write to ask me what was in it. I shall write back and tell him it was detailed plans on parchment for a new attack on the Japanese with things that burrow underground and come up behind them and he will say, ' Sad, sad,' and not bother any more. But I don't think the Knight of Gloucester will ever know anything about it. Nazi officials are very chary of interfering even with the best intentions in any business between one Knight and another, and no one even as high up as a Knight's Marshal is likely to look into your sack. Get some twigs as from the Holy Forest and a stone or two as from the Holy Mountain."

" I have some genuine ones."

" What for? "

" A man asked me to bring some back. A homesick Nazi."

" Oh, poor lad! Well, I hope they'll make him feel better. And what are you going to do with the book instead of taking it to the Knight of Gloucester? "

" I'm going to put it underground until it can come up behind some Germans. Now I'll tell you something very secret, a real English secret, and you won't be able to say you've heard *this* in Saxony. You know Stonehenge, of course? "

" Yes."

" Did you by any chance notice a little chalk quarry, or what looks like a chalk quarry, about due east, a quarter of a mile, not far from those old ripples that must have been a trench system? "

" No."

" A sort of raised lump with a chalky face one side ? "

" Wiltshire's so covered with lumps.   No, I don't remember it."

" Well, it's a burrow all right, but not a primitive one. It's an old gas chamber or dug-out.   A concrete room, a big one, underground."

" Don't the Nazis know about it? "

" No. Its front fell in, either in some bombardment or a chalk slide in bad weather.   It was blocked up.   I was poking round about Stonehenge ages ago, when I was only nineteen, and I fell through this loose bit of chalk into the entrance of the dug-out.   I was half killed.   But I got out all right and told no one, and then I made a tunnel through the chalk into the dug-out and concealed the end of it."

" And what did you find, gas? "

" No.   The air was just plain bad, but with the hole in the chalk it gradually got better.   After a while I could go in safely.   I found a decent big dug-out, a little room off it and eleven skeletons.   Mouldering skeletons.   Just slightly unskeletonish.   They didn't smell bad exactly, but very queer and musty.   But I put some disinfectant on them and they soon settled down again."

" Why didn't you put them out?   It's quite likely they died of plague influenza."

" I couldn't put them out.   Supposing I carted them off to bury them and some Nazi sergeant saw me and said, ' Hi, Englander-schwein, where did you get those bones? ' No, I kept them in.   But I wanted a two-way run to my rabbit-hole, so I told another fellow, a young chap of my own age who worked in the Armaments in Salisbury.   He stole some explosive and we blew a bit out of the corner of the big dug-out.   At least we cracked it up and then we could make a small hole."

" Did he know anything about blasting? "

" Not very much.   But we didn't stand and throw matches at the stuff, we fixed it with a decent long fuse and waited for a thunderstorm.   A beauty came at last, at night fortunately, and I rushed up there from Bulfort and fired it. It didn't blow up much of the top part of the dug-out, but when I was waiting for the thing to go off, lying outside in pouring rain, I got the most terrible fright we might have put far too much in, and then the whole dug-out would go up and perhaps about half a mile of country and Stonehenge too. I was very young and stupid, and we knew really nothing about explosives. And there came the most terrific bang of thunder and I thought, ' Oh, God, there's Stonehenge gone.' I never thought I'd be gone myself. Well, it was all right and there was just a nice little thump, quite un-noticeable in the storm, and when we could next get there together we saw it was all right. So we tunnelled through the chalk and made a much better concealed entrance the other side of the lump where there were some little juniper bushes. Then we got all these stiffs, and wired them up."

" Wired the stiffs? What's that in German? "

" Wir haben den Draht durch die Skelleten gerannt. There were eleven of them, ten men and one little one. Must have been a child, though what it was doing there I can't think. There was an old machine-gun, all hopelessly rusted and jammed up, and some rifles."

" ' Arms from thy choicest store,' " said the Knight, sardonically.

" We had a good laugh over that," Alfred admitted. " But we found out what liars *you* all were, anyway. The Germans have always told us that all the old dug-outs and concrete stuff, and the old holes under London, were made by *them*, hundreds of years ago, to protect us and themselves against the Japanese. And we found on the concrete, painted with everlasting paint, ' No Smoking.' In English. A give-away, was it not? But I didn't believe in Hitler any longer, neither did Tom, my friend. I stole lengths and lengths of wire little by little from the shop and we wired the skeletons together, leg-bone to leg-bone, and arm-bone to arm-bone, to make them firm, you see, and dressed them up again in their bits of rags and other clothes we made out of anything we could find. We set the machine-gun up in the entrance with four men and made each skeleton be in its proper place doing what it ought. We gave the other men their rifles and leaned them up against the wall at stand easy, propping their toes with stones. They look fine by torch-light. It took us about eighteen months to fix those stiffs, because we could only go up there at night. But we got them all set at last, and those ten Englishmen will guard that place better in their death than in their life. Nazis are afraid of ghosts in England. Did you know that?"

"I know they're afraid of Stonehenge. Yes, it's a good place, where your dug-out is. What did you do with the child?"

"We buried him. He was a very little skeleton; we dragged him out of the back hole and buried him a little way off. At least we buried him thinking he was an English *boy*, but I'm a bit doubtful now. There was some long hair— about, not exactly on his head. I think he must have been a little girl. Well then, I made a great wooden shield or door for the little room in the dug-out and took it up there in bits and painted it muddy colour. It looks exactly like the rest of the dug-out by torch-light. So that's where I shall keep the book. The Nazis will never find the place itself, because they don't like fossicking about near Stonehenge, and there is nothing to look for there. If they find the place they won't like those grim soldiers all set up near the entrance. They'll just say, 'Ach, Hitler!', and leave them there, doing no harm to Heilige Deutschland. And even if they should get past the soldiers they won't find the inner room."

"And what about your friend, Tom? Is he absolutely trustworthy? Does anyone else know?"

"No one. I thought, there *may* be a time when this'll come in handy. But not while we're all just not believing in Hitler and singing 'God send our King' on the downs at night. We must be doing more than that. So I didn't tell anyone."

"And what about Tom?"

"Tom's very trustworthy. He's dead. He got in a fuss with some Nazis at the Armament, and they kicked him to death."

"Ach!" said the Knight.

"You ought to be quite pleased. Tom was very dis-loyal."

"Well, I am not pleased. He was a brave lad, and brave boys should not be kicked to death."

"Oh, well, it was a long time ago," said Alfred, comfortingly. "Tom wouldn't bear any malice. He was very bloody-minded, and would have liked to kick the Knight's Marshal of Salisbury to death five times, to start from perfect health every time. But he was a pleasant lad. The fun we had over those poor stiffs! They all had names, and we laughed at them, but we thought about them when they'd been alive too. Until it made us too savage and gloomy."

"How do you think they died? How did you find them?"

"Just lying about. The child had died with her head on a dead man's shoulder. At least he hadn't moved afterwards. They weren't broken, except King Nosmo, who had the top of his head bashed in."

"King Nosmo?"

"No-Smo-King. Nosmo our King. King Nosmo. Like King Alfred."

"Is that a typical English joke? I don't think it's very funny."

"It was funny to us. We nearly choked ourselves, because we didn't dare to laugh very loud, just in case someone was going over the top and could hear us. King Nosmo was our pet skeleton, and he looks the ghastliest of all because of his head. The others I think must have been gassed or died of disease."

"Well, it really does sound a fairly safe place, though not a quarter as safe as if you were a Knight and left the book unlocked in a drawer in your writing-table. But how about the Christians in the district? Are there many? They're always about at night setting snares and taking them up."

"There are some Christians at Amesbury."

"That's very close. They'll be out after hares and rabbits on the downs."

"Well, I know, but I don't think they've ever found the place. You see, no one can find it accidentally, so to speak, any more. When I fell through, all the chalk settled down firm and no one can fall in again. The hole that end doesn't look as if it went anywhere. The other hole is always blocked up unless someone is actually inside. It's blocked with a stone too big for a boy to move. I've got awful work to move it myself. It's a piece of that big solitary stone outside the main part of Stonehenge that's all smashed up."

" I know it," said the Knight. " That stone must have got a direct hit with a bomb or shell."

" So it doesn't look really very odd for a comparatively small piece to be a bit farther away than the other lumps and fragments. We lugged it over one night. And I hope it'll guard the book as well as it did whatever it was supposed to do when it was joined on to the big one and standing up."

" Are the Christians afraid of Stonehenge? "

" No. But they're superstitious about other things. If one of them does find the front entrance he won't like those old soldiers. And besides, even if Christians did find it and found the book and everything they wouldn't do anything about it. They can't any of them read. They'd know it was either an Englishman's burrow or a very queer Nazi's hide-out, and they'd never interfere or even say much about it. Christians attend strictly to their own business—praying to Jesus, mourning the Sin, poaching, carving wood, making whistles and baskets, brewing herbal remedies and engaging in illicit buying and selling with the future denizens of the fiery lake."

" Yes," said the Knight, " I am so thankful that it has always proved impossible to prevent all trading with Christians." He rose and opened the door of a little cupboard in the wall. " I have here the best collection of Christian whistles of any Knight in the Fatherland. When I am dead and my property reverts to the State, some zealot will probably feel himself impelled to burn them all. It will be a great crime. I have them in every key, and there is not a German one among them. The Christians must have a secret method of treating the wood before they make the holes that gives the whistles that peculiar sweet bird-like tone. It is a fascinating little primitive musical instrument. There is a kind of music you really cannot play satisfactorily on anything else. Listen to this."

The Knight selected one of his whistles and played a delicious cool little air on it.

" You hear, Alfred? That is not primitive music, but it is the thought of a man with his head full of bird-song. So the

Christian whistle is the suitable instrument. No nightingale—
no blackbird—could sing more sweetly and purely. You
know that bird-music in what we erroneously call the Siegfried
Symphony of Wagner? It is not a symphony at all, but an
opera, of course."

"Yes, I know it."

"That bird-music should always be played on Christian
whistles. It can be done perfectly well. It would not *fit*
with the more sophisticated instruments, any more than a
bird's voice fits with anything else in the world. It just would
be birds, unfitting, startling and delicious. But unfortunately
I have never dared to suggest that it should be even tried.
There are so many things a sensible man would like to do but
which cannot be suggested. Many things." The Knight
sadly put his whistle back and closed the cupboard.

"How did you get all the whistles, sir? You can't go to the
Nazi go-between and say, 'Get me a Christian whistle in
C major.'"

"No, no. My people bring me the whistles. Every now
and then at long intervals a man will let me know he has a
whistle. I send for him, and I say to him, 'You are sure this
is a German whistle?' He says, yes he is sure, he knows the
man who made it. Then I hear him play, and if, as occasionally happens with the tone-deaf, it is a German whistle
I give it him back. It is not the key I want. It is very childish
and stupid, for they all know I won't buy anything but a
Christian whistle, and a good one at that, but formalities must
be preserved. And, of course, it is very wrong and irreligious
of me to collect Christian whistles. I ought not to allow such
unclean things inside my house. And I am indirectly encouraging trade with Christians which it is my duty as a
Knight to put down. But they forgive me all that part. For
one reason, they are mainly musical men themselves, and
for another, I am von Hess. When I was away from
home on foreign duty in England and Persia and France
and Egypt I had to be more careful, but here, even though
it is within a walk of the Holy City, I do what I like.
Feudal aristocracy, for ours is in feeling feudal, has great
advantages."

"Yes, for the Knight," said Alfred, with a grin.

"And even for the Nazis too."

" In keeping them boys and not allowing them to be men."

" They cannot be *men* while they are still under discipline of any kind. I cannot be a man myself if I swear *blind* obedience to der Fuehrer and really mean it. But my not-men, my Bavarian Nazi boys, are better off under me than under the Army Knights and sergeants. That is a cold, uninterested discipline, mine is a paternal rule. Until men can rule themselves, a father is a better thing to obey blindly than a government."

" It depends on the fathers. All Knights, I suspect, are not like you, even in their own home districts."

" No. There may be bad fathers. Cold, unaffectionate, unjust, more cruel than even our religion permits. But a government *must* be cold."

" But not necessarily unjust. The Nazis should be the government themselves."

" What, all of them ? "

" No. Selected ones."

" Who is to select them ? "

" The Nazis."

" And who is to be der Fuehrer ? "

" The selected ones would choose der Fuehrer."

" Now think of them all as English and not German, and if England was free, would you promise *blind* obedience to any man, always, even if he had been selected by Englishmen ? "

" No. I should have to be the Leader myself."

" Without knowing anything about democracy you have found the flaw in it. In a democracy no man of character is willing to give up his right of private judgment, and as he cannot blindly trust his leader, knowing him to be of the same clay as himself, *he* must be the leader. So government becomes exceedingly difficult. Because while there are many men of character, and democracy encourages them, there is also the large mass of weaker men, who must be told always what to do and what not to do, and cannot be trusted to live rightly without laws. So the end of democracy, von Hess says, is always the same : it breaks up into chaos, and out of chaos comes some kind of authoritarian government, a Fuehrer, an oligarchy, government by the army, or something of the kind. Now I am not so contemptuous of democracy as he is, because I have seen the ultimate natural decay of authoritarian government, which is complete stagnation. But I still do not see how democracy can be made to last long enough to develop character in a sufficient number of people. That will be the problem of your great-grandsons, Alfred, for once truth has come back to the world the authoritarian form of government must collapse."

Alfred was deeply interested, frowning with concentration.

"I don't think people ought to chuck—what did you call it? democracy, just because it's *difficult*," he said. "They ought to be so certain it's right that they can face any difficulties. If they persevered with it, it would get easier and easier, after a time. Did they ever try it for very long?"

"Well, no, because of the menace of war. Soldiers cannot be democrats, and armies, even the armies of democratic countries, were always authoritarian."

"Soldiers cannot be men of character, of course," said Alfred. "They can't be *men*. They must always be boys. I've always seen that."

"And again an authoritarian government behind the authoritarian army gives a nation enormous advantage in time of war. The democratic countries, when war was threatening, were panicked by their severe handicap, and loss of faith in the form of government was inevitable."

"Then what it really means is that democracy is too difficult to be persevered with when war is likely to happen, not that it is actually too difficult for human beings to cope with."

"I expect that is it."

"And there is another thing. Has a democracy ever started in a community, a nation, where the men all really considered themselves equal, no one fundamentally and *unalterably* superior to any other?"

"I should think it most unlikely. Democracies rose on decayed aristocracies."

"But you see *we'll* start fair from the bottom. In Germany there'll be numbers of discontented Knights, disgusted at the loss or sharing of their privileges. But not among *us* once the Empire has broken up. All Englishmen are so low in your

eyes that they're equal, and we feel equal in our own estima-
tion too.   There is no *class*, as there is in Germany.   There
are only men who can read and men who can't.   *That*
doesn't really matter."

" No.   When there is nothing to read but the Hitler Bible
and absurd legends about the heroes and technical books,
literacy has an entirely different significance from that which
it had in old time.   A boy who is to be a technician learns
to read just as part of his job, it causes no jealousy among those
who do not want to be, or are not fitted to be, technicians.
Hermann has the Bible read to him in church, and saves his
eyes.   And there are advantages in not reading.   Hermann
sees far more than you do.   He notices things about weather,
about nature, about animals, and all movements and changing
aspects of the world he lives in that you would never see.   The
illiterate eye and brain are different from the literate, but unless
the man is half-witted, they are in their way just as good.   It's
not only that Hermann is a farm-worker.   I've noticed the
same thing in illiterate factory workers who tend the simple
machines.   They see things differently.   But you will have to
teach your young men to read, Alfred.   They must read von
Hess for themselves."

" Fred can read, and speak baby-German, but he doesn't
know much grammar yet."

" You must teach them to read German.   Von Hess is not
difficult.   But don't try to do things too fast.   Neither Jesus
nor Hitler nor their best disciples could convert Europe in
their lifetime.   If you can make twenty men really understand
before you die you will have done well."

" I don't understand about Jesus.   Where did the Jews
come from ? "

" They were an Eastern Mediterranean people, not black,
but dark, and I gather a little like Arabs to look at."

" But where are they now ? "

" They don't exist.   They were either absorbed into other
nations or wiped out.   There were a few left in von Hess's
time.   The Palestine Jews were killed, massacred to the last
man and the last child, when the Imperial German Army took
Jerusalem.   The German Jews were killed in various pogroms
both during and after the Twenty Years' War.   The Jews in
other countries were harassed first by the anti-Semitic authori-

tarian war governments of those countries, before Germany
conquered them, and were much reduced in numbers, and
then were harassed over again by the German armies of
occupation. But how the last remnants disappeared I don't
know. It happened after von Hess's time, as did the segrega-
tion of the few faithful followers of Jesus. The end of the
Jewish tragedy is in the gulf of our darkness. There must be
plenty of men of Jewish descent, particularly in Russia and
America and England where they had mixed more with the
indigenous people, but there are no Jews as such. They were
an unlucky people."

" After they killed Jesus? "

" No, always. Enslaved by the Egyptians, then by the
Babylonians, then by the Romans. Then the massacre of
Jerusalem and the dispersion (like a whole nation going into
Permanent Exile), then the Christian persecution. And
hardly had the Christian persecution, which had a religious
motive, stopped, than the racial persecution started. And
hardly had a little portion of the Jews made a new home in
their old home in Palestine, than the Germans pushed the
Empire down there and killed them all."

" Why did everybody hate them so much? "

" I cannot make out," said the Knight. " Von Hess does
not know. In his time there were too few of them for anyone
to wish to do more than despise them and leave them alone.
There were none in Germany then. Von Hess had read a
great deal about the Jews, but said that even in his day it was
not possible really to understand anti-Semitism. They had
the unpleasant characteristics of all people who are persecuted
persistently and made to feel aliens in the country where they
live, but they had brilliant qualities. And they were fanatically
brave if once they started fighting. They resisted Titus
heroically, and they resisted the German Imperial Army.
Titus rewarded them with crucifixion, and we more mercifully
shot them and clubbed them. I think that the whole world,
not only the Germans, must somehow have been afraid of the
Jews. But von Hess could not feel the fear, and so he cannot
understand the hatred. Now no one is ever afraid of
Christians. We look on them rather as we look on wild
animals. If they got savage they would be shot, but as
they're harmless they can be left alone."

"But there are so few of them. When there were a lot and they were preaching Jesus against Hitler, weren't men afraid of them?"

"I don't think so. Not in the same way. Von Hess says that the Christians in his time had most of them no heart for their religion. Germany was not Christian, it was without religion except devotion to Germany, and the subject races were for the main part only Christian because to be so was to be anti-German. There were tough ones among them; Christians are everywhere in Europe, even in Germany, but the majority had no heart for it. Now Jews always seem to have had a good will to be Jews, and to contain in their Jewishness something very menacing. But then they were a race, not only a religion, and perhaps Blood will tell. Sometimes. And perhaps Christianity came too soon. Perhaps it was too difficult, like democracy. Von Hess, writing with his martial side uppermost, despises it. He says it is an effeminate religion."

"What does that mean?"

"Like a woman."

"How could a religion be like a woman?"

"It made men be like women."

"They couldn't ever. Oh, well—I did think that perhaps Hermann—oh, yes, I see. It's because the women were more like men. But too soon? Do you mean Christianity will come again?"

"I don't say that. But rejection of war must come again. I mean a conscious rejection, not this dreary involuntary starvation. Now von Hess would have said when he started writing that any man who denied the glory and goodness and beneficence of war was effeminate—that is, like a woman."

"Well," said Alfred, "if I had him here, and saving your presence, highly-born, I'd knock his head off."

The Knight smiled, and then sighed.

"I shall miss you, Alfred. I shall miss von Hess, and I have to assist at the formal disgrace of one of my own Nazis. It's a wretched end to an old man's life. Well, here you are. Our time is up."

The Knight had drawn from the desk a very imposing-looking parcel covered with seals, and most carefully addressed in his meticulous German writing:

From Friedrich von Hess, the Knight of Hohenlinden in Bayern, to the highly-born Wilhelm von Hodenlohe, the Knight of Gloucester in England, by the hand of the bearer, Alfred, E.W. 10762, Englishman on pilgrimage in Germany.

Alfred stared at it and said nothing.

" The photograph is inside the book," the Knight explained. " I have not put the plate in. I shall break it. That print is good for a hundred years if you keep it out of strong light, and before that time someone will be able to make a new plate from it. Take care of it. It is not as important as the book, but it has significance."

" But, sir, you said you *were going* to pack the book up. Do you mean I've got to go now, altogether? "

" Yes. But I did not want to spoil our last conversation with thoughts of parting."

" But why can't I come again? I don't *half* understand things yet. You say you can do what you like."

" Up to a point. But when the others know, as they will to-night, that Hermann has gone to jail, then I cannot see you any more. They will know afterwards *why* Hermann went to jail, and that I, as Knight, am from this evening in a sort of shameful mourning because one of my men, a Nazi personally known to me, is disgraced. I could not be expected *then* to pay any attention to an Englishman, however mad I was, and if I did go on doing so there would be definite suspicion of something odd about the whole affair. You see? "

" Oh, I do. But it's very upsetting. I shan't be able to understand the book."

" Von Hess says a half-witted man can understand it. If there are, as there must be, words that are lost now, you will guess their meaning from the context. Hermann will perhaps be able to help you at first with bits of German you can't understand. But, indeed, though your accent is deplorably British, your command of German seems to be quite good."

" Nothing like as good as yours of English. Oh, the things I meant to ask! I never thought of this because I know it's all put up about Hermann. And can I walk right out now with this parcel under my arm? And of course I can't come with Hermann to-night because he's going to make his foul confession to you."

" No. But you can walk out now with the parcel and show it to the whole village if you like, though I shouldn't do that, and then I think you had better get your sack and walk on somewhere else. To Munich, I think. You must finish your pilgrimage properly. You see, I have done all this with a light heart because all I know so far is that Hermann has accidentally killed a boy whom he swore was interfering with a Christian girl. But after to-night I am not light-hearted any more, and it might be as well if you were started on your journey, and had separated yourself from our affairs."

" I'm not very light-hearted now," said Alfred. " Can I say good-bye to Hermann? "

" The more affecting and public your parting is the better. If Hermann could weep it would be an excellent thing. He is already working himself up to come to me to-night with his horrible tale."

Alfred was standing up, his precious package under his arm. He was staring at the Knight intently, as if he were trying to make a clear photographic image in his brain. He sighed, and presently looked down at the desk.

" When I was a young man," he said, " I used to get little Fred out from the Boys' Nursery in my free time, and take him a walk down the Avon or somewhere, and we used to play a game: ' I love my love with an A, because he is Alfred. I hate him with an A because he is an ass, or annoying, or angry,' or something bad, you see, and then young Fred used to do it to me. All through the alphabet, and sometimes in German, to teach him a few words.'

Alfred looked up at the Knight again.

" I love my love with a G," he said slowly, " because he is good. I *hate* him with a G, *because he is German*. If I could only remember your face and hair and the shape of your beard, and your eyes, and forget that blue tunic and the cloak, and those silver swastikas on the collar! You have done us a very great harm, because now we can't really love all through, as we should like to, even the best German, not even the *best man*, if he should be a German, in the world."

" Well," said the Knight, with a little cough, " I agree that it is lamentable. But you think too much of me,

Alfred. I am not the best man, I am merely a man with special advantages. A lucky man, and that is not admirable. I pass my luck to you and I hope it won't kill you. So good-bye."

He held out his hand, and Alfred shook it, wondering with half his mind how many centuries had passed since an Englishman had thus been treated as the equal of a Teutonic Knight.

The Knight sat down again, and said, " Attention. I must summon Heinrich."

Alfred stiffened and stood staring into vacancy above the Knight's head till Heinrich came in.

" My lord," he said, saluting.

" Take this man out, and inform the Knight's Marshal that I am ready to see him now."

" My lord," said Heinrich.

Alfred and he saluted, but Alfred walked out in a very slummocky English way, with his head turned over his shoulder. The Knight did not look up. He had his long slender old hands before him on the desk, and was gazing down at his ring.

CHAPTER EIGHT

ALFRED arrived in Southampton in the early afternoon of the last day of his pilgrimage. His pass gave him till eight o'clock on the next morning, when he must report to his Nazi foreman at the aerodrome. He dawdled about in Southampton till the evening, with plenty to say to the English dock-workers about his travels in the Holy Land, then he walked out on the Salisbury road and presently hailed a passing lorry.

" Where to? " he asked the driver, a German.

" Bulfort. Any good to you, Englander? "

" Nein. Danke schön."

Alfred walked on, the weight of von Hess's enormous tome pressing into his shoulders through the straps of his sack.

Soon another army lorry came bumping along behind him. Alfred thought: " If this one is going up to Bulfort, I'd better take it even if it is a German. Or I'll get on it and go as far as Salisbury with him anyway." He stopped it.

" Where are you going to? " he asked in German.

" Bulfort, you son of a million pig-dogs," said the driver in good Wiltshire English. " Jump up, Alfred, and don't talk German to me, please."

" Oh, what luck, Johnny! I couldn't see you properly. Oh, that's grand! Now I can go to sleep. Wake me up at Amesbury, will you? "

" Won't you tell us about your pilgrimage? " the driver's mate asked.

" Any time you like but now," said Alfred, yawning. " I was sick all the way from Hamburg. I'm short of sleep."

He wedged himself comfortably between the driver and the youth, his mate, with his precious sack down on the floor where he could feel it with his feet. He leaned towards the youth in order not to interfere with Johnny's driving, and was almost instantly fast asleep. The lorry noisily sped on through the darkening landscape. Johnny presently switched on his headlights. When they got to Amesbury it was quite dark. Johnny woke Alfred up with a dig in the ribs.

" Amesbury, Alfred. D'you want to get down here? "

" Please. I've got an appointment with some ghosts up at Stonehenge."

Johnny laughed, and threw Alfred's bulky sack down to him.

" Hitler! What've you got in that sack, Alfred? "

" Stones from the Holy Mountain. Good night, Johnny. Good night, Charles. See you soon."

The lorry drove on, and Alfred turned his face to the west. Charles said, " He can't really be going up to Stonehenge this time of night."

" Not he," said Johnny. " Though I know he likes the old place. He's probably going to see a man in Amesbury and walk up. And I bet it isn't stones from the Holy Mountain in that sack, either. Alfred's a damned old hypocrite.

I'm twice as religious as he is, and I don't get pilgrimages chucked at me."

Charles laughed. " The pious ones don't need pilgrimages," he said. " They think Alfred's faith wants strengthening."

" It does, and how," said Johnny.

At four o'clock in the morning Alfred reached his own house in Bulfort where he lived with Fred and James, his two eldest sons, and Thomas, his younger brother. His sack was considerably lighter. He went quietly into the room he shared with his boys, pulled off his boots and coat and lay down. Fred heard the little narrow bed creak.

" Father, is that you ? "

" Yes, my lad. Don't wake Jim up."

" I was afraid you were going to be late on report," Fred whispered. " We've been expecting you any time all day. Young Jim's been as nervy as a cat about you. Just let me wake him up and tell him. He's probably having bad dreams."

" Bosh," said Alfred. But he got up and went over to the younger boy's bed. " Guess who's here, Jim," he said, shaking the boy's shoulder.

Jim woke up, and greeted his father so demonstratively in the dark that he managed to give him a hard box on the ear.

" Damn you," said Alfred. " There, go to sleep again." He kissed Jim and went back to his own bed.

" Why are you so late, father ? " Fred asked.

" Tell you some time. Not now. Go to sleep, Fred. We've got to get up in less than three hours."

Next day Alfred did his work with only half his mind. He did it automatically well, but he could not keep his whole attention really on it. He had meant just to leave von Hess's book in the inner chamber of the dug-out and go straight home, but when he got to his secret place, and found everything undisturbed, the dead soldiers still on guard in their accustomed positions, the pile of flints and crumbled chalk he and Tom had scraped out of the back tunnel the same as it had been, he had succumbed to the temptation to sit down on the old pile of sacks he and Tom had brought there years ago to rest on and read a little in

the book by the light of his torch. He had read until the
torch began to dim, and he came to himself with a terrible
headache. He decided to bring candles up for general use.
There was a draught through the dug-out when both ends
of the runs were open, but he could sit and read in the inner
room where they would not gutter, and keep the hinged
wooden shield open to have some air. He put the book
away, crawled down the tunnel and stopped up the end
of it with the old piece of stone. He stumbled back across
the downs to Bulfort with his knees failing and his head
full of confusion and glory, and the wonder of the vistas,
like jewelled fairy caverns, faintly revealed by the little light
von Hess had been able to leave still burning. And to-day
how could a man think whole-heartedly of mechanism,
even though it was his proper and satisfactory job, when
by walking a mile or two and crawling down a hole, he could
get in touch with lost civilisations and the thought-mechanism
of complex human beings?

At dinner-time in the English mechanics' mess his absorption did break up. The meal was finished and the men
were idling about ostensibly listening to the news on the
loudspeaker until the whistle should blow that would send
them back to work. A man called Alfred aside from the
group he was addressing on the subject of his pilgrimage, which everyone found more interesting than the
news.

" Alfred," said the man, " your woman, Ethel, has had
her baby, and it's only a girl. It's about three weeks old
now."

" Oh, I'd forgotten about that. Well, can't be lucky
every time, I suppose. Thanks, Henry. Have you taken
your son away yet? "

" No. Margaret'll have him for another six weeks."

Alfred said no more, but he grew thoughtful and un-
responsive to the other men.

When his work was finished and he had taken his evening
meal at home with Thomas and Fred and Jim, he put on his
coat again. He had been sitting comfortably in his shirt
sleeves.

" You're not going out, father? " young Jim pleaded.
" You haven't told us anything hardly yet."

Fred said nothing. He was a patient lad, a tall lanky fair creature, not at all like his father, with deep-set intelligent blue eyes.

"I am going out," Alfred said. "I'm going to be here the rest of my life, Jim. You'll hear my tales so often you'll be sick of them."

"If you're going to be here the rest of your life you can stay with us this evening," said Thomas reasonably. "Where are you going?"

"To the Women's Quarters."

"Oh, well," Thomas sounded resigned. "Did anyone tell you that baby of yours is only a girl?"

"It was born three weeks ago," snapped Alfred. "I suppose I can go and see Ethel if I like?"

"Certainly, certainly," said Thomas, peaceably. "No one is trying to stop you."

Alfred grunted and went out. The Women's Quarters was a large cage about a mile square at the north end of the town. The women were not allowed to come out of it without special permission, which was very rarely granted. They had their hospital inside it, and their house of correction, where they were sent if they injured each other or failed in perfect humility. Their rations were brought to them every day, and once a day all women and girls who were not in late pregnancy or ill were made to do some gentle feminine physical exercises under bored male instructors. Otherwise they could do what they liked, but they had nothing to do except nurse their small children, cook their little rations, and quarrel. Their clothes were made for them and doled out like the rations. Once a month they were driven out of their enclosure and up to the church, and that was the only time they were allowed to walk in the streets of the town like the men. They did not relish this privilege at all, because the Worship made them cry. They got on better living their stupid lives in little groups of two or three women with their daughters and very tiny sons, who lived each group in the small wooden separate houses. They hardly knew that there were women who could move about freely, the Christian women; because they never saw a Christian. They knew vaguely that there were some horrible things called Christians, and that they were not required to be submissive to the male monsters among them, but temptation was kept out of their way. No Christian would come within half a mile of the sentry at the gate of the Women's Quarter in any town or village. Other men were allowed to go in at any time, so long as they were over the age of sixteen. To prevent incest, which was considered weakening to the race, a certain house (or houses) was pointed out to the son by the father as barred. The women in those houses were not for him. The sense of taboo was so strong on the sons that they usually avoided that part of the cage altogether. None of the women found their lives at all extraordinary, they were no more *conscious* of boredom or imprisonment or humiliation than cows in a field. They were too stupid to be really conscious of anything distressing except physical pain, loss of children, shame of bearing girls, and the queer mass grief which always overtook them in church.

Alfred made his way through the girls' playground where a crowd of small children, too young for the dullness which overtook all women at puberty, were playing like puppies; not a recognisable game—there was no one to teach them any games—but just chasing and fighting and tumbling. If they got in his way, Alfred moved them out with his foot or hand, not ungently.

He came to the house where his woman, Ethel, lived with her sister Margaret, who belonged at the time to the man called Henry. He walked straight into the living-room. Henry was not there, neither was Margaret, unless she was in one of the bedrooms. Ethel was there, looking dully unhappy and not well. The new baby was nowhere to be seen. When Ethel saw Alfred she got up weakly, bowed before him, and began to move towards the door of one of the inner rooms. She would not speak unless he did.

"Stay here, Ethel," Alfred said. "I don't want that."

Ethel began to cry.

"Master, I am ashamed," she said. She was about as unhappy as a woman could be. She had offended Alfred by bearing him a girl, now he would take the white armlet off her jacket which showed she was one man's present property, and some other man would take her. Alfred was never unkind; he never beat her or kicked her or even cuffed her. She might do so much worse. She might even have to go to the big house where the Nazis went, and though that would mean a long rest from child-bearing, for the German men were taught how to prevent racial calamities of this kind, the prospect never rejoiced any woman's heart. They had no national feeling, all men were equally lords, but they could not understand the Nazis, and the Germans were also inclined to be physically more brutal than some, at any rate, of their own men. Ethel would cheerfully have borne Alfred a child every year till she died, in order to be kept by him away from the Nazi house. But Ethel felt all this in a vague dull way, as she felt her weakness and a dragging pain in her back. She was wretched and she was ill, but she knew it hardly more than an animal would have done.

" Sit down, Ethel," Alfred said, seeing her begin to shake as well as cry. " You're not well yet."

Ethel sat down. Alfred looked at her, and thought of the German girl in the photograph.

" I shall find it easy enough to leave you alone till you're quite strong," he said, more to himself than to Ethel.

" Master, I am ashamed," Ethel sobbed.

" It's not your shame," said Alfred. " It's ours."

Ethel didn't even try to understand this, but she felt a little happier. Alfred had not touched her armlet yet.

" Woman," said Alfred after a long silence, " where is my daughter ? "

Ethel stared at him. Alfred had used the form of words spoken by a father fetching his holy male child, and had applied them to a girl !

" Well, where is she ? You haven't drowned her, I hope ? "

" No, master. She's asleep in the bedroom."

" Fetch her."

" You—you want to *see* her, master ? "

" Ethel, if you don't get up and fetch my girl quickly I'll clout you one over the head. If I get her myself I may break her."

Ethel threw herself on her knees before him and clasped her hands.

" Oh, master, I am a shameful woman, but I have borne two sons. Do not hurt the girl, oh, do not hurt her ! "

" You want to have one to keep, eh? I'm not going to hurt her. *I want to see her.*"

Ethel, completely bewildered but obedient, went to fetch her baby-girl. She hesitated half inside the door of the living-room with the little bundle clutched in her arms.

" Bring her here," said Alfred.

Ethel came a little closer.

" Put her in my arms."

" Master, oh please——"

" I'm not going to hurt her. There, that's right. Is that the way to hold her? She seems quite placid. Is it a strong baby ? "

Ethel hovered near with a terribly anxious look in her eyes, like a bitch whose new-born puppies are being handled.

" Yes, Master. For a girl. Please, could I—could I have her now ? "

" No, sit down. She's quite happy with me."

Ethel sat down. Her anxiety was beginning to abate. Alfred's actions were wholly incomprehensible, but she was at last aware that he did not mean to hurt the child. Alfred sat with the little ugly still new-born thing in his arms, thinking very strange thoughts. The baby had quite a crop of dark brown hair, which would, of course, fall off, to be replaced by baby down. Then, when she was older, and had some real hair, it would be shaved off and kept shaved like Ethel's ugly little head. This was the only skill the women were allowed to acquire, shaving each other's heads with a safety razor, because of course no man would undertake such a humiliating job. But it had to be done under super-vision, and the women were not allowed to keep the razors. They might use the little blades in fights. Alfred was thinking, if I took this baby away from Ethel and from all other women and never let her see a man or a boy and brought her up by myself, and taught her to respect herself more than she respected me, I could turn her into a real woman. Something utterly strange. Beautiful perhaps, like the Nazi girl, but something more than just being beautiful. I could make a new kind of human being, one there's never been before. She might love me. I might love her. Or would she by heredity be like Ethel? No, because Jim and Robert aren't like Ethel, dull and stupid. It's not in the womb the damage is done. Ethel can't despise the child in the womb because she doesn't know what kind it is. This little thing could be made into a woman, but it'll grow up to be exactly like Ethel.

" Ethel," he said, " how would you like it if I took this child away and brought her up myself, and she turned into something quite different from you? "

Ethel only understood that Alfred was for some utterly incomprehensible male reason threatening to take her girl away from her.

" Oh, Master, no," she whimpered. " I am a shameful woman but not wicked. I swear to you she's only a girl. I can keep her, dirt though she is."

" No more dirt than you are," said Alfred sharply, and of course stupidly. But he was upset. The feel of the baby in his arms, its very tiny weight, its placidity (it was still sound asleep), and the queer longing he had to give it a different kind of life from all others of its sex made him feel almost as if he and his little daughter were a unit, belonging together, while Ethel was an outsider.

" Of course, Master, no more dirt than I am," said Ethel, in meek apology. " We are all dirt."

" Well, I can't really take her away," Alfred said regretfully.

He sat silent again, very still on his hard primitive wooden chair, in order not to move his arms and wake the baby. He was thinking about family life. In past times he might have been sitting as he was now, with this little thing——

" Have you called her anything yet? " he asked.

" Edith, Master."

And there would be Fred and Jim and Robert, as well as this very small Edith, and Ethel, all sitting in one room like Christians. Alfred could not imagine it. Even now, though he liked to hold the baby, he was feeling restless at being so long in the same room with Ethel. A man could sit with a dog quite indefinitely, but he could not stay with a woman except to satisfy his natural needs. When the boys had been old enough to recognise him and take some notice of him he had always taken them out into the open or sent Ethel away somewhere while he played with them. He had never thought of the unfairness of robbing a woman of precious half-hours of the short time she could keep her sons with her. He wondered why women made men restless. They did not criticise any more than a dog would. They were quiet. They never spoke unless the man spoke first. And yet one couldn't stand it. One had to get out by oneself or go back to man's company. "We are all ashamed," he thought. "We don't know it, at least only the Knight and I know it, but all of us are ashamed of this low vile pattern that has been set them to live. Their appearance and their manner are criticism as loud as if they screamed at us, and we can't stand it. Men could perhaps have sat with that Nazi girl without wanting to rush away. But even that was only a pattern, not women themselves. I could take notice of Edith when she gets a little older. Play with her like I did with the boys. Then Ethel wouldn't despise her so much, and she wouldn't despise herself so much, and she'd be bound to grow up different. *Different*. Unfit for the Women's Quarters. Unfit for the cage. Oh, God, I wish I'd never had to think about women! I can't do anything for her at all, if I ever take any notice of her it'll make her consciously unhappy. It doesn't matter holding her like this because she'll never know about it. It is the same as with the boys. The women may love them so long as they're young enough to forget about it. I can love Edith—love Edith—love a little girl? How strange that is! As long as she never knows. I couldn't love Ethel. No. It's impossible to love women as they are. But *this* thing isn't anything yet. It's just Edith, my child. Ah, von Wied, a million years in the Christians' fiery lake wouldn't be too long for you." Alfred unconsciously gripped the child tighter at the thought of von Wied, who had driven girls like the Hitler maid off the face of the earth and had made it impossible for a man to love his own daughter. Edith began to whimper, then burst into a little thin angry cry like the impatient mewing of a cat.

" Master ! " said Ethel, jumping up quickly in spite of her weakness.

" Sit down ! " Alfred said sharply.   " She's quite all right.
She'll stop in a minute."

But Edith did not stop. She went on mewing, and waving
her small arms about in feeble protest. Alfred rocked her
gently, as he had seen Ethel do with the boys. Edith went on
crying.

Ethel stood it in silence as long as she could, then, with
agonising audacity, gasped, " Master, forgive me, but I think
she's hungry. She's been asleep a long time. If I might
have her—just for a little while. She doesn't take very
long."

Alfred surrendered the baby. He walked up and down the
room while Ethel fed her. He could not bear to see this
natural process. He was in a fantastically upside-down
state of mind. He ought to have taken no notice whatever of
Edith ; he ought to have been disgusted at her sex. In the
morning when he heard she was a girl he had been disappointed,
but then all the afternoon he had wanted to see her. And now
he was far more advanced in his unmanly doting, for he was
furious with Ethel for being able to do something for the baby
he could not do himself. Edith, he felt, was entirely his, no
one else ought to touch her. For he alone knew what
Edith was *now*, not dirt at all, but the embryo of something unimaginably wonderful. Ethel was not fit to touch
her.

" Master," said Ethel presently, " do you—do you want to
have her back ? "

But Alfred's mood had changed again. A black despondency
had come over him, and he wanted now to get away. He put
his finger into Edith's palm, and the baby's hand curled itself
round weakly, but with a noticeable little pressure.

" You keep her now. Look after her well, Ethel."

" Yes, Master. And you will not take off my armlet ? "

" What ? " thought Alfred, " have some other man coming
in here and making Ethel neglect the baby because he wants
her so often and for so long at a time ? Not likely ! "

" No," he said. " I've nothing to complain of."

" Oh, thank you, Master. I am not worthy, but I swear our
next child shall be a son."

" It shan't then ! " snarled Alfred. " I'll see you don't have
another child at all till Edith's three years old. I know how

the girls are kicked about and neglected when a boy comes along."

"Master, how can it be otherwise?" asked Ethel, in such amazement that she even dared to seem to argue with him.

"I don't *know*!" shouted Alfred, "but it's bloody well got to be otherwise *some time*, and if you don't take proper care of Edith I'll beat you till you can't stand up!"

"Master, I will. I—I will care for her always as if she were—were a boy," said Ethel, greatly daring.

"All right then," said Alfred more gently. "I'll come again soon."

He went out, and crossed the now dark and empty playground towards the gate. There were a few lights, not on the playground, but between the little rows of houses, and as he passed a certain small street, or rather a little square, for the houses were built round an open space as broad as it was long, he saw a Knight leave a house and cross the square towards him. Alfred saw his face for a second under a lamp. It was one of the Army Knights. The most vigorous and healthy of the young girls were picked out for the Knights, and become Knights' women. After that, when the Knights were tired of them, Englishmen could have them, or they could go to the Nazi house. Knights' women carried a small swastika on their white armlet, and it was very perilous for any Englishman or Nazi to interfere with them. But few girls really liked to go to the Knights' square. They could not have children, and they were more afraid of their noble lusters than of common Germans or Englishmen. They lived in a terror which was spiritual as well as physical, because the Knight they lay with at evening, might bellow and storm at them in the morning in church, if it was the right day of the month.

When Alfred saw this man striding across the Knights' square towards him he fell into such a reckless rage that he trembled and the blood sang in his ears. Here was the enemy who had done all this to him and Edith, here was the descendant of a man who had helped von Wied to put his filthy plan into action, here was *Germany*, to be loathed now for a new reason, one he had never dreamed of before he had started to think seriously of women and had held in his arms a girl of his own. The Knight came closer and Alfred grimly waited for him. He even moved towards him, into the Knights' square. He forgot about the book, and that he had not yet told a soul in England where it was ; he forgot all old von Hess's solemn warnings about the stupidity and evil of violence; he forgot even his own genuine inner conviction that the forceful way is not the way to get good things done. He had no thought in his mind except that the Knight was alone, and that he, Alfred, could, if he were quick and clever, severely mangle him, perhaps even kill him, before help would come. He gripped his stick and waited. But as the Army Knight came swinging along towards him, Alfred was reminded, with deplorably weakening effect, of that other Knight, who wore a tunic like this Knight's with silver swastikas gleaming on the collar, whose cloak had shaken so gracefully back from his shoulder when he played the violin. Alfred groaned inwardly in despair. " Now, even their clothes, the clothes that mean all that is bad to me, must remind me *of him*." Alfred sank his stick to the ground. It was almost as if old von Hess were standing behind him, saying in his pleasant way, " Alfred do not get so heated." The Army Knight, who seemed preoccupied, suddenly looked up and saw Alfred standing quite close to him, inside, well inside the Knights' square.

" What are you doing here, Kerl? " he asked harshly. " Are you a stranger? "

" No, highly-born."

" Get out," said the Knight, and with no more words passed on his way. He never looked round to see if Alfred followed him, so certain was he of instant obedience. Alfred did follow him with no more thought of violence, much relieved now that he had been saved from committing so vast and irremediable a folly. " It's this place," he thought. " Once you've started to think about women, it's intolerable. It has the atmosphere of a stinking bog, heavy and evil and sickening. And Edith must live here all her life. I hope she'll die." But he felt better when he had passed through the gate and was in the men's world once more. He realised how little and unimportant was his personal emotion about the baby girl compared with the task von Hess had set him. Truth, first guarding it and then spreading it, must come before everything. " All this woman business will be broken up once the German idea, the force idea, is smashed. I must be more careful when I go there again and try to think straight." He went home, thinking now about Hermann.

When he reached his home, Jim, the thirteen-year-old, had gone to bed. He worked long hours in the Technical School and was generally very tired at night. Thomas had gone out somewhere. He never went to the Women's Quarters. His whole sexual and emotional life was lived among men. No stigma attached to it, and the German government had nothing to say against a whole-time homosexuality for Englishmen. If they had no children it was their own look-out. Alfred, who was as normal as it was possible for a man to be in such a society, had never blamed or envied Thomas for his way of living, but now when he came into the kitchen and found Fred alone, reading a book on engineering, he did suddenly wish he had grown up like Thomas. *He* wouldn't be in the sickening atmosphere of the Women's Quarters, worrying about his baby daughter and being sorely tempted to beat up Army Knights. He'd be off with the friend of the moment, free to go where they would, with the whole clean night-country before them. But then as he looked at Fred, studious, absorbed, patient, with only his father knew what a solid gritty character behind his intelligence, he ceased to envy Thomas entirely. A son like Fred was worth any frets and difficulties.

"I suppose a Red German didn't turn up while I was out?" Alfred asked, sitting down.

"No. Have a cigarette, Father." Fred pushed one little cigarette across the table.

"Where did you get it?"

"A fellow gave it to me."

"Nazi?"

"No, English."

"Smoke it yourself, lad."

"No, do have it, Father. I meant to try to buy some for you but I simply couldn't save the money. Thomas doesn't manage the food like you do. We went pretty short at times. Jim always had enough, though. Now smoke it, Father. I don't really care about it."

"Thank you, Fred. Well, it's nice to have a whiff."

"What do you mean by a Red German?"

" A German in a red uniform.   A Permanent Exile."

" I've never seen one."

" Well, you'll see one soon.   It's Hermann.   Do you remember a Nazi, a young soldier, who used to come here a lot about five or six years ago? "

" I remember Hermann, of course.   What's he done? "

" He hasn't really done anything.   But we've got to pretend that he has, because no decent Englishman would have anything to do with a man who tried to ruin a boy for life maliciously."

" But what did he really do? "

" Oh, he really killed the boy.   But I'd better start and explain properly.   Shut the door."

Alfred told his son about Hermann, the chorister, von Hess, the flight in the aeroplane, and the book.   Fred was utterly absorbed.   He made no comment at all, but occasionally put a question.

" When can I see it? " he asked, when Alfred had given a very concise *résumé* of his adventures, and had stopped to get a drink of water.

" To-morrow I must go and see Andrew, the foreman up at Long Barrow farm.   He'll be glad to do me a favour if he can.   I want him to take Hermann on.   He's got a bargain in that boy.   He can work any two Englishmen to a standstill. Then, though I may be allowed for sentiment's sake to keep a disgraced Nazi who was once a friend of mine from starving to death on an old woman's ration, after that we mustn't see him, not publicly, I mean.   Of course we shall see him.   I must do that to-morrow, because Hermann may turn up any time, but the night after to-morrow we can go up to Stonehenge and you shall see the book.   But at present I shall have to read to you, translating as I go, because you can't manage the black letter or grammatical German yet.   I can see I've got to get out of my sleepy ways.   There's another fund of information I haven't half worked properly yet and that's the Christians.   I was interested in them, but I always thought their old tales were primitive superstitious nonsense.   But now we shall be able to compare their legends with what von Hess says.   We must go down to Amesbury one night and see my old friend Joseph Black.   You know I used to think he and his family were called "black ' because they're so dirty, but it isn't, it's a surname like a Knight's. We all had them once. Now only Knights and Christians have. Hullo, is that Thomas?"

But the step outside the house, after pausing a moment, went on down the street. Alfred went to look, thinking it might be Hermann.

"No, it's nothing. Just a fellow looking for a number," he said, when he came back. "But I don't want Thomas told, yet. It isn't that he isn't with us against the Germans, and a stout unbeliever, and all that, but von Hess told me not to hurry. I want you to understand thoroughly first. And don't say a word in front of Jim. He'd be as loyal as you or me, but he's too young and excitable. Some boast might slip out. So don't say anything except to me and carefully, at present. And don't talk much to Hermann. He'll be in a queer mood, I've no doubt."

"That isn't a safe place, Father," Fred said after a long silence. "Not really safe."

"Did *you* ever know or guess that lump had a dug-out under it?"

"No. I dare say no one does, and no one but us ever will. But it's not safe, for all that. Because someone *may* find it. And you can't *absolutely* trust to the terror Nazis have of Stonehenge and ghosts generally."

"But what would you do, Fred? Where in all England could you put a book where the Germans *couldn't* get at it?"

"I don't know," said Fred. "There is no place. Only it's terrible trusting to such a lot of chances like we shall have to."

"Well, it's no manner of use worrying," said Alfred, philosophically. "Von Hess couldn't keep it, and so we must. God will look after it so long as we do our best."

"Do you believe in God?" Fred asked dubiously.

"More and more. But not to say He's German or this and that. And now I'm going to bed. We must sleep while we can."

CHAPTER NINE

THE foreman up at Long Barrow was a practical man. When Alfred next evening put his proposition before him he said that if the four arch-fiends in the Creed knew anything about farm work he would employ any two of them.

" I'm so short of labour I don't know which way to turn," he said. " I've complained to the Knight's Marshal, and he says that labour is to be sent up from the East, where they've got a few more than they want, but the labour ain't *come* yet. Nor will it for a few weeks. The government is sure enough, but it isn't always as fast as a hare. So send your wicked Nazi up to me as soon as he comes, and I'll see that he sweats some of it out. There are too many boys being let into the Technical Schools, Alfred, and they're starving the land."

Alfred nodded gravely at this ages-old complaint.

" It suits me they are," he said. " I wouldn't like this fellow actually to starve. He's a great big hulk; he can't exist on an old woman's ration. And you might drop a hint to the other men that he'll be in a desperate mood, not caring much whether he lives or dies, and he's very strong. If they pick on him he's liable to kill a few before they down him."

" They'll let him alone," said Andrew. " They'd be ashamed to fight him. Civilised men ought to stick together about Christians. If one doesn't—well, then," Andrew spat on the ground contemptuously. " But work ! He shall have that."

In three days more Hermann arrived. Alfred found him in the kitchen, alone with Fred, when he came back from work to his supper. Neither man was speaking. Hermann looked up. He still did not speak. He looked huge in his red uniform—red breeches, red coat, red cap—but older, and ill. His broad shoulders sagged despondently, his eyes looked dull and lifeless.

" He has been through it," Alfred thought. " Worse than I thought. Oh, my poor silly Nazi, it's I that brought you to this."

He laid his hand on Hermann's shoulder.

" I've got you work, Hermann."

Hermann's eyes did not brighten. He mumbled something Alfred could not hear. Fred brought his father's soup and Alfred sat down to eat it in silence. When he had finished he got up.

" Come on, Hermann. Back to the farm."

" Can't he stay here to-night, Father? " Fred asked.

" No. Officially we can't sleep in the same house with him."

Hermann got up and followed Alfred out without a word. His head nearly touched the top of the doorway. Such a large man had probably never been through it before. And yet he was no giant. He fell seven inches short of the legendary Hitler. Presently they were out of the town and walking up to Long Barrow farm, out of step, as usual. When they turned in to the lonely downs road that led to the farm, Alfred took his arm.

" I'm sorry I brought all this on you, Hermann."

Hermann said nothing.

But when they were very near the farm Hermann said, very slowly, " How shall I see you again? "

" Go down to the end of the lane to-morrow night after your supper, when it's dark, I mean, and we'll come. We go up to the dug-out where the book is. Only Fred and me. The others know we're doing something, but they don't know what. And pull yourself together, man. You've done nothing you think's wrong, and von Hess is trusting you to help us."

" I shall be all right," said Hermann, still in that slow voice, " when I can work. You stay here now. I'd rather go in alone."

Alfred watched him go to the farmyard gate and swing it open, then shut it carefully and go round the corner of some barns.

" Why is red their colour of disgrace? " he wondered. " Christian crosses are red, and Permanent Exiles wear red. There must be some old reason they don't know themselves. Perhaps I shall find it out."

Alfred found out this and many other interesting things during the end of the summer and the autumn and the winter, in session with old von Hess, the Knight of the Inner Ten.

He and Fred and Hermann went up to the dug-out roughly
one night out of every three. As autumn came on they could
go up earlier, but the dug-out began to get very cold and they
could not stay such long hours. They all three spent every
penny they could scrape together for candles, and Hermann
was as single-minded in this as the others who could read the
book. Alfred took up a little stool each for himself and Fred,
and a tiny rough table was transported up in pieces to hold
the book and the candles. Hermann usually stretched himself on the pile of sacks, which he added to whenever he could
conveniently steal an old one from the farm, and went to sleep.
He was tired out after his day's manual labour, and he had no
absorbing interest, as the other two had, to keep him awake.
Sometimes they woke him up to ask the meaning of a German
phrase or word, or to tell him a really interesting piece of news
about his country.

" I say, Hermann, wake up. Now what do you think
of this? Do you know what the Teutonic Knights *really*
were? "

" Hitler's Knights."

" They weren't. They were much older than that. They
were German Knights who went to convert the heathen
Slavic Prussians to *Christianity*. Now what do you think of
that? "

But Hermann was too tired to think. So long as he might
stretch his huge form between Alfred and the entrances
whence might come an enemy to him and the book, Hermann
was content. He was unhappy in the daytime because the
other men on the farm, though they let him alone, despised
him without concealment, and sometimes it was hard to
believe that he was not really what he seemed to be, a Permanent Exile in a red uniform, or shortly, a Red. But on one
night in every three he was happy, as whenever he woke from
a doze he could see Alfred's dark head and Fred's fair one
bent over the book, and hear the mumble of German and
English in Alfred's voice. They never heard a sound from
outside except sometimes wind. They took endless pre-
cautions, going separately and meeting at different places.
No man was allowed to wear his boots within two hundred
yards of the entrance, in case a track was left. Smothered
curses were constantly heard, every time someone trod on a

thistle. There seemed to be more thistles than grass on that particular bit of down. Sometimes one member of the reading party did not come at the appointed time. That meant he had met a poaching Christian or someone else too near Stonehenge and had walked on in some other direction and had then gone home. But no catastrophe happened, and through coldness and weariness and eye-strain, because they had to be careful about candles, Alfred acquired knowledge and translated it to Fred. Fred pretty soon began go be able to read a lot of the book for himself. Then Alfred just read on in German until Fred stopped him. It was a great night when they had got once all through the book, having carefully considered every sentence to try to draw from it its deepest meaning. Alfred suggested they should have a rest from reading for a little while, and spend more time with old Joseph Black, the head Christian of the Amesbury community.

" No, don't do that," Hermann pleaded. " I can't see you then."

Alfred thought it better not to take Hermann to Joseph Black's house, though since the enlightenment in Germany he had let Fred know that he was acquainted with Christians and had taken him two or three times to see Joseph. But Alfred had not had much leisure in the last four months. If he were not struggling to understand von Hess he had to see his friends, visit little Robert in the Boys' Nursery, go to see Ethel and brood unhappily for a little while over the baby Edith, and pay some fatherly attention to his adoring second son, young Jim. He had to do his work and have some time for sleep. So Joseph, who was a mine of interesting but mostly inaccurate information, had been rather neglected. Alfred's acquaintance, or really friendship, with this Christian had been the result of an accident. He had been returning late one night from a meeting of the Brotherhood of British Heathens, the official name of the anti-Hitler secret society. There were branches all over England, and in Scotland and Ireland and Wales, and though members could not move about freely news of progress did filter through from other branches, so that the leading men had an idea as to how the society was growing. Alfred was returning from this seditious conspiracy across the downs with two other men when at least three miles from Amesbury they heard something crying, and found a very small Christian boy of not more than five years old, quite alone and half-frozen. The other two men, who included in their anti-Hitler feelings no toleration at all for any other kind of religion, and had a rigid conventional contempt for Christians, whom they considered more unclean than ordure, told Alfred to leave the brat, as it was too tough to die, and would certainly be presently found by its own people, and what did it matter, anyway? But Alfred had reacted so strongly and logically against the Hitlerian virtues of bloodshed and brutality and ruthlessness that he was already developing shoots of their opposites. He would not leave the little boy, but parted from the other men and carried him over to Amesbury. Joseph Black, the father, received the child, his youngest son, with unashamed transports of relief and joy, and told Alfred that the boy might well have been out all night in the frost, and possibly the next day too. Owing to a misunderstanding as to the direction in which he had strayed the Christians were all searching the wrong part of the downs. But Joseph, while very grateful, remained aloof and unapproachable, and Alfred, though he was immediately interested in the Christians, whom he had up to then regarded as something quite negligible and rather disgusting, could not make him talk. But he came again, ostensibly to know if the little boy had since died of pneumonia, and let Joseph understand that he was anti-German and did not believe in Hitler as God. On that Joseph opened his heart to him, and talked freely enough about everything except the deeper mysteries of his religion, though, he warned Alfred frankly, " It makes no difference in the Last Day whether you believe in the foul fiend Hitler or no. The Lord will not ask you whether you believed in this evil man or had lost your faith in that one; He will ask you whether you believed in the Lord Jesus, and it's no good thinking you can get out of it by lying, for God can read all hearts." But Alfred was not concerned with the last day, and was much pleased at Joseph's change of attitude. All that was long ago now; the little boy was a sturdy lad of sixteen; Joseph was nearly old, and head of the settlement.

Alfred said to Hermann, " We must stop reading for a bit, old lad. Fred's eyes ache so that he can hardly do his work next day. We need a rest. You can walk down to Amesbury with us at night if we don't go on the road."

" When will you go on with the reading? "

" We'll start it through again in about a fortnight, or perhaps sooner if our eyes are better. And, Hermann, you mustn't come up here protecting the book by yourself."

" Or looking at the Nazi girl," said Fred gravely.

" I'll clout your head, mein Junker," grumbled Hermann. " I didn't leave Germany to be preached at by a boy who can't grow a beard at seventeen. Well, Alfred, then it must be a fortnight."

" You can have nice warm sleeps every night instead of getting so stiff with cold you can hardly walk home."

" I'd rather be cold," said Hermann.

So Alfred and his son put in a few secret visits to Joseph, at night, going and coming carefully, for they were most anxious not to lose their reputations as normal English people.

Joseph always received them with pleasure in his filthy hovel, and immediately turned all the women out of the room, for they were not fit to listen to men's conversation, even though two of the men were condemned unbelievers. Joseph's father, a very old man and rather deaf, generally stayed there, polishing a newly made whistle or some such old man's job. The sons were usually out of the way, setting or taking up snares, stealing vegetables from the fields, or getting a nice chicken from some outlying run. Alfred often had a better meal with Joseph Black than he could afford to buy with his wages. The Christians were allowed no rations by the government, and they could do no work. They lived on the country or starved on the small proceeds of their illicit sales, and most times of the year they lived fairly well.

Joseph would sit on his stool and talk for hours in the most dogmatic way about everything on earth and in heaven. His expression was an extraordinary mixture of religious fanaticism and humorous slyness; his person was very dirty; his long hair was greasy, grey, never washed and rarely combed; his teeth were perfect and very white, and his small dark eye could see stars in the sky where Alfred could see none.

Alfred would question him, "Why do you think women have their heads shaved, Joseph?"

"I don't know why *your* infidel women, whom you keep shut up in pens like bitches on heat, have their heads shaved, for a superficial following of the blessed Paul the brother of our Lord will not save any of you in the Judgment. But *our* women are shaved because the blessed Paul said, 'A woman's hair is her shame, therefore let her be shorn.' And its truth is evident in the fact that a man's hair is his glory and his strength lies in it, like Samson in the den of lions."

"What would happen if men cut their hair off or shaved their heads?"

"They could beget no children and would come to a deserved extinction."

Alfred looked at Fred's solemn young face, and caught the ghost of a twinkle in his eye. Both of them knew the truth about the shaving of women's heads, and the consequent pride men took in their hair and beards.

"If a woman grew her hair as long as it would grow would she be barren?" Fred asked.

"A woman's hair *cannot* grow beyond the bottoms of the ears," Joseph stated. "But even that is a shame to her. Women are hairless. Why, if they were meant to have hair on their heads they would have it on their faces. Have you ever seen a woman with a beard like mine? Sometimes they grow a little hair, but only when they are past child-bearing. But this is a very trivial matter for talk between men, even between Christians and unbelievers, whose fate is worse than a woman's. For she merely parts and disperses asunder, atom from atom, drop from drop, in a wholly painless fashion. Nothing she is and nothing she must become."

"But men must burn for ever in the fiery lake."

"That is so, Alfred. In that day before the eyes of the faithful remnant then alive, and all the glorious hosts of the Christian dead, Hitler the foul fiend and all other false gods shall plunge at the head of their reprobate followers into the lake of fire."

"Joseph, if you could, would you overthrow the Germans by violence?"

"By violence the Jews killed our Lord. By violence we, the disobedient, persecuted and killed the Jews, forgetting the commandment, ' Christians, forgive them, they know not what they do.' By violence the Germans and all other followers of Hitler have persecuted us. Shall we then add sin to sin, and calamity to calamity? "

" But then," said Alfred, " if you were to forgive the Jews for not knowing what they were doing, ought not you also to forgive the Germans? For just persecuting Christians can't be such a great crime as killing the son of God."

" It is not for us to forgive *them*. We have not been told to forgive them, and disobeyed. We have not persecuted the Germans, nor offered them any violence. It is for God to forgive them, but *He will not*," Joseph said very firmly. " We have sinned, and they aré the instruments of our punishment, but they are willing instruments, bloody and deceitful men."

" They *were* deceitful, certainly," Alfred murmured. " Joseph, what was there in the world before there were Germans? "

" Jews and Christians. But first there were only Jews. The whole world of men descended from the blessed race of Jesus. Why, how could it be otherwise? "

" But the Japanese are yellow, and Africans are dark, and we are white," said Fred, looking at Joseph's grey and filthy skin.

" And why should not Jews and the descendants of Jews be of different colours? Your hair is nearly yellow, Fred. Alfred's is brown. Are you not his son? "

" I believe so."

" Then there is no difficulty. There is no difficulty about anything unless the eyes and the mind are made filthy and dark by unbelief."

" Joseph, do you think Christians could ever read? " Alfred asked.

" No. Reading and writing are heathen. The truth must always be passed on by the words of the mouth. Does God *write* to us to tell us what He wills? Do you think that in the Last Day God will send you little notes to let you know of your damnation? He will *tell* you, in a voice louder than the thickest thunderclap. You mock, Alfred. You think I don't know why you come here, to mock and tease the old Christian."

" Joseph, you know perfectly well I come here because I like you. So does Fred."

Joseph smiled, his sly humorous smile. " I know it, Alfred. You saved my child, you are a very good man for a damned one, but I shall crow over you in the Last Day like the best cock in the yard——" Joseph stopped, looking a little confused.

" Why, what's the matter? *I* won't mind, Joseph. If you're right, well you are right   I shan't blame *you*."

" It's not that. I was inadvertently speaking not *of* holy things, but rather near them."

" Oh, dear," said Alfred to himself, " now we shall never know about the cock. But I don't suppose it is important. Joseph, what is there besides this world? "

" This world is a round ball with the shell of the sky outside it. The stars are all the other worlds."

" And what is on them? Christians, Germans? "

" Angels and spirits and ministers of flaming fire."

Joseph went to a box by the wall and drew from it a bottle, very black and dirty on the outside, and after a little searching among the litter of the untidy room he found four earthenware mugs. He poured the contents of the bottle into the four mugs and took one to his father. There was a low mumble of words Alfred could not catch, then Joseph came back to the table, made the sign of the cross on his breast and picked up his mug.

" Now drink, Alfred, and Alfred's son."

They drank. It was something very potent, and a very little of it made Fred's head swim. He had never drunk anything but water. Even Alfred who occasionally had beer did not want more than half the contents of the mug.

" What is it? " Alfred asked. " It's very powerful, Joseph."

" It is a wine we make out of sloes and wild honey, but the strength comes with keeping it in the cask. Is it good? "

" Very good."

" All the fruits and beasts of the earth are for man's use," said Joseph, taking a good sip of the wine. " The Lord Christ came eating and drinking, not like the fiend Hitler upon whom the rich and blessed viands of this world had such a

retching effect that he could keep none of them in his foul
stomach. Now, because *he* was so unnaturally wicked that
even the dead flesh of beasts and the wine of grain or fruit had
to shrink from him and eject themselves from his company, the
heathen say that if a man would please God he must eat little
or no meat and drink nothing but watery beer. It is not *those*
questions the Lord will ask in the Last Day."

"But surely the Germans would be worse if they were
drunken?" Alfred suggested.

Joseph took another sip.

"Nothing could make them any worse," he said. "Neither
can anything ever make them any better. The Lord's
mercy is not extended to them. Now if you, Alfred, were
convinced of sin and believed in the Lord Jesus Christ, the
Son of God, I could receive you into the fold of Christianity
and in the Last Day you would be saved." Joseph looked
across the table a little wistfully. "But I am not at all
hopeful, because I am not a fool. But as to the Germans and
the Japanese they are damned already. If their highest
Knight, the man whom they call der Fuehrer (though he
leads them nowhere), if he were to come to me in sincerity
and humility to be absolved and blessed and received into
the arms of Christ, I could not do it. We have no power to
turn back the judgments of God."

"It is extraordinary, Joseph, you despise him, and he
despises you. No, it isn't extraordinary. It's right."

"It is right. His contempt for me is part of our Atonement,
and is the will of God. Mine for him is because we are the
Lord's people, though suffering and sinful, while he is one
of the damned."

"Joseph, what happened *before* Jesus was killed? How did
the world start?"

"God made it to be the habitation of the Jews. They lived
a thousand years without sin. Then Cain killed Abel his
brother."

"Why?"

"Because they both wanted to be the King of the Jews.
Then sin was there, the sin of pride and power, and all the
other sins sprang from that one, and the Jews lived in sin
for a thousand years."

"How did they manage to *think* of the sin when

there was no sin there before?" asked Fred, deeply interested.

"It is a mystery," said Joseph, shaking his head.

"You mean it's a religious mystery and you can't tell heathens."

"No. I mean it's just a thing no man can ever understand, why there should be sin when God is good. At the Last Day *we* shall understand that mystery, you of course will not. But that was how sin started, with a killing. With violence between man and man. Then they lived for a thousand years in sin, and then Jesus was born to save them from their sins and make the world as it had been before Cain and Abel. But the world was only half of it willing to forgo sin, which they had come to like. Half the Jews wanted to do without sin, and half of them wanted to go on with it. The half that was unwilling to part with it crucified Jesus, through their leader who was called the Pontifical Pilot— which is a name of a certain though not really holy mystery," Joseph added, again looking a little worried. "But the others who accepted Jesus and wished sin to depart were called Christians. So the Second Great Sin was committed, and Jesus was killed. Then the Christians being enraged at the death of this just man——" Joseph paused. His eyes neither shone with fanaticism nor twinkled with slyness. His face was quiet and strangely ennobled. He was in a dream, and he saw something better than himself, and yet approachable. Alfred thought, "I'm sure Joseph has all this Christianity muddled up. I *know* he has. He's a superstitious ignorant old Christian, and yet something of the real Jesus still reaches him. Ah, there was a Man."

"Yes," said Joseph, coming to himself, "they chased the Jews to the ends of the earth, wherever they stayed, wherever they had their houses and set their snares, the Christians chased them out of it, and spat on them and killed them and tortured them. All in Disobedience, for they had been told to forgive the Jews. And that was for a thousand years. Then came the Punishment. The Christians had persecuted the less stalwart Jews into the extreme filthiness of becoming Germans or Japanese, and the more courageous among them became French or English or Russians or what you will. But because a snake is more dangerous in its bite than a dog, these very low Jews became our chief persecutors, while the more bravely born among you, that is the descendants of slightly less cowardly Jews—you, Alfred—have never been so apt at rubbing in our transgression as the Germans. Not that that will save you in the Last Day."

" And that will be when you have been despised for a thousand years."

" Yes," said Joseph. " There are three hundred and five more years of the Punishment."

" But we say it is now 721 years after Hitler."

" Your times are wrong. There are three hundred and five years and some months still to go."

" Then the world altogether only lasts four thousand years? "

" Yes. And the third thousand was by far the most evil and unhappy. For besides the Disobedience, the Christians in those days were given over utterly to terrible sins, worse than the sins of the old Jews, to witchcraft and magic and idolatry and dissensions among themselves so that they tore each other limb from limb."

" But you sell charms now, Joseph? "

" We do not. We sell herbal remedies which you could very well make for yourselves if you were not all so ignorant, and if they sometimes work like magic it is either that the heathen really has the disease he thinks he has, and so the remedy fits it, or else he has such faith in the remedy that it will cure any illness that springs from a disordered mind. That is a thing you cannot understand, but half your heathen ailments are caused by the deep wretchedness of being cut off from God, and by your sins. Faith in a Christian remedy has in itself a healing power, and some of you will overcome partially your contempt for us, being driven by distress, and take our physics with a sturdy faith worthy of a better object. But the Lord will not ask, ' Did you believe in Christian *medicines*? ' any more than He will ask, ' Did you have a hare or only potatoes in the pot? ' "

" What was the idolatry the Christians went in for? " Alfred asked.

" They worshipped images, and idols of unworthy substance in exactly the same way as the Hitlerians do. It is hard to believe it," said Joseph meditatively. " It seems impossible that they should have fallen so low as to crawl on their bellies in front of idols. But they did."

" And what was their magic? "

" It was worse still. For it was only a pretence. Now when I say I could receive you into Christianity, Alfred, I do not mean that only I in this Amesbury Settlement could do it. I am head of the settlement because in practical matters there must be one man who in any discussion has the final word. But any man who is beyond childish age, and who is not afflicted like poor young William Whibblefuss, can celebrate the mysteries and receive you among us. The power is the power of Jesus, and no mere man is more holy than another. Such a thing is heathenish, as when Germans conceit themselves to be more sacred than the English, or when the Knights in their vanity and blindness think themselves of different clay from the common Nazis. But in the thousand years of Error some Christians were set high above others in the mysteries and dared to say, ' Ours alone is the power, the Lord Jesus Christ will come to you only through us.' Which error was the end of all brotherhood and love between Christians, and led to the most bloody and cruel dissensions among them."

" So that as well as killing the Jews they killed each other? "

" In the thousand years of Error, yes. Since then no Christian has ever killed another."

" Not even in personal private fights? "

" We never have fights," Joseph said.

" But how do you manage not to? "

" We never have fights because we love each other. Why, see, Alfred, if you have some kind of dispute with Fred, do you fight him? You argue, you finally agree, or you leave the matter unsettled, each holding to his own opinion. You do not rush at each other like two cats and tear each other's eyes out. All Christians are like father and son, brother and brother, because they are purified, not in Error, and though under Punishment and with no hope that their chastisement will be abated by a single day they have now nothing to cause anger one with another. Killing men, like reading and writing, is a heathen activity, and that it was once a Christian pursuit is our constant shame."

"I wish I could bring you acquainted with an old German I know," said Alfred. "You have so much in common."

"Impossible," said Joseph, without resentment but inexorably. "Unless of course he is a Christian you met in Germany. But then you should not call him a German."

"No, he is a real German. But if you should meet a Christian who had been born and brought up in Germany, would he be as much your brother as the Amesbury people?"

"Of course. Every man who wears the cross is my brother, and until he could speak English or I German we should exchange in love the holy words we both know."

"Are they in a language you both know?"

"Yes."

"And do any of *us* know it?"

"God forbid! It is the language of Christ Himself. No one knows the holy words but Christians."

"Could you say some?" Alfred asked tentatively.

"No. It is blasphemous to say any of them before heathens."

"Oh, I'm sorry, Joseph. I didn't mean to be offensive. But where is the rest of the language gone to? Why are there only a few words left?"

"It was lost," said Joseph sadly. "For our great Sin the most part of the blessed language of Jesus is lost. Not till the release and glorious enlightenment of the Last Day shall we recover the rest of it. Then these heathenish tongues which we have to use will disappear like the women, and we shall great each other and praise God in His own speech. Ah!" cried Joseph, quite carried away by enthusiasm, "O death, where is thy sting, O grave, thy victory? *Then* we shall sing *Laus Deo* and many many other things besides. Er—h'm." He coughed as he realised his blasphemy.

Alfred hastily passed on to something else.

"Joseph, is even the mother of Jesus to disappear?"

"She *has* disappeared, one thousand six hundred and fifty years ago. Women," Joseph stated firmly, "are nothing but birds' nests. What use is an old bird's nest? Does anyone value it, would anyone preserve it? Does the bird even care about it? And what can you say even of Mary

except that in her nest was laid an exceptionally divine egg?
How could Mary be alone in heaven? If she were there all
the other women would have to go too."

"Yes, I see. But what do you mean when you say they're
birds' nests? You think they contribute nothing towards the
physical child?"

"Nothing at all. The whole child, whether male or female,
is complete in the seed of man. The woman merely nurtures
it in her body until it is large enough to be born."

Alfred was very much interested, as von Hess had mentioned
this very ancient biological error as one of the causes of the
lower patterns of behaviour which had been imposed on
women.

"*We* don't believe that," he said. "Whether we believe
in Hitler or not. The mother contributes part of the
child."

"None of the child," said Joseph stolidly. "You are in
error, but why should you not be? If the child is to be male,
it has its soul from the father in the moment of conception,
but if it is to be female it has none. It is born nothing, like
all other women, even Mary. In Christian families we call
our eldest girl Mary, in remembrance of her, but no Mary is
presumptuous enough to think she is any more *something* than
any other woman."

"Why should sons sometimes grow up to look like their
mothers?"

"Because the food the mother gives him affects his physical
shape."

"Oh."

"And why," asked Joseph, carrying the attack into the
disputant's country, "if you hold such a fantastic belief as
that women actually help to form the child, do you treat your
women so badly? Keeping them shut up in pens and robbing
them of their little sons, which is the most ghastly cruelty that
any man can do to a woman?"

"I think it is wrong, Joseph. I like the way you treat your
nothings better than our way. Before you turn the women
out of here to go to one of the other huts I've seen them
laughing and talking with you. And not only the little girls.
Our grown women never laugh."

"Our women are treated as if they were good and well-loved dogs. We are fond of them, they play with us and are happy with us. If we have food they never go short while we are filled, they obey us and they love us. Our hands are never lifted against them unless they transgress, and like all decent and trustworthy dogs they are free to come and go where they will when they are not working. And they repay us for our care of them, in picking all our herbs and making our medicines and our wine, in getting wood for the fires and cooking our food, and even the preparing of the wood for whistles is not beyond one or two of the cleverest. Whereas your women are like ill-bred weakly and half-witted puppies which any sensible man would drown."

" But you've never seen any, have you, Joseph? "

" I have seen them in Bulfort driven to your heathen temple like cattle from one field to another. And I know they can do nothing, and that they are not happy. The Christian way of treating women is the only possible way. It was laid down once and for all by the blessed Paul, brother of our Lord, and even in the thousand years of Error Christians did not depart from it."

" Didn't they? "

" Never."

" That's rather curious."

" Why, Alfred? The Error and the Disobedience were among men. Such matters are too high for women, who can only err as a dog does against his master, but not against God. So, as the Error was not their fault, why should they be punished for it? God cannot be unjust."

" But then why should our women be unhappy for what is not their fault, either? "

Joseph was rather gravelled for once. Then he said, " They suffer as a dog does with a bad master, but you cannot say that it is *God* Who plagues and beats and starves the dog. It is the man. Your women are plagued because you are all filthy heathens, but the time of *their* suffering has an end. It ends with their death, and even for those who are alive at the Last Day the Dispersal is painless. Your suffering has no end, for at the Last Day all of you must come up out of your graves to be judged."

" Well, it is late," said Alfred with a sigh. " We must go, Joseph. I should like to talk to you for hours."

" And when will you come again? "

" Not for a little while, I think. Perhaps in another three months."

Joseph nodded, his eyes intelligent and sly, without any gleam of fanaticism.

" You must come and go as you will, Alfred. My house is always open to you, day or night, but of course night is best for you, as you are ashamed to be seen coming."

" I'm sorry, Joseph. If I could do what I like I'd come in broad daylight and march straight up to the Settlement under the eyes of Englishmen and Nazis."

" I understand."

Joseph let them both out and then called Fred to come back.

" Fred," he said, " your father is doing something dangerous."

" How did you guess that, Joseph? "

" I am a man of God, but besides that I am a man of perception, and I never cloud my natural abilities of mind with reading and writing. A Christian child of any intelligence would know it from his manner. And I want to tell you, Fred, that I love Alfred as much as it is possible for me to love a heathen. He saved my son, he has long ceased to despise us, neither has he ever gone to the other extreme and cast lustful eyes on our girls. He has eaten our bread and meat and drunk our wine, and I would put my body between him and his enemies, and between them and anyone who was dear to him, or anything which he wanted to keep safe, even weapons of war. If he wants a refuge it is here, with me or with my sons, or my sons' sons to the twentieth generation. There is friendship between my family and his family, I swear it before God. Ingratitude is not a Christian sin, Fred, but if I tell your father all this he is likely to laugh, as he is in a way modest, and not take it seriously. Now you understand."

" Yes, Joseph. I shan't forget it."

Fred ran after Alfred and presently caught him up.

" What did he want? " Alfred asked.

" He was telling me he loved you and was grateful to you."

" He's a nice old man, Joseph is."

" Do you trust him, Father? "

" As far as *he* can see *me*," said Alfred laughing. " That's a long way, but not right round the world."

" I believe you could trust him."

" You can't really trust any man who is religious. If your interests conflict with the religion the man breaks his word and betrays you and thinks he's right to do it. But Joseph's a good man all the same."

Fred was silent and thoughtful and he said nothing more about Joseph.

Presently Alfred said, " That language they've lost nearly all of must be Latin, the Romans' language. Von Hess says it was dead long before Hitler except as a written language and in the Christian Church. They must have some of the old Church bits which have come down from mouth to mouth. Then that's interesting that he knows about the priests and the religious wars. Fred, we must get back to von Hess again in a day or two. I'm sure we'll get more out of it the second time through. And Hermann'll be so pleased to be on guard again, poor old lad."

" I hope he'll never have to do anything except sleep," said Fred. " Father——" he began, but he changed his mind, and kept his own counsel.

CHAPTER TEN

FIVE Nazis in the charge of a corporal were returning to Bulfort from a job on the telephone wires a little way down the Amesbury–Exeter road, about two miles west of Stonehenge. They had worked till it was nearly dark, and then had piled into the small lorry that carried their kit and tools, to drive back to Bulfort. The lorry would not start, and on investigation was found to have a broken connection in the feed pipe. It was tiresome and difficult to manage a makeshift in the dark by the light of torches, so the corporal ordered the party to march home. None of them minded the walk, it was a mere trifle to tough young German soldiers, but they did mind the course of this particular evening stroll. They must go right past Stonehenge, in the dark, on their feet. However, they strode along singing, until they got near the stones. Then they fell silent. The corporal did not urge them to start again; he would not have admitted it aloud for gold or torture, but he too felt that there was no reason for making a loud German noise outside that peculiar English place. Marching quietly past Stonehenge was not against any army order that he had ever heard. So they marched quietly, and had nearly reached the angle of the rough stone wall which enclosed the place when a terrible loud high screaming, just behind the wall, only a few yards from the nearest man, made everyone jump and shiver and earnestly desire to hurry on. But their discipline was fairly good. They only quickened their pace just a little. The screaming went on, and with it a sort of chuckling leering sound, like a very inhuman laugh.

"Ach, Hitler!" burst out one of the men. "It's the ghosts! The ghosts of Stonehenge!"

"Halt!" said the corporal. "You fools, it's only a hare! There's someone there killing it."

He was over the wall in a second and, in the light of the moon just rising, the party saw something jump up and rush away, with the corporal after it, towards the stones. The lust of catching and seizing was so strong on the corporal that he would probably have followed it right into the circle, but he didn't need to, he was a noted runner, and he caught it before it got there, took something away from it, and dragged it back to his party of Nazis. They flashed torches on it to see it better. It was a Christian lad, obviously half-witted. The noise he had allowed the hare to make as he took it out of its snare, when he must have heard the feet of the soldiers on the road just by him, proved that. The hare, which he had finally killed the second before the corporal sprang at him over the wall, hung limp and peaceful, its troubles done, in the corporal's hand. The lad was dressed in nothing but a filthy woollen shirt and breeches, though it was a sharp spring night of east wind. The cross on the breast of his shirt was plain enough, though. The corporal gripped him tightly and he rolled his eyes in terror.

"We'll have the hare, scum," he said. "Fall out, men,

get round him. We'll teach him something about poaching our hares. You know all the hares belong to Germany, don't you, scum?"

"Nein verstehen," gasped the poor lubber. "Ich sprech Deutsch nicht!"

"No, I should say not. German wouldn't come well out of that mouth," and he gave it a light flick. "Do you understand English then? The hares belong to us. All the hares, all the rabbits, all the everything."

The men roared with laughter at the poor half-wit's terrified expression. They were relieved from fright, but they were angry, a little angry, with the Christian boy for causing it. If their discipline had failed they might have killed him, but as it was they just gave him light stinging little taps on his face and ears, pushing him from one to another across the circle. It was only horse-play and teasing, and they would soon have got tired of it and marched on, but the poor lout got more and more frightened. His mouth hung open and dribbled, his eyes shone wildly in the increasing moonlight.

"Mein Herren! Mein Herren!" he screamed. "Oh, nicht, oh, nicht. Oh, let me go! Oh, let me go. I'll show you where the ghosts are, Mein Herren! And the guns—the lovely guns to shoot hares with, but I daren't take them. I'm afraid of the ghosts."

"What!" cried the corporal. "Leave him alone. Now, you, what do you mean about ghosts and guns? How many guns?"

The idiot began to count on his fingers. "Five, six, seven, ten, sixty, *a thousand*!"

"He's not all there. He's making it up to get away."

"He's too half-witted to make a tale up, I think," said the corporal. "I think we'd better look into it. Though if it is anything it's probably only some old truck that was never cleared away. Where are these ghosts and guns, Kerl? Over there? In Stonehenge?"

"Nein, nein, Herren. This way, over there. Now let me go!"

"Not on your life. You come too and show us the ghosts and guns. And if we don't find any you're for it. Bring him along, Karl."

The Christian boy led them to the chalky face of the dug-out lump. His wits were more astray than usual, but he had a vague idea that if he could induce the Germans to enter the tunnel the ghosts would eat them up. Then he could run away very fast in case the ghosts came right out and ate him up too, though he knew a man with a cross on his breast was far more ghost-proof than an unbeliever. Still he thought the ghosts might be a little angry with him for sending a party of infidels into their shrine, as angry as they would have been if he'd taken the guns, which to his uncritical eye were sound and useful property. So when he had all the Germans round the entrance to the tunnel and was explaining that they must go in there, and all were leaning forward to look he wriggled furiously and broke his jailor's grasp. The man made a clutch at him but got nothing but a piece of shirt which tore like cobweb. The boy was off, half-naked, running at a pace none of them except the corporal could emulate in their thick boots and heavy clothes and equipment.

"Oh, never mind him," said the corporal, when he saw what had happened. "This is a tunnel all right. It goes round the corner. Give me your torch, Karl. Has any other man got a torch?"

"I have, but it doesn't always work."

"Then forward into the earth, single file," ordered the corporal, laughing. "We'll find these ghosts and guns or stick in the runway."

Inside the dug-out Alfred and Fred were so utterly absorbed that they heard nothing, no murmur of voices. Perhaps the bitter east wind was snatching them up and carrying them away. They heard nothing until the scraping sound of the first man coming along the tunnel on his belly and feet and elbows struck on Fred's sharp ear.

"There's someone coming, Father."

Alfred woke Hermann, who was as usual asleep on the pile of sacks, with one kick.

"Someone coming, Hermann, Be quiet. Fred, take the book—here, put the photograph in—go out the back way and put the stone over." Alfred blew out the candles.

Fred breathed in his ear. "Can't you come too?"

"No. We'll never all get down there before they see us. Go, Fred, quick."

"Make them think you and Hermann are here because you wouldn't like to be with him where anyone might find you," whispered Fred very rapidly, but quite unflustered.

He was gone. Alfred listened to scraping sounds in the front of the dug-out, but he could hear nothing of Fred's exit. He stood with his back to the hole in the corner of the dug-out to wait what happened next. There was no time to pull the door over the inner room. There was no time to do anything. He could just hear Hermann's breathing. Perhaps the ghosts would stop whoever it was at the entrance. A light flashed on and someone said, "Ach, Hitler!" Then someone else said, "Ach, Himmler!" and there was a sound of confusion. Alfred for all his anxiety and tension could not help wanting to laugh. He imagined Germans, not knowing what was there, pressing on in the tunnel, and Germans knowing what was there, wanting to get back. And it was true that even the corporal, for a second or two, very much wanted to retreat before those grim skeletons. Then, being a brave man, he pushed one of them, and it fell down on the concrete floor with a bony clatter.

"Come on, you fools!" he roared, his voice echoing queerly in the hollow place. "They're only old corpses. And, by Hitler, someone's been putting them here like this."

"All up, Hermann," Alfred breathed, gripping Hermann's arm. "That fellow's not afraid. Fred said you couldn't trust to it."

Hermann's arm swelled inside Alfred's hand. The muscles felt like living things, things with a fierce uncontrolled life of their own. Alfred thought, "Now Hermann will go mad. But I mustn't."

The corporal strode round the machine-gun party and flashed his torch on Alfred and Hermann, who were standing together at the back of the dug-out.

"Ach," he said, "there's something here besides those bones!"

Hermann went into action. He seized a large flint from the pile of chalk and flints and hurled it with perfect aim and tremendous force at the torch. There was darkness and hubbub. Hermann was fighting, there was no doubt about that, for there were grunts and groans and gasps. Skeletons crashed about, the snapping of their dry bones making a

staccato macabre accompaniment to the more homely and human noises. Alfred did nothing. If he went into the fight Hermann would be confused. As it was he could hit, kick, bite and gouge anything that was not himself, and know that he was doing well for his side. There was a constant stream of oaths from someone who seemed to be enough outside the fight to have some breath. Then, after what seemed an eternity of confusion, a light flashed on. The corporal was standing quietly out of the fight with his revolver drawn, unwounded except for a bad cut on his right hand. Hermann was still on his feet, streaming with blood. The corporal shot him, twice. Hermann collapsed, like a great red tower, and lay so still that Alfred wondered at it. The next minute he had to laugh at poor King Nosmo, who had fallen over the machine gun in the attitude of one who is very sick indeed. His shattered head had in the fight become still more shattered, his head was just an open bowl, and yet he looked like a person overcome with sickness. Hermann was dead; he looked dead, and yet King Nosmo, who had been dead no one knew how long, looked just sick.

" It's their positions," thought Alfred. " A man ought to lie down when he's dead."

Hermann had downed two of his enemies. One lay quite still but breathed stertorously. The other was sitting against the wall of the dug-out, dazed. Two were on their feet, both bleeding copiously, and the only uninjured Germans were the man who had been struggling with the obstinate torch, and the corporal, who had only been cut by the flint. He had waited coolly for the light when he could safely use his weapon. The smoke from the revolver cleared away and the stunning reverberations died down, leaving every man with a sensation of deafness. There was dead silence except for the panting of the Germans. The corporal kept Alfred covered with his revolver, but he took no notice. He was looking at Hermann, and thinking of him and von Hess. " *With his heart's blood.*" Poor brave, stupid, sentimental Nazi. But that last wild fight must have been a tremendous relief to him after his tragically peaceful short life. For a few minutes he must have been completely happy.

" It's the Red!" someone said at last, in a tone of surprise.

" I knew that," said the corporal. " You there, who are you? "

" Alfred, aerodrome ground mechanic. I've got some candles here, corporal. Shall I light them? "

" Yes. Keep the torch on him, Adalbert. I have you covered, Alfred. Don't do anything funny."

Alfred, followed by the torch beams, lighted the candles. All was well. There wasn't a trace of the presence of a third man. Two stools, the little rough table and the long pile of sacks. Fred had got a splendid start. When Alfred had lit the candles the corporal moved up to look. He took in the arrangements at a glance.

" Anything under those sacks? " he asked.

" They're just to lie on," Alfred said.

" Search them, Karl," the corporal ordered the uninjured Nazi. The sacks were scattered and nothing was found but one minute cigarette butt and a couple of match-ends.

" A boy told us there were some guns here."

" So there are," Alfred said. " There's that machine gun in the entrance, and those men by the wall there have rifles."

" That's old stuff."

" Very old," agreed Alfred.

" Where does that chalk come from? " the corporal asked, looking at the big pile.

" From the other tunnel. There's the hole."

" Does it go right out? "

" Yes, but you can't go that way. It's got a stone over the end."

" Karl, take the torch and go down the tunnel till you come to the stone. Feel about well. You other two poke this chalk about a bit with your daggers."

" Karl won't be able to turn round," Alfred said.

" Don't be funny, Alfred. It'll be best for you not to speak unless I speak to you perhaps."

No guns were found hidden in the chalk, and presently Karl came painfully back out of the tunnel hind end first.

" Nothing there, corporal, except the big stone. You can't move it from this end."

" You and the Red always used the front entrance? "

" Yes."

" Who made the back tunnel and this false wall here and put the skeletons in position? "

" Someone who hadn't much else to do, I should think."

" You found the place like this? "

" It's always been like this since Hermann and I have been using it."

" Who told you about it? "

" A Christian," said Alfred, guessing at his betrayer.

" And you came here with this Red because you thought some decent Englishman or Nazi might catch you above ground? "

Alfred looked ashamed.

" I knew him a great while ago, when he was doing his military training. He wasn't a Red then."

" You've got filthy tastes, Alfred. Filthy even for an Englishman. But that's nothing to do with us. Karl, bring those candles down here and we'll see to these men."

The corporal put his revolver in its holster, and the whole party moved down to the entrance of the dug-out with the candles to see how badly injured were the victims of Hermann's berserker rage. All the Germans were quieting down after the nervous excitement of the fright by Stone-henge, and the stimulation of the struggle in the dark with such an adequate foe. There is little doubt that the affair would from then have passed off peacefully had not the six old soldiers at stand easy by the wall chosen this moment of all their years of duty to fall down. One, touched perhaps in the fight, slipped and fell against his comrade, he against the next, and with the added weight of their rifles—which were bound to their right hands—they made a loud and ghastly Quakers' wedding. The sight and sound of these frightful, half-dressed skeletons moving and falling about in the dim light, without any human agency empowering them, was too much for the most highly strung and nervous among the Germans. He jumped and screamed. The other men laughed at him, a roar of laughter, with more than a touch of hysteria in it, and he, to relieve his feelings of shame and fury, kicked savagely at Hermann's dead face which lay conveniently close to his heavy boot. Alfred lost control completely for the first time since his boyhood, and taking his hand from his pocket he dealt the Nazi a smashing blow on the mouth. After that as far as he could make out the dug-out collapsed on him.

He came to himself on a bed, in great pain. There seemed to be no part of him that did not hurt, but the worst pain was in his chest when he breathed. He thought each breath must kill him with its agony, and yet he went on breathing. Once he tried to stop, but couldn't, and only made the next breath a more fiery hell than those that had gone before. After what seemed a year when he could do nothing at all but suffer, the pain got a little better or he became more used to it. He found he was thinking. He was in hospital and therefore must be in a bad way. He remembered everything. He must see Fred. He must call someone and ask if he would be allowed to see Fred. He tried to make a sound. Some blood came up in his mouth, and the sound was not very loud. But a Nazi orderly with a handsome wooden face like an old rough carving presently was bending over him. Alfred had one eye out of bandages, which could still see, though mistily.

" Am I going to die ? " Alfred whispered, articulating each word with incredible effort.

" Ja," said the Nazi. Then he added, " Probably."

" Then I want to see—Fred, my eldest—son. Can I ? "

" I don't know. I'll see."

The orderly went off and Alfred again concentrated on breathing as little as possible. He felt a lot of strength had gone out of him just with those few whispered words. But he was still conscious and carrying on pretty well when Fred came. He sat beside his father and took his right hand which by some miracle was whole except for a cut on the knuckles.

" You talk, Fred," Alfred whispered.

" All right. I must talk very low. If you can't hear me, move your hand a little. The Nazis went mad when you hit that man and beat you up. The corporal didn't try to stop them. He helped them. Now everyone's rather sorry, in spite of your bad behaviour with the Red. The ground-foreman at the aerodrome is furious, and all your German friends are upset. You've been unconscious for two days and they've had time to think it over. No one has the faintest